# THE
# NUDE
# DIANA

SHE WAS EXQUISITE.
BEYOND REACH.
AND A FRAUD.

"A most delightful novel, that is also a drama of the
modern world of art and art fakes, of the wild way with
sex in today's fast spinning world of change and greed.
Rowe knows his setting well—the world of art dealers,
painters and their women, and the very intimate desires
and habits that have begun to stain the existence of all
of us. The novel has literary merit . . . a good story, interesting characters and situations of true drama."
Stephen Longstreet, author of
*The Kingston Fortune* and *The Pedlocks*

# HUNTER ROWE

# THE NUDE DIANA

## HUNTER ROWE

**AVON**
PUBLISHERS OF BARD, CAMELOT, DISCUS, EQUINOX AND FLARE BOOKS

AVON BOOKS
A division of
The Hearst Corporation
959 Eighth Avenue
New York, New York 10019

ISBN: 0-380-00677-4

First Avon Printing, July, 1976

AVON TRADEMARK REG. U.S. PAT. OFF. AND
FOREIGN COUNTRIES, REGISTERED TRADEMARK—
MARCA REGISTRADA, HECHO EN CHICAGO, U.S.A.

Printed in the U.S.A.

# The Present

From their table on the balcony of Shorts, Andrew and Gail watched the activity on the floor below.

"Look," Gail said. "That man in the plaid jacket." She pointed him out with a red-nailed hand. "What's the matter with him? He looks desperate."

The man she indicated was frantically pushing and elbowing his way through the seething mass of bodies. He looked as if he were fighting to get out. But at the bar he stopped and spoke to a dark-haired girl. Andrew had noticed her earlier. She had danced several times but always came back alone to the bar and sat just a shade too casually over her drink, chain smoking.

Now she nodded as the man spoke to her, and her hair caught a gleam of light. Her bored expression did not change. They went to the floor and danced. They didn't talk. The man was already looking round for another possible partner. At the end of the number they separated. The girl went back to the bar.

"What's the matter with her, I wonder?" said Gail. "She looks all right from here."

From the balcony, in the subdued, pinkish light, everyone seemed attractive.

"Perhaps there's something the matter with him," Andrew said.

"Maybe she has bad skin. Or no ankles."

"Perhaps she's hoping she'll find someone she actually likes."

"It is a funny place, isn't it?" she said, ignoring the distaste she could hear in Andrew's voice.

"Funny? This place? It's pretty damn peculiar, if that's what you mean."

"Oh, I think it's great. It's funny."

"Shopping for sex. You call that funny? It's pathetic."

"Oh Andrew, don't be so *English*." She laughed and reached across to put her hand over his.

"I am English, for heaven's sake."

"Yes. But most of the time it doesn't show. Only when you're like this. Most of the time you're—well, you're sort of New York!"

"I've been here for three years."

". . . and suddenly now and then you come on like Queen Victoria—really English, with these snappy remarks."

"It's still shopping for sex."

Andrew's fair hair was thinning. The lines were stacking up at the corners of his eyes. Gail was younger. She could have given him ten years, and he would still have been ahead.

"Oh Andrew." She laughed. "You are being English. Pretending. Playing games. Everyone's after the same thing. Even the real English must have sex sometimes. I'll bet you've been hunting here yourself."

She looked to him for an answer, but he met her eyes with a defiantly blank expression.

"Have it your own way." She nodded towards the floor below. "All the dating, the dinner parties—sex is what they're really all about. This is just more honest. I'd rather have this than all that damn polite conversation. There's no pretense in this place."

"I don't like it."

"You *are* Victorian."

It was true, he did disapprove. He didn't know why. There were plenty of things he had done he was not too proud of. Maybe sometimes, in business, he had cut corners. But that did not touch him as a person. It was a race, a competition. Whatever he'd done, he had kept alive the capacity for personal relationships. He liked to think he had. The pairings on the floor below were not personal. They were inhuman.

"It's so crude," he said.

"It's honest."

"Take your choice. That's why there's chocolate and vanilla."

"You're a hypocrite, Andrew my friend. A damn English hypocrite. Why don't you admit it—you're only after me for my money?"

"That's right."

"If you didn't know I have a daddy who is super-rich, you'd be down there yourself, wouldn't you now, doing a little shopping?"

"If you say so. But not for money. For the money I'm up here with you."

"Well, that's a comfort. I thought maybe you wanted me only for my body."

They were smiling and looking into one another's eyes, in case one might take the other literally.

"Well," the girl went on in a more serious tone, "I suppose I should be glad in a way. Three years ago—I never thought about it, it just seemed there would always be money. Everyone knew Arthur Peters. Everyone in California, anyway. Now ..." She opened her hands in a small hopeless gesture. "I don't have a cent, and I never will. Not even when Dad—when Dad goes away."

"Dies, you mean?"

She lowered her eyes. "Yes. Now you're being crude, Andrew."

"No. Honest, not crude."

"All right." She brightened. "Anyway, he's not going to, to die for ages, so there's no point in talking about it."

"And meanwhile, you're poor as a church mouse."

She smiled. "Practically." After a pause she asked, "What happened to that girl you used to go around with—Corinna?"

"Corinna?"

"Oh, Andrew, don't look so guilty, dammit. I'm not jealous. I hardly knew you then. I liked her, that's all. What was it you used to call her? You didn't call her Corinna?"

"No. Fidget. It was ..."

"That's right. Fidget. That was it. She was a really nice girl, Andrew. I'd like to see her again."

"She's left. She's gone back to Europe."

"Oh. That's a shame. She was such a nice girl."

"Yes."

"She wasn't like the others on the scene. You know, most of them are in it either for money or for the fun—you know, the whole social bit, the openings and the parties. But Corinna wasn't like that. You sort of felt, you know, she cared about *painting*—you know what I mean? She didn't care about all the games that went with it."

"She did care. She didn't care *for* them. She didn't like them."

"Yes. Sure. That's what I meant. She was on the scene, because that's where the painting was at. But she didn't really care for the rest of it all."

"That was her trouble. It's a very naïve attitude."

Andrew was beginning to feel stifled. He had to get out. The air conditioners were at balcony level. Smoke rose on the heat from the floor below and passed over them like fog, visible in milky streaks above the red-shaded lamps at each table.

"Okay, it's naïve. It's also very attractive. Naïve can be right you know. I mean, most of the people on the scene are phony as hell. They don't give a fig about the paintings. They're there for every other reason, but not because they care about painting. She did, Corinna did. She was a nice girl, Andrew."

"All right, I know. You don't have to tell me. She was a nice girl. I said that. Her trouble was, she was too nice, that's all. She was too sensitive. . . . Look, do we have to talk about this?"

"No . . . No, but . . ."

"We didn't agree, let's put it that way. We didn't agree."

Gail shrugged. "Okay." She smiled at Andrew. "So that's why there's chocolate *and* vanilla."

"You know," said Andrew seriously, "I always choose the chocolate. But sometimes I wonder if I don't really prefer vanilla."

"So?" Gail said. "What's the problem? You have both. Chocolate *and* vanilla. That's the beauty of it. Chocolate. Vanilla. Chocolate and vanilla. It's a three-way choice."

"I suppose so," said Andrew without conviction. He could feel the familiar sensation, the depression gathering like rain clouds at the back of his head. "She wouldn't have both, not together. She said you couldn't taste one from the other."

"She? Who?"

"Corinna."

"Oh. Hey, she really got to you, didn't she? I think I shall begin to be jealous."

"Look, it was a bad time in my life. I behaved like a fool, a damn fool."

"Yes. I can't say I liked what you did to Lennox."

"No. I know. I'm not too proud of it myself. I really don't like to think about it."

"I never understood why you should do a thing like that. I didn't know you too well but I—well ..." She reached over and touched his arm lightly. "... You seemed a nice guy. I mean, you were tall and fair and handsome and you looked like a surfer,"—she was smiling now—"and that counts with us California girls: but you were nice to me. ..."

"I liked you."

"Yes. I don't mean that. I mean, you were considerate. I'd have trusted you."

Andrew was turning his cigarette pack over and over on the marble tabletop. "I don't know. I got it wrong, I guess."

"But why did you do it?"

Andrew looked at her seriously, frowning slightly. "I've thought about it a lot. I guess it was envy. Plain envy. I don't know why. My family were poor, but, you know, not on the bread line. My parents had really boring lives. I hated that. But a lot of people come from poor families. There's probably some more complicated reason. If I went to a shrink, he'd find something. Toilet training, or penis envy . . ."

Gail laughed. "A penis you have."

"You know what I mean. Anyway, I don't need to know the reason. I know I *was* envious."

"What of?"

"Of all those people who started off ahead of me. I sort of saw it as a handicap, and they all started halfway round the course, just by being born with money, or connections—being privileged. I suppose I got obsessed with it. It really ate me up. I had to find a way to catch up. . . . Well, it didn't work."

"It certainly didn't. But . . ."

"I mean, I'm glad it didn't work. I still am envious. I always shall be."

"But it doesn't mean anything. Look at Dad. Money—it comes and goes."

"Look, I've never believed that. You have to understand, everyone always believes: *I* am the one person in the world who can handle being rich; give me the chance, *I* wouldn't make those mistakes. I still want the chance. I'll always be envious. So I'll be ambitious. But I think I've learned to handle it."

"You learned your lesson?"

"I don't know. I suppose so. I know it was a lousy time, if that's learning a lesson."

"Why don't you tell me about Corinna? I'd like to know. Really."

"It's a long story."

"That's all right. There isn't any hurry. We're going to have a lot of time."

"Yes. Well . . ."

"Tell me about Vanilla."

"Corinna."

"Corinna." She laughed. "God! Vanilla! I mean Corinna. Tell me about Corinna. I never heard what happened to her. She disappeared. She used to be around, and then suddenly you never saw her anywhere. There was a lot of talk. . . ."

Andrew broke in impatiently. "There always is a lot of talk on that scene. You can't believe the gossip of those gallery queens."

"Oh, sure," the girl said lightly. "Still, you know what they say. Where there's smoke . . ."

With nervous movements Andrew took a cigarette from the pack on the table in front of him. The bar's matches were in the shape of a pair of shorts, and the striking strip ran down the fly.

Gail was watching him. "The talk was," she started, "oh, I don't know. Some fishy business about a Rembrandt, a family painting: Christie announced the sale, but it never showed up. Everyone said Corinna and her mother . . ."

"Corinna was nothing to do with it. Absolutely nothing to do with it." His voice was thick with suppressed anger.

"All right. All right. Have it both ways. You sound like a lawyer—it isn't true: and if it is, my client has nothing to do with it." A smile played on her lips. "Aren't you going to offer me a cigarette?"

"I'm sorry." Andrew handed her the pack.

"Your eyes change color when you're angry, did you know that? They turn gray, cold and gray." She shivered and put her arms around herself.

"You enjoying yourself?"

"Oh Andrew. What happened to your sense of humor?"

"I never had one."

"I guess not!" She shrugged. "Well, you can't have

everything. We'll have to play it straight. Tell me what happened. Where did it start?"

"It started when Rembrandt painted the *Diana*—three hundred years ago."

"Let's skip that bit."

"It's still a long story."

He didn't want to talk about it. He wanted to forget it all—to forget all that part of his life. In those days he had got everything wrong—himself, and where he was, and what he wanted. Now it seemed that he had the chance with this girl to get it right. The best thing to do with the past was to forget it.

But she was determined. "You said that already. Now tell me the rest. From the beginning!!"

## 1944

THE ANCIENT THREE-TON truck, camouflage paint flaking from the hood, rattled between the high, overgrown banks of the narrow road. Before they set out, the men in the back had rolled forward the canopy, and now they stood hanging on to the metal frame, turning their faces to catch the breeze. The leaves on the trees were motionless; the grass on the banks ahead of them stood straight and still—but as they careered past, it bent and eddied like reeds in a torrent.

One of the older men spat over the side of the truck and nodded forward to indicate the driver. "*Stupido*," he said. "*E stupido. Pazzo.*" Madman.

Some of the younger men laughed. They had unbuttoned their shirts, and the wind filled them like sails. "*E fresco*," said one. "*Non te piace?*"

The older man spat again. "*No*," he said gruffly. "*No.*"

The truck swept around a corner and swerved violently to avoid an old lady leading a white goat on a rope.

In the cab the man beside the driver gasped. "Blimey!" he said. "Mind where you're going, mate."

The driver laughed. "Never mind," he said cheerily. "Get her on the way back."

"I shouldn't be surprised," said the first sardonically. "There's no bleeding hurry, you know. We're not going down to the pub."

"No such luck," the driver said, putting his foot down to make speed again. His shirt was hung over the back of his seat, and he leaned his elbow casually out of the window of the cab.

The man beside him was in shirt-sleeves. A rifle was propped against the back of the cab beside him, and his battle-dress jacket hung from the handle of the cab door. Private Greene fished in the top pocket, took out the green NAAFI packet of Woodbines, and shook two into his palm. He lit them both together from a cylindrical metal lighter and held one out to the driver.

"Here you are, mate. Woodbine for you."

The driver let go the wheel and took it. "Ta," he said.

For five minutes they smoked in silence, while the hedges and trees flew past. Occasionally they caught a brief glimpse through a gateway of fields and the distant rolling landscape, but mostly they sped along the narrow green corridor without sight of anything beyond.

Then the truck braked suddenly and slowed into a gateway. The men in the back were thrown forward. They cursed vociferously in Italian, calling on God and the Holy Mother herself to do their worst to the driver and his relations.

The driver leaned on the horn with the heel of his hand. A little girl of six or seven, wearing only a pair of brief pants, ran from the lodge to open the gate. The younger men in the back of the truck leaned over the side, whistling and catcalling.

Private Greene leaned out of his window and shouted. "Shut up. Shut your mouths, you dirty wops. Dirty sods. You'd better behave your bloody selves, or I'll have the lot of you on the fucking latrines."

The Italians stopped calling. They could hear from the tone of his voice that Private Greene was threatening, but they did not understand what he was saying.

"Thanks, darling," said the driver as he passed the little girl. "I like your bathing suit. Where's your Mum today?"

"She's up at the house. She'll be back after dinner. It's her half-day."

"Good. Look after yourself then. See you later."

As usual the girl waved to the prisoners as they passed. It was the same every morning. They shouted and whistled as the truck drew up. Then Private Greene shouted at them, and they were quiet. Then, as they passed, she waved to them and one of them threw her some chewing gum or a toffee.

"Dirty sods," Greene said again, without feeling, as they drew away up the long approach to the back of the house and the stable yard.

"Oh, you know Italians," said the driver. "Very fond of children, the Italians."

The truck bumped over a humpbacked bridge. On the lake below swam dozens of brilliantly colored ducks.

"Beats me," said Private Greene sourly, "how her

ladyship manages to keep them so healthy-looking. The rest of us has a job just feeding ourselves."

"Gives up her bread ration, I shouldn't be surprised."

"Well *I* should, I can tell you. From what I hear, there's not a lot she'll go without, wartime or no wartime."

"Don't blame her for that, do you? When the cat's away ..."

"I do blame her, yes, I bloody do. Disgusting. How would you like it if your missus was carrying on here, and you was stuck in a bloody P.O.W. camp in bloody Italy?"

"I haven't got a missus."

"*And* with a bloody Eyetye, what's more, carrying on with a bloody Eyetye P.O.W."

"I got more sense."

"I think it's disgusting."

"She never asked you up to see her etchings, that's what's niggling you."

"I shouldn't go if she did, I can tell you. Bloody aristocracy."

"She's French."

"What's the difference? She's still aristocracy. They're all the same."

They lapsed into silence. Beyond the lake and the rich green lawns, the house glowed in the morning sun like a golden wedding cake. The personal standard of the de Boys hung from the flagpole on the west tower, waiting for a breeze to display its device—three oaks, silver and black on a red ground, below a thick zigzag gold line.

At either end of the travel forecourt stood a great stone urn. Between them was situated a vast Henry Moore bronze. It consisted of several holes, joined by vaguely female shapes of breasts, hips, head, and thighs. A peacock was standing on the hip. Thickly encrusted droppings covered the side of the statue.

The truck now swung away around the west wing of the house. It made a long sweep that took it past the walled kitchen garden, the old home farm dairy, and through a formal stone arch into the stable yard.

As the truck drew to a sharp halt, Private Greene jumped to the ground, slinging his rifle casually over his shoulder.

"Right, you lot," he shouted. "Let's have you. Form up in rear of the truck. Come along now. Look sharp. You're not on the bloody Riviera now."

The Italians ambled down from the back of the truck. Private Greene always shouted, and they always took their time. He didn't expect anything else. Over six months they had come to this tacit agreement.

While the others had stood hanging on to the metal canopy frame, or sat on the side benches and leaned out from the truck to catch the breeze, Franco had sat silently on the floor with his back to the driver's cab. He didn't feel like joking or joining in the game of insulting the English with Italian names they did not understand. It was not that he disliked the other prisoners, or that he disapproved of their being high-spirited, while their relatives were engaged in a hopeless battle for their fatherland. A week before, on the 4th of June, the American Army had entered Rome, and Franco's reaction on hearing this news was sheer relief. Soon there would be an end to the fighting and killing. He certainly had been glad to escape from it himself when he was captured in North Africa—even if it had been at the cost of a shrapnel wound in the head. He had almost died from loss of blood. But that had healed now, and his hair had grown over the scar. Perhaps in time the wounds of war would also be covered.

Yet he found himself more and more often overtaken by these fits of depression. At times he was convinced that the head wound had affected his brain. He refused to allow himself to admit that his depressions were connected with two things that, for him, were themselves connected: the fact that the war in Europe was evidently in its final stages, and the fact that every morning as the truck turned into the gates of Boys Hall and he caught the first sight of that flag flying on the west tower, Franco's heart filled with mixed emotions—excitement and fear in equal parts.

"Right now. Fall in," Private Greene shouted.

The prisoners shuffled roughly into two ranks. Greene watched them with contempt. Fourteen apathetic men. It was hard to think of them as soldiers, let alone enemies. The washed-out gray desert uniforms, with the giant P stenciled on the back, were frayed and stained. Their boots were dirty, the leather scuffed and cracked. They had not bothered to button their shirts. It would be stupid even to try to drill men like that.

The truck jumped forward with a spurt of dust from its tires and bucketed out of sight through the archway with its horn sounding. Franco took his usual place on the left of the second rank—the least obtrusive place in the squad. He looked miserable, and he felt it. He hated this moment, the worst ordeal of the day. Every morning, as it approached, he wished he could shrink his tall frame and creep away without being noticed.

"Right," said Private Greene. "Ruggero. Interior detail. Fall out. Report to Lady de Boys. Back here sixteen hundred hours. Ruggero— Fall out!"

Franco turned quickly to his left and walked away across the yard towards the kitchen entrance.

The other men scarcely took any notice. One or two of them smiled, or put on expressions of mock disapproval. But Franco's "interior detail" had become part of the daily routine. While they worked in the kitchen garden under the direction of an old gardener, Franco reported to Delphine de Boys in the house. They did not resent this privilege. Their own work was easy enough. They planted potatoes and cut spinach, weeded the asparagus beds, hoed between the rows of raspberries. . . . Three-quarters of the produce from the Hall went to the camp, and the rest was kept for the house. In that way the prisoners had a certain amount of fresh vegetables; the camp commandant had a constant supply of unaccustomed luxuries— asparagus, artichokes, white raspberries, alpine strawberries—and the Boys Hall gardens were kept in reasonable order, as well as supplying sufficient produce for the wants of the wartime household.

Even if his fellow prisoners felt resentment against Ruggero, there was something about his manner that prevented mockery. He would not have noticed if they had tried it. He lived more and more in a world of his own. They had seen a difference in him in the last six months. He had always been quiet, a dark, thin, serious Florentine. They knew he was an artist, and artists are "sensitive." But he had seemed to enjoy their high spirits, had always smiled at their jokes. Now he was completely silent. He never smiled. They began to wonder if "interior duties" was actually the sort of activity their ribald jokes had suggested. But

Franco said nothing. After a while they began to call him by a nickname—*La Sphinge*. The Sphinx.

As Franco reached the door of the kitchen entrance he heard Private Greene shouting again. "Right now, the rest of you. Brace yourselves up. Squad. Squad, atten . . . *shun*. By the left . . . qui-ick *march!*"

Chatting cheerfully to one another, the prisoners ambled off towards the kitchen garden.

Inside the lobby, with its flagstone floors and white-washed walls two feet thick, it was suddenly cooler. Franco went through to the kitchen.

Marjorie Baxter, at a long table at one side of the great, vaulted room, neatly chopped the legs from a rabbit and began to peel the skin from its back. The corpse of a second lay already skinned, pink and shiny, on the wooden table beside her.

"Morning, Mr. Franco," she said.

"Good morning, Mrs. Baxter," Franco smiled shyly.

"Fancy a nice bit of rabbit pie for your dinner, do you? Fresh as a daisy. Old George brought them in this morning."

"Old George?"

"George the gamekeeper. You know. Lives out in the North Lodge."

"Oh yes. Yes. Good. Rabbit very good."

*More than I can say for your English,* Mrs. Baxter thought to herself. But she said, "See my Carol, did you, when you came in?"

"Your Carol?"

"Yes. My little Carol. Down at the lodge. Didn't she open the gate for you?"

"Oh yes. Yes. Very pretty." He smiled. "She have some shooing gum."

Marjorie Baxter laughed. *"Chew*ing gum," she said.

"You never learn, do you? I tell you that twice a week, I'm sure. It's *chew*ing gum. You'll have to work a sight harder at your English lessons, Mr. Franco." Then she blushed suddenly, realizing the remark might be misinterpreted.

On the table in the center of the kitchen stood a tray elegantly set with breakfast things. The coffee pot was silver, and so were the sugar bowl and toast rack; the cup and plate were of fine Dresden china with the de Boys arms and the Proudfoot motto—*Diligentiae Praemium.* The reward of hard work. The hard work, in fact, more than four hundred years ago, of Martin Proudfoot, founder of the family, whose single-minded pursuit of Spanish treasure benefited the coffers of Elizabeth I by many thousands of pounds, and also left sufficient profit for him to build himself a residence suitably magnificent for the earldom she conferred on him—Boys Hall.

Marjorie Baxter noticed Franco's glance momentarily on the tray. "Madam hasn't rung for her breakfast yet," she said. . . . She pronounced it clearly so that he would understand.

"Oh? No?" He seemed embarrassed. "I go to work," he said suddenly. "I go to work."

"Right-oh," said Mrs. Baxter. "Oh, and Mr. Franco —could you leave the shooting room unlocked when you get your stuff out? Only George, old George, he says he needs to have a look over his lordship's guns in there, give them a bit of an oiling."

"Guns? What do you say, Mrs. Baxter? I do not understand."

"George," she said, mouthing the words at him. "*George.* He wants to go in the shooting room. *Shooting room . . .*"

At noon Delphine rang down on the house phone from the drawing room to the butler's pantry.

"Maitland?"

"Madam?"

"Maitland, Mr. Franco and I will have lunch at twelve-thirty."

"In the dining room, Madam?" Maitland asked, with affected obsequiousness.

"Of course in the dining room," said Delphine sharply. "Where would you expect? You can leave everything on the hot plate. We shall serve ourselves."

"Very well, Madam."

"And we shall have coffee afterwards in the Red Drawing Room."

"The Red Drawing Room?"

"That's what I said, the Red Drawing Room. It's cooler there. And quieter." She sounded displeased. In moments of anger a faint trace of accent revealed itself in her voice. "I shall be giving Mr. Franco his English lesson."

*Talk about the blind leading the blind,* Maitland thought. He was leaning back in his chair with stockinged feet on a tapestry stool in front of him.

"We shall not want to be disturbed. You can leave the tray and a flask of coffee."

*I'll bet you won't want to be disturbed,* he thought. He smiled to himself. But his voice was heavy with respect. "Very well, Madam," he said.

Delphine understood his tone perfectly well. Since her husband had joined his regiment—he had set out, with a formal leavetaking of the entire staff, like a medieval crusader, on the first day of war—and left her in charge of the Hall, and even more since Franco had become a regular visitor, Maitland had perfected a tone of obsequious insult. But he was making rope for his own neck. She would tolerate him for the time being—she did not have any alternative. But there would not be such difficulty with staff after the war. Then she would heave him out of the Hall like a dead rat. She smiled to herself, enjoying the sweet prospect of revenge. And even more the fact that at that very moment Maitland should be polishing the silver and setting a place at the dining table for the man she intended to take his place.

She knew Franco would have no idea of the time. When he was working, he became so absorbed he could have starved to death without noticing a pang of hunger. She glanced at the young boy playing quietly at her feet on the floor, patiently but unsuccessfully attempting to build wooden bricks into a tower. The bricks were painted in bright colors with pictures of strange creatures—owls with triangular beaks, and bulls, and horses with wings, and Minotaurs, the bull-headed men. These bricks had been given to Delphine at the birth of her first child, Giles, by her friend Pablo Picasso.

"Now Timmy," said Delphine. "It is time for you to go with Mrs. Baxter, to play with Carol."

Timmy looked up at her and smiled. Sometimes he did not seem to understand what she said. Perhaps at the age of three she should not expect too much. At least he was quiet and unobtrusive. He seemed to take after his father in that as well as his coloring. She wished he had been dark like her. She did not much like these blond English complexions that scorched in the sun. But Timmy would probably grow darker as he got older.

She lifted the phone again and dialed.

Marjorie Baxter answered in the kitchen. "Yes, Madam?"

"Oh Mrs. Baxter, Timmy is with me in the drawing room. You'd better find a pullover for him in the nursery on your way up."

Timothy cried when Mrs. Baxter carried him off.

"Take him quickly," Delphine said. "He'll soon get over it."

Almost immediately after they had gone, Delphine herself left the room by the opposite door. She passed through the library, with its bookcases and priceless, calf-bound volumes, each embossed with the family crest, and the great desk, decorated with gold eagles, that once belonged to Napoleon; then through the Italian Drawing Room, with its painted paneling, decorated in the eighteenth century at the height of the Pompeian craze, when the ruins of the ancient city had recently been discovered buried under the lava of Vesuvius. It was a temptation, Delphine was thinking to herself, to dramatize oneself in such surroundings, hurrying through these rooms with their priceless paintings, their historic furniture, to a *rendezvous* with a handsome Italian painter....

Delphine looked out from the window across the park. On the lawn by the upper lake strode the spindly Giacometti *Walking Figure*, one of her recent acquisitions. She smiled to herself. So many people disliked it, had even seemed to go out of their way to tell her how much they hated it. But if there was one thing she was sure of, it was her taste in art. In many things she was frightened and insecure, however bold a face she put on it. With art, she *knew*. It was almost a physical feeling, that sense of joy, of excitement, and also of fear, a feeling in the gut as well as the mind. When she felt that, she had no doubts.

Even years of familiarity with the treasure of Boys Hall had not stilled the excitement Delphine felt before a great painting. Stepping out on to the landing at the head of the staircase she saw before her those incomparable pictures—the Rubens, the Van Dyck portrait of the third Lord de Boys, the famous Rembrandt; and down below in the Great Hall, with its tattered battle standards and the historic wooden screen carved in the high style of the English Renaissance, the other Proudfoot treasure, the Raphael *Madonna Dolorosa*. The sight of these riches never failed to move her.

Before the Rembrandt, Franco had set up his easel.

"*Buon giorno, Franco,*" she said quietly. In the public parts of the house they always spoke formally, even though they spoke in Italian. Delphine's Italian was fluent and Franco's English stumbling. It also made doubly certain that the servants did not understand their conversation.

"*Buon giorno, signora,*" Franco said.

They stood facing one another, three feet apart, for this formal greeting, but their eyes exchanged looks as intimate as caresses.

Delphine nodded towards the easel. "How is it coming along?" she asked.

"Oh, it's difficult. It's so difficult." He walked towards it. "To get it exactly right, it's impossible, without the right materials, without the same materials *he* used. I'm trying for the flesh only for the time, but that's the most difficult."

"We'll get whatever you need," said Delphine. "Just tell me and I shall get it—whatever it is."

Behind Franco's easel the painting hung on the oak-paneled wall. It had been bought by the Proudfoots at the sale of Charles II's paintings after the Revolution of 1688, and ever since it had been the jewel of the family treasure. Known worldwide as

*The Nude Diana,* it depicted the goddess reclining on a grass bank after bathing in a woodland stream. There are only three known life-size Rembrandt nudes—this; *Bathsheba After the Bath,* which is in the Louvre; and a painting of *Danae* in the Hermitage in Leningrad. And this, the *Diana,* the only Rembrandt nude in private ownership, was by far the most sumptuous of the three. Diana, plumply female, covered not even with the scant draperies of the other two paintings, reclines in a luxurious pose, exuding an air of sensual satisfaction. No wonder, Delphine had often thought, such a painting should appeal to "the Merry Monarch," famous for all those mistresses and all the illegitimate children he fathered on them. Women were more generously proportioned in those days. She guessed the portrait must have reminded him of a particular favorite—Nell Gwyn, perhaps.

"The flesh is so difficult," Franco was saying in his serious manner.

Here and there on his canvas were odd patches of dark color, olive greens and khaki browns. And on these he was attempting to reproduce the exact tones of the Rembrandt masterpiece, the particular pale succulence that conveyed with such subtlety the chastity and the physicality of the Goddess of the Hunt.

"*E difficile,*" Franco muttered again. "*Molto, molto difficile.*"

"Leave it now," Delphine said tenderly. "Leave it and come for lunch."

"It's lunchtime already?" Franco asked, with a slightly startled look.

"Yes, already," said Delphine, smiling, She loved to see that expression on his face, when his dark eyes, with their enviable dark lashes, opened in such innocent surprise. "I knew I should have to remind you of the time."

Franco began to wipe his hands with an old rag.

"Good," he said. "Luncheon is served."

Delphine was smiling. "No," she said. "Lunch will be ten minutes."

"But you said ..."

"No. I wanted you to have time to clean your brushes."

"Oh, that's not necessary. They'll be all right just while I have my lunch."

"But after lunch I give you your English lesson. Remember?" She was seeking his eyes with hers, but he was avoiding her gaze.

"Oh yes. But that's all right. The brushes will be all right until I get back."

"You might not come back. You might not be back before the truck comes."

"Oh no. There will be time ..." Franco began. Then he realized what she was implying. A flush spread up in his face, visible clearly even beneath his dark complexion. He appeared confused, but he immediately looked up and met her eye, with a small, daredevil smile.

"So. Perhaps you had better clean your brushes."

"Yes. Perhaps. Perhaps I'd better."


The dining room had been redecorated in the eighteenth century by Robert Adam at the height of his popularity. He had indeed decorated a suite of three rooms, but they did not suit the gothic extravaganza of Victorian taste—of which the Proudfoot family were eager followers—and the ninth Lord de Boys had had the other two rooms completely refurnished in a style of crenellated Camelot fantasy. He

had been arrogantly certain of his own good taste.
And somewhat eccentric. He had had a dozen portraits of earlier members of the family burned, because he did not like their faces. Mercifully, funds
had run out before he reached the dining room, and
Adam's original scheme, the cool, pale green and
white, and the clean bare lines survived.

Here Delphine hung the cream of her collection of
modern paintings. In 1939, as the prospect of war became inevitable, Delphine had set out boldly against
the tide of European refugees, determined to save
from the advancing armies at least some of the masterpieces of modern art. She had to travel, not to a
single sale, but, in the chaos of a threatened country,
to galleries, private owners, the *ateliers* of artists
themselves. And they, facing the prospect of actual
invasion, the possibility of confiscation, and certainly
no sale for their work, took the opportunity of some
ready cash. Many indeed also considered that the
chances of war might mean that these paintings
would be the last examples of their work to survive
for posterity, and they parted with their best works to
Delphine at a fraction of their usual price. At enormous cost—far more than many of the paintings themselves—she had bought a vast Citroën, and she drove
about Paris, and sometimes deep into the country,
piling her priceless cargo on the back seat. She
scarcely took her eyes off the car and at night insisted
on sleeping doubled in the front seat, wrapped in a
military greatcoat. War had been officially declared,
and the German army was deep into Poland while
Delphine was still in Paris.

On the 6th of September, alternately bluffing and
pleading, in French and English, shamelessly using
her husband's title, as well as her own armory of fem-

inine tears and a persuasive tongue, she got the Citroën with its precious cargo on a boat across the Channel. She never understood what it was that gave her such energy. For ten days she existed on sheer determination, and little else. German planes passed overhead and they had to sail by night without illumination. Delphine was terrified but also excited. She drove home at reckless speed, nonstop from the Kent coast, and when she reached the lanes near Boys Hall she found herself singing at the top of her voice the old French songs she had learned as a child. Finally she drove the car into the stable yard—and collapsed over the wheel. She slept for two days.

But it was worth it. In this room she had hung one major work from each of ten great modern painters. Opposite her at the other end of the room hung a masterful Braque bird. Elsewhere, an important Picasso from his early Cubist period, Leger, Cézanne, Van Gogh, Matisse . . .

Maitland had set places at either end of the long table.

"Come and sit beside me," Delphine said to Franco. "Bring your things and sit here."

The rabbit pie was on the hot plate, and the vegetables—minted peas and new potatoes from the garden. Franco put the vegetable dishes on the table and served a portion of pic on to the two crested Sèvres plates.

As he put her plate in front of Delphine, he asked, "I am learning to do it properly?"

She smiled briefly but said nothing.

Delphine refused potatoes, took a small spoonful of peas, maneuvered them around her plate a little, ate just a few—then she sat back abruptly in her chair, with an expression of disgust.

"Ugh. It's no good. Food is disgusting. Eating is such a disgusting habit."

Franco had in front of him a good helping of pie.

"Oh, don't let me put you off," Delphine said quickly. She filled Franco's glass from the decanter of claret. "I'm sure the food in that camp must be dreadfully unhealthy."

She put her hand on his thigh for encouragement. But Franco could feel his appetite drain away. He felt Delphine's eyes on him as he struggled through a few mouthfuls. It tasted like sawdust.

Delphine was sipping her wine and looking around the room with a proud expression. She pushed back her chair and stood up. She went and stood before a large painting of random shapes, bright colors against a plain ground. "Oh, this is my favorite," she said. "This is such an *important* painting. It is historic." A strange expression crossed her face. "If he were not to survive the war, this painting would be the most important painting in the house. It would be priceless."

Franco watched her. In her soft shoes and simple gown she herself could have been a girl from a Botticelli painting.

Delphine smiled. "*Today* it is my favorite. Today Matisse is my favorite. On other days I have other favorites. I am a *woman* after all. I ought to change my mind."

Franco was unobtrusively eating some more of the pie.

"What a shame you don't appreciate my pictures. I wish you liked my lovely pictures."

"I don't dislike them," he said. "They're very pretty."

"Pretty? They are certainly not pretty! They are magnificent. These ten paintings have a place in the history of art. Whatever happens, they will remain a part of history."

But Franco, quiet and stubborn, said, "I think they're pretty." He wished Delphine would not make these extravagant claims. Everything she was even slightly connected with had to be in some way extraordinary—the most beautiful, the most important, the most valuable.

"Oh Franco, my dear." She came up behind his chair and held his head affectionately between her hands. "I know you believe that every painting later than 1750, almost without exception, is decadent art—if it deserves to be called art at all. Art doesn't stand still, you know. Those painters of yours are great painters. Of course. They were masters. But there are masters also in our time. Art progresses. Botticelli, Leonardo—they were revolutionary also in their time."

"I know," said Franco, with a trace of anger in his voice. "I know that."

"Of course. Of course," said Delphine, running her fingers through his cropped hair. "You know it better than I."

As part of his training at art school in Florence, Franco had been sent to copy paintings in the Uffizi Gallery. He found that he had some natural gift for it. He had a sympathy with those old masters that enabled him to reproduce the manner in which they painted. It is the tiny variations in technique that are most difficult to reproduce. Mastering the exact angle at which the brush is held, the pressure and rhythm of the strokes—the secrets of those details is the art of a good copyist.

But Franco also found it depressing work. In the permanent presence of these great paintings, he soon realized that he had no chance of even approaching their standard. And, even if he had, he began to feel that there was nothing left to say in painting—at least that he himself might be able to express—that had not already been said for all time by these men. It was a depressing thought, and it persisted. He could not shake off the depression. It affected his work. The instructors had had high hopes of him. His portfolio for the entrance examination had been so brilliant that they had seriously wondered if he could have done it himself. But his work soon proved his ability—and then, in his second year he came to this sudden halt. He just could not find the inclination to carry on his own work. He would sit for hours in front of a pad or canvas on the easel and not have the courage to make a mark on it.

At first his tutor thought it was a temporary block. He urged Franco to force himself, to draw or paint anything, merely to reestablish contact between himself and the canvas. So Franco went back to the Uffizi. He set up his canvas in front of Botticelli's *Spring*. And he never went back to art school.

"I tell you though, my darling, this is only the beginning." Delphine was stalking around the room now, and she indicated the paintings on the wall with a sweeping gesture. "Already there are painters who would call these old-fashioned, *decorative*." She pronounced the word with scorn. "I don't happen to agree with them. But I understand what they are saying. Art does not stand still. It must not stand still. It must move."

"I don't see why," said Franco. "I don't understand why *movement* should be so important. There is too much to see already. No one looks at pictures properly as it is. No one looks long enough, or deeply enough, to understand what they say. More art is less appreciation."

He was thinking of the people who had bought his copies of Old Masters, of the many times they had come back to tell him how, by having a painting in their house, living with it and looking at it daily, they had begun to learn from it in a way that was never possible in a gallery, where it hung beside hundreds of other pictures. Franco was glad to make that revelation possible. He had accepted the fact that he had not the genius of an original artist. But he had the satisfaction of knowing that his copies were probably more like the original painting, as the artist had intended them, than even the originals themselves after three, four, or five hundred years. And they were *real* paintings, layers of pigment, brush strokes—living creatures almost, responding to gradations of light, age, atmosphere. Prints are dead things, but these were alive.

He loved the paintings, and he knew this showed in his copies. In those two years before the war, he had finally been happy again. His technique improved. There was a long waiting list of clients for his copies. He could have spent his life in this practical act of worship. He never thought of politics or international affairs. The war had started before he had even known it was a possibility.

But Delphine was not in the mood for this sort of romantic philosophy. She was in an excited state. She could not keep still. Franco suggested she sit down and eat some lunch, but she said, "No. No. I'm not hungry. I don't want anything. You know I don't like food. But you have some. Help yourself to some cheese." But she did have another glass of claret.

And she continued to circle the table as she talked.

"Don't you see?" she said. "For us, for the family, here in this house, there is a *duty*. Here in this house is represented the taste of every century since it was built. Every generation has wanted to add something or dress up some part of their inheritance in the fashionable style."

Franco looked up. "You are going to refurnish the Victorian rooms?"

Delphine had not expected to be interrupted. She looked at him suddenly, and said somewhat sharply. "No. No, of course not. That's the point. We know better now than they did. They were too arrogant. David's grandfather was actually mad. He burned a lot of family portraits. But they all believed that what they liked was right and what was unfashionable would never be heard of again. We know better than that."

"Do you think those Victorian rooms will come back?"

Delphine looked at him impatiently. "Not in a decorator's sense they won't come back. But they're important. They're the real thing. Thank God they didn't get to this room. This room should never be touched. We know that, but they didn't." She lifted the lid from a crystal cigarette box on the table. "Do you mind if I smoke?" she asked, and began to light a cigarette without waiting for an answer.

"Of course not," said Franco. "So, you will have to build on, you have to make additions. Very expensive."

"But don't you see? If we don't do this, the house ceases to live. We cease to live. It is a museum. All the great houses are becoming museums. Why, most of them were last altered in the last century. Have you ever seen a 1920s drawing room, Art Deco rooms? Art Nouveau even?"

Franco laughed. "Very few of my friends live in such houses as this," he said.

"No, of course," Delphine said. "But I assure you it is so. And it must not be allowed to happen to Boys Hall. I do not intend to allow it to happen."

"It will be difficult."

"Of course it will be difficult. But I shall do it. I shall fight for it. You know I'm rather good at getting what I want."

"Yes," said Franco quietly, looking down at the table. On his plate a few crumbs remained, sprinkled over those words written in the ancient language of his own country: *Diligentiae Praemium*.

Delphine saw his expression. "Oh Franco, my love," she said. "Am I so terrible? I'm good to you, am I not?"

Franco held the hand that she slid down over his shoulder. "Yes, Delphine. You are good to me. I am happy with you."

And it was true, he thought to himself. He was happy with her. Yet, to tell the truth he was also somewhat frightened of her. He had never realized before that that combination was possible.

"You'll see," said Delphine, tightly grasping his hand. "I have it all planned. There are people working in America now—painters, sculptors, architects—who will be the masters of the future. We shall build here in their style. We have had Classical, Renaissance, Oriental, Gothic, styles from Italy, France, China—but never yet from America."

"But how can you build for them? They are so different from—from all this." He had a sudden terrible vision. "Rembrandts don't go with skyscrapers."

"Why not?" Delphine said. "Well, perhaps not a skyscraper." She took another cigarette and walked to the window, as if she could picture what she planned taking shape there outside. 'You know what we shall do? We shall find a great architect, a great man who understands this new language, and he will build us a bridge, a screen between the East Wing and the West Wing. Out there. We shall enclose the courtyard again, as it used to be—you know they knocked it down in the nineteenth century? They were so cowardly in those days. And there we shall house the *new* masters."

"It will be expensive," Franco said.

"Oh Franco, don't be so *practical*. You sound like *them*." She turned from the window to face him. "They are always talking about cost. They don't understand what it is to realize a dream. They'll do anything to stop me. They cannot abide new things. They are so *old*," she added contemptuously.

"Who are 'they?' "

"Oh, David's parents. You know. At the Mill House. It's so typical. They give David the house, but they try to make sure he only does what *they* want with it. They watch us like hawks. And David is still frightened of them. It's ridiculous. A grown man. An officer. Fighting for his country." She noticed Franco's look of embarrassment. "Well, I'm sorry, my love, but it's no good pretending things are other than they are. That's the irony of war. You're a prisoner here, and he's a prisoner in Italy. It is pointless to let ourselves be embarrassed by it."

"I hope he is well treated."

"So do I. Poor David. I do hope so. He's not very good at coping for himself. But anyway, he's still frightened of his parents. And I know it was. *they* who talked him into thinking we should not build the new wing. Do you know what he suggested? That I should have the stables converted to a gallery, if I wanted somewhere to display my paintings. As if I was a child with a hobby, to be carried on in the stables. That was *their* idea, I'm perfectly sure of that."

"The stables are nice."

"Yes, Franco. Yes, they are nice. But they are not part of the house. To put my things in the stable—that would be apologizing for them, you know, saying that this is just a little hobby. Oh no. That is not how it will be. You will see. You will see, Franco. Boys Hall will be famous."

"It is famous already."

"Yes. But it will be more famous. It will be famous for its present as well as for its past."

Franco looked at her admiringly. "I believe it will. Because I believe you can make it so. But," he added sadly, "I doubt if I shall ever see it."

Delphine came immediately to his side. She looked deep into his eyes. "Franco! What are you saying? What do you mean? My love, you will be here. You will help me. Do you think I could ever let you go?" She was running her palm over his chest and pressing her body against his arm as he sat in the chair. "Oh Franco. You must not say such things." She took his hand and pulled him up from the chair. "Come. Come. We must give you your English lesson. Otherwise, when the time comes, you will not be ready. Come."

She led him by the hand along to the Red Drawing Room. She allowed him to pour her coffee, but she did not touch it. They sat beside one another on the sofa, but neither had the patience to concentrate on the English grammar.

"Knee," she said, placing her hand on Franco's left kneecap. "*Ginocchio*. Knee."

"K-nee," said Franco, purposely mispronouncing it.

"*Rotula di ginocchio*. Kneecap."

"K-nee k-nap." Franco was laughing.

Delphine, laughing too, silenced him with a kiss. She drew away her lips. "*Bocca*," she said. "Mouth."

"*E labbri?*"

"Lips. *Labbri*, lips." She slowly approached her mouth to his again. "And tongue," she whispered. "*Lingua. Leccare.*" Their tongues touched. Franco felt the urgent response of his body. They kissed deeply.

But Delphine broke away. "Come," she said. "Come." She led him by the hand. "Not here. Not here."

She led him again along the corridors hung with family portraits, past the cases of priceless porcelain. Franco held back, but she urged him on. "There's no one in the house," she said. "Only Maitland. He has little enough sense, but sufficient not to come up here. No one will see us."

In Delphine's bedroom, with its incongruous mixture of styles—a large and quite erotic Picasso painting behind the four-poster, with its white silk summer hangings—she and Franco embraced silently. But she sensed some reluctance from him, an almost imperceptible, but still physical restraint.

"What is the matter, Franco? *Caro?* What is the matter?"

"Nothing. Nothing is the matter."

But she still felt a tension in his body. She pressed herself against him, against his chest, thrusting her hips with gentle pressure against his groin.

"Something is the matter. I know something is the matter. Do I not please you?"

"Oh yes."

"You are tired of me, is that it?"

"Oh *no*." Franco sounded shocked. "Never. Never." He bent his head to reassure her with a kiss.

"Then why do I not please you?"

"But you do. I love to be with you."

Delphine drew back from him. "Oh Franco. A woman can tell when she does not please a man." With a single movement she dropped her gown to the floor. She stood naked before him. "There. Do I please you or not?"

"Oh yes. Yes. It's not . . ."

But Delphine stepped to him and silenced him with a kiss. Then she began to unbutton the faded gray shirt, stroking his nipples, smoothing the hair on his chest with the palm of her hand.

"I am so glad you are dark. English men are so—so *pink*." Franco smiled and gripped her shoulders. Her skin was smooth and warm to his touch—and its tanned olive color as always reminded him of the flesh of Rembrandt's *Diana*. Perhaps that was why he loved the painting so much.

Delphine unbuckled his belt. "It pleases you?" she asked. "*Te piace?*"

"*Oh sì, sì,*" said Franco, his voice now thick and hoarse. "*Me piace. Molto. Molto.*"

They made love in unison, to a rhythm they had perfected together, admiring and caressing one another in turn, moving without haste to union, and to climax, in a smooth uninterrupted sequence that drove everything from Franco's head but the sensations of his own flesh.

Afterwards they lay in the bed, with the white hang-

ings like an embroidered tent. Franco could see the
rising ground of the parkland, crowned by a clump of
oaks round a mock-classical temple. And then the
feeling of apprehension returned to him. Afterwards
is always a bad time, he told himself. But he knew it
was not simple after-love depression. It was deeper,
more permanent than that.

As he had lit her cigarette for her, Delphine had
said, "You do it so well. I shall have to give you regular employment." Then she laughed and briefly
touched him. "I don't mean that. I mean the cigarette.
You will be such a good butler. I shall be so proud of
you—my tall, handsome Italian butler. Everyone will
be madly envious."

Franco had not even smiled.

"What's the matter, my love?" she said. "Don't you
want to stay here? Don't you want to stay with me?"

"Yes. Oh yes—of course I want to stay. . . . It's just
. . . well, just that I am not really sure that you want
me to stay."

Delphine had cried, "Oh Franco! Franco! How can
you *say* such a thing." She had fallen on his body
with kisses and caresses, from head to toe, as if she
would devour him. "How *can* you say such things?"

And Franco knew that what he had said was not
what he meant to say. At least, not what he wanted to
say. But before he could bring himself to think exactly what he had meant, let alone express it, Delphine's caresses, and the reactions of his own body, had
driven it out of his mind again.

Again they made love, with practiced elegance but
perhaps, Franco thought even as he let slip the con-
trols of his mind, with rather too much control.

After they made love Delphine always smoked a
cigarette.

"They tell me I shouldn't use these things," said Delphine, indicating the embroidered curtains with her cigarette. As she drew it down from above her head it left a tiny ring of smoke, and she idly repeated the gesture, leaving two smoke rings, like white halos above them. "They watch me. In my own house I feel I am watched all the time. The old people out in the Mill House, Maitland—they're watching me all the time. They disapprove of me, of what I do. They hate the Hall to be used. They want it to be *preserved*, like one of those damned birds. They'd have it stuffed, if only they knew how." She angrily blew smoke from her lips, and dispersed the thinning halos. "But that's not right," she continued. "They were made to be used. Four hundred years ago they enjoyed them for what they were. They probably even got a little tired of them. Then when they were finished, they threw them out and replaced them."

Suddenly Franco turned and clung to her, as if in terror. With his mouth at her breast he was murmuring "*Cara. Cara mia . . .*" over and over like a child.

With his back to the driver, Franco squatted on the floor of the truck as it bounced down the Boys Hall drive towards the West Lodge. His fellow prisoners were cheerful, enjoying the cool air of the fading afternoon, pleasantly tired after the day's work in the open air. They left Franco alone with his gloomy thoughts. They had some time ago ceased to make pointed remarks about how tired he looked, or, sniffing suspiciously, enquire of one another what was that peculiar smell? Scent, was it? Or—something else? They left him alone now. He seemed so worried all the time, they had actually begun to feel sorry for him.

And Franco was sorry for himself. Crouched on the floor, hugging his knees, he repeatedly told himself that he should be happy. He was young and healthy, and he had the love of a beautiful woman. Could anyone ask more than that? Yes, indeed a man did need something more than that, something before even any of those things—his pride in himself, his self-respect, his dignity, if you like. And that Franco had lost. When he was away from Delphine—here, on the floor of the truck—he saw it so clearly. What would he tell any other man to do? What would he tell his best friend if he came to him for advice? There was only one possible answer. If he did as Delphine planned, what would he be? A gigolo, waiting at table and serving on demand in the bedroom. If she really loved him, if she cared about him as a man at all, she would not want to put him in a position like that. There was only one answer, and he should insist that she accept it. If she loved him she should go with him, give up her wealth, and her rank, and her grandiose schemes, and go to live with Franco the simple life of an artist's wife. If she wanted a Latin lover, then doubtless she could find a substitute for Franco from among the hundreds of sex-starved young Italians in the P.O.W. camp with him.

The truck slowed at the gates and the children, Timothy and Carol, came out to wave. The men threw them cherries they had picked from the trees that grew against the walls of the kitchen garden. "*Ciao*," they called. The children replied solemnly, "Chow."

Franco heard but did not see from his seat on the floor. Timothy was a beautiful child, a miniature

blond version of Delphine. What beautiful children
they could make, he and Delphine, beautiful dark-
eyed Latin children! Could she not be happy to be
his wife and have the pleasure of bringing up such a
family? But he knew it was a hopeless wish. Every
time he saw Delphine he planned to say these things,
to insist that she make the choice. But in reality he
did not have to ask; he knew what choice she would
make. And for the time he had not the courage to
face it.

*1973*

# 1

GAIL PETERS was surprised when Andrew called to ask if she'd go with him to an opening at Wetherby, London. A Wetherby opening in New York was quite an event.

"Oh—well, yes, I'd adore to," she said. "But, I mean, don't you—isn't there someone else you'd rather take?"

Andrew laughed. "I'm asking you," he said, "because I'd like to take you. Don't you want to come?"

"Oh yes. Yes. It's just ... I'm sorry. Yes. Thanks. I'd really like to come."

Gail on this, her first visit to London, was spending the summer with friends of her parents in their apartment in Eaton Square. She had met Andrew when he was working in New York, at Parke-Bernet Gallery and she and her parents had been there on a trip from California. They had dealt with him when they thinned their collection and sold some modern paintings they no longer had room to hang.

After two years with Parke-Bernet, Andrew returned to London as Exhibitions Assistant at the London

National Gallery of Modern Art. It was a good job, not too well paid, but it gave him the entree to every last corner of the British art scene. Gail guessed that when she came to Europe her mother dropped Andrew a line and tactfully suggested that Gail might appreciate a little attention.

But Andrew was really nice to her. She had remembered he was tall, but not that he was so good-looking. She guessed he was one of those men who looked better as they grew older. He had probably been a pretty boy, with round cheeks and bright blue eyes; now the bones of his jaw and cheeks were clearly defined—in twenty years he would probably have a haggard look—and the blue of his eyes was less intense, almost gray. His body was lanky, but he moved it easily, like a tennis player—or a surfer. He took her up to Bond Street in his green MG sports car. He looked after her at the party, took her around with him and made sure she knew who everyone was.

And it was a very stylish opening. They were greeted effusively at the door by Pearl Skipton.

"*Andrew.* How *nice!*" she exclaimed in her low, intimate voice. "Bob will be *so* pleased you've come."

Andrew introduced Gail. "How *nice.* I'm *so* glad you came," Pearl said. She emphasised random words, drawling them to an absurd length. But she conveyed a sense of real feeling—a genuine eccentric, in a wide-brimmed hat and a startling dress of floating violet material.

"How is it going?" Andrew asked.

"Oh marvelous," she said quickly. "*Marvelous.* All the crits have been. We're *thrilled.* You *must* have a glass of champagne."

"Thanks."

"We're *thrilled,*" she repeated. She seemed at a loss

for anything else to say. "You *must* ask Dominic. He's over there with our protégé."

"He seems busy," said Andrew. "We'll talk to him in a minute."

"Oh yes, do. You *must*." She still seemed to be looking for something to say. "Do you know our protégé, our young Philip? Do you know his work?"

"I saw him at the College show."

"Yes, of *course*. Everyone saw his work there. He was quite famous even before he left! We're *so* thrilled to have him. *Everyone* knows his work."

"He's very talented."

"Oh yes, he is *ta*lented."

Two years before, Dominic Skipton had been teaching at the Royal College of Art. The young Philip had indeed been a young *protégé* of his. But he had gone off to live with a rather well-known painter who was old enough to be his father. Rumor had it that Dominic was heartbroken. Little wonder Pearl had such a nervous manner.

"I hope you're going to tell your *people* to *buy* him," Pearl went on. "He's going to be *very* important. You should buy him while he's still cheap."

"I'm sure you're right," Andrew had said noncommittally. Pearl had thankfully turned to greet another arrival:

"*David! How nice! ...*"

Andrew grinned and raised his glass to Gail. "Just like America," he said. Gail looked around the crowded room. "It looks a whole lot more respectable than an American opening."

"Deceptive," Andrew replied. "You know how the British are about appearances."

"I like Pearl."

"Yes. Everyone likes her. She does a really good job

managing this place for Bob Wetherby. Knows every-one. Her husband helps too—he teaches at the R.C.A. This guy"—he nodded to the paintings—"is one of Dominic's finds."

"He's lucky to get a show with Wetherby."

"Yes. But he's one of those people—he's been fa-mous since he was just out of school. He had plenty of offers. I guess I shouldn't have said he was a 'find.' " He told her of Dominic's involvement. "It's sad," he said.

"Who for?" she asked.

"For all of them. Isn't it?"

"Yes, of course. If we're going to be serious . . ."

"You're right. We shouldn't. Come and meet some of the more respectable British. If we push hard we might even get to meet the artist."

It was hot and noisy in the room. But everyone seemed in high spirits. Wherever she looked Gail saw smiling faces, heard laughter.

She was trying to distinguish exactly how it was that the noise here was different, had a different qual-ity from the noise of a New York party—it was no quieter, but somehow in a different key . . . when An-drew took her glass from her hand, neatly exchanged it and his own at the same time for a full glass from the tray of a passing waiter, and leaned to speak in her ear.

"This," he said conspiratorially, turning his back on him and indicating the man to her left "is Timothy Proudfoot. We were at Cambridge together. Both read History of Art. The girl in the blue thing is his girl—fiancée by now, I shouldn't wonder."

Andrew and Timothy saw one another infrequently at this sort of party. Tim's girl, Sally Marchant, worked in the Old Masters department at Christie's.

He himself was somewhere on the fringes of the art world. For ten years he had been hanging around the Chelsea scene. He still had not quite decided "what to do." With his beat-up old sports car, his apartment in Cheyne Walk, he led a pleasant enough life, just supported by a legacy left him by his Aunt Jane. But Andrew guessed he was beginning to think of settling down. Recently Andrew never saw him without Sally.

Andrew turned and introduced Gail to the group. They all together inclined their heads and said, "How do you do." Gail almost laughed. Timothy Proudfoot was tall, with sandy hair already thinning. He peered down at Gail, and his arms were too long for the sleeves of his dark suit. Sally seemed specially constructed to avoid attracting attention—medium height, medium build, medium coloring—and she dressed to match. Andrew noticed that, compared to Gail's natural vitality, she seemed dull and prematurely middle-aged.

They seemed to have stopped a conversation.

"Well, it looks as if everyone's here," said Andrew, to break the silence.

"Now that you've arrived, they are," said Sally, in a quietly venomous voice.

Andrew laughed. "Everyone that can get asked comes to Bob's parties," he said. "But excuse us—I want Gail to meet Bob."

"Well," said Gail as they moved away. "That girl doesn't lose any love on you."

"No. It's so bad, she can't even control herself."

"What have you done to her?"

"Nothing. It's Timothy. She knows I have designs on Timothy . . . no, don't try to look broadminded."

Gail laughed. "I did wonder exactly what you did mean."

"Sally knows I want to go into partnership with Tim."

"What in?"

"A gallery. His money. My knowledge. He wouldn't have to work too hard. Just right for him."

"He has money?"

"Must have. If he hasn't, he can raise it. His father's a lord. Lord de Boys. One of the old families. Huge estates. Paintings—Rembrandt, Van Dyck, even a Raphael. Must be plenty of money about."

"And he doesn't want to?"

"He doesn't know what he does want. But Sally doesn't want him to. And now it looks as if she's permanently on the scene." He took Gail's arm and steered her through the crowd. "So that," he said bitterly, "is just another of my famous enterprises that will never see daylight."

Gail was going to make some polite denial, when they stopped at another group.

"And this," said Andrew, "is the man himself. Bob Wetherby. The greatest dealer in the West!" Bob threw him a suspicious glance. "Bob, I want you to meet Gail Peters."

Gail found herself shaking hands with a small bright-eyed man with a trim dark beard and mustache. His handshake was limp, absentminded. But when Andrew said, "Gail is from California. I think you know her parents," he leaned forward and said, "I'm sorry. What was your name again?"

"Peters. My father is Arthur Peters. He bought . . ."

"Of course." He clasped her hand again with both his. "Of course, my dear. How good to see you. I remember you with your parents—you came to the gallery. How long have you been in London?"

"Ten days."

"Ten days already? Why didn't you come to see me?"

Gail smiled.

"Well, I hope Andrew's looking after you. I hope he's taking the trouble to show you the real London."

With Bob Wetherby was a young couple. The man was wearing paint-stained Levi's and tennis shoes.

"Hello, Max," Andrew said.

"Hi man."

"You two know one another?" Bob Wetherby sounded surprised. "Oh, of course. You were involved in that show of Max's last year." He made it sound like something to be ashamed of. "And you know . . . er . . . He'd already obviously forgotten the name of Max's girl.

"Yes," said Andrew. "Hello. This is Gail Peters."

"Hi," said the girl.

"Hi," said Max, looking Gail up and down slowly and deliberately.

"When are you giving Max a show, Bob?"

"As soon as he has the work to put in it."

Max looked directly at Andrew. "Man, that show of yours, it really screwed me up. That was a bad scene. You really fucked that one. After that crap, I guess I thought I'd never work again. But Bob here's been great, really great."

"Well, good luck," said Andrew brusquely. "Both of you. Now I'm going to try to get Gail near enough to see one or two of Philip's paintings. She's never seen his work. She must be the only person in the room who hasn't."

"Oh, no," said Bob. "A lot of friends from New York are here. And Paris. We haven't shown Philip in

New York yet. You'll be one ahead there. You should
tell your parents about him. But it's not the best way
to see them. You should come back tomorrow."

"Maybe I will," said Gail. "But I'd just like to get
an idea right now."

"Well," said Andrew. "I'm not too welcome around
here this evening. Depressing, isn't it? You'll be getting a bad impression."

"Well, it wasn't exactly for my own charm that Bob
Wetherby was so attentive."

Andrew stopped and took her arm. He spoke with
an urgent sincerity. "No. And in case you think I'm
only interested in you for your parents' sake, I'm not."

It had occurred to Gail that this might be the case.
There was no other reason he should ask her, after
all. But she believed him. "That's okay," she said. "I
believe you."

"Remind me to tell you later about Max Marske,"
he said. "It's a long story."

He was beginning to feel that dangerous and familiar depression, the gripping at the back of his head.
He had to admit Bob Wetherby did this thing rather
well. There was a real party atmosphere in the gallery. An international feeling—it could as well have
been Paris or New York or San Francisco. Some well-
known faces. Some film people. Some Beautiful
People. Some "characters." The people turned their
backs on the paintings and gathered away from the
glare of the lighting in the center of the room.

"At least the paintings can't insult me."

"At last," said Gail, laughing, "a painting."

"To tell the truth," said Andrew, "—this really isn't
my evening—anyway, to tell the truth, Philip's work
gets worse every time I see it. It ought to get better

and it gets worse." They were standing in front of a large canvas, divided into lozenge shapes, painted in clear paint-box colors. "Not very exciting, is it?"

"It has a title," Gail said. " 'Acronym.' What does that mean?"

"Search me. Sounds sort of right, though, doesn't it? Perfect painting for penthouse flats. Young executive art. Goes with the chrome and the glass-topped tables. . . . It's a shame. Three years ago Philip had a couple of paintings in the Diploma show at the R.C.A. He was years ahead of the rest of the kids there. He knew about painting—what it is, what was happening. You can go a long way into painting without finding out these things. And he knew everyone. He got around. Very popular. And all he's done is go on repeating himself for three years. Every other artist paints like this now. It's not difficult to do it quite adequately, and you have to be way ahead for it to show. . . ."

"They're not that bad," said Gail.

"Really? You really think so?" Andrew asked her seriously. "I mean, I wish I thought so myself. You like them?"

"No," said Gail quietly. "You're right."

On the other side of the room Dominic Skipton was standing with his hand on Philip's shoulder. He caught sight of Andrew and Gail in front of the painting and made his way across.

"Andrew!" he said, grasping his elbow affectionately. "How *are* you?" He and Pearl, Andrew had noticed before, caught habits from one another. He supposed it happened often enough in marriage, but with the Skiptons it seemed more noticeable. They overadvertised their unity.

"Fine," said Andrew, controlling the urge to remove his arm. "How are you? Gail, this is Dominic. Gail Peters."

Dominic nodded briefly and immediately turned to Andrew and said, "Tell me. Tell me *hon*estly, what do you think of Philip's work?"

"I . . ."

"We have such high hopes for him. He's going to be *very* important," he echoed Pearl. "But *tell* me, Andrew. Tell me, *hon*estly, what do *you* think of him?"

Andrew was not in the least affected by this somewhat desperate sincerity. "I like them," he said, looking around. "I like them a lot."

"Oh, I'm so glad. I'm *so* glad." Dominic's pressure on his elbow just perceptibly increased. "You know how much we respect your opinion, Pearl and I. I *hope* you know how much we respect you."

"Selling, are they?" asked Andrew. He couldn't resist this jibe. The pressure on his elbow relaxed.

"Well," said Dominic, laughing rather falsely. "Money has not actually changed *hands*. But, you can see, we have several reservations."

"I'll bet at least one of those is for Gerry."

Dominic released his arm. He flushed deeply. "*You* know how it is with a *first* show. Even with Philip. It is his first *commercial* show. Everyone waits to see what people are going to do. But we are *absolutely* confident. It's really a very exciting time."

He sounded as if he were trying to convince himself.

"Excuse me," Dominic said, "I must circulate."

"Nice to see you," said Andrew. He decided it was time to go. He was getting that suffocated feeling.

"How are you feeling?" he said to Gail.

"Fine."

"Ready to go?"

"If you are." She sounded slightly surprised.

"Okay. Let's go then. Sorry you didn't get to meet the artist. I think I've had as much of this as I can stand."

"That's all right."

As they passed, Timothy Proudfoot drew back a step from his group to speak to Andrew.

"Oh Andrew, I forgot. I've been meaning to telephone you—but you know how it is. . . ." He smiled indulgently, as if he had learned to tolerate his own ineffectuality. "You must come for the weekend."

"Oh thanks," said Andrew coolly. "That would be nice. I'd like to."

"I've been meaning to ask you for ages. You know how it is. Mother keeps saying, 'When is that charming friend of yours coming for the weekend again?' You must come again soon. You were a great success with Mother."

"Tim, I have to go. Why don't you call me at the office?"

But Timothy was already fishing in his inside pocket for his diary, insisting that they must arrange something then and there.

Behind him he could hear Sally say, "Poor old Gerry. He never learns."

"Oh, don't be so *mean*, Sally," said the girl.

"He can afford it," said the man.

"Well, I like Gerry," said the girl defiantly. "I think he's a darling. Anyone can make mistakes."

"No one can make them as often as Gerry."

Andrew fixed with Timothy quickly to go out to

Boys Hall in two weeks' time. But he almost gagged as he did so. It was a physical sense of revulsion. He was nauseated by those people, by the whole scene. He knew what they were talking about. Mel German, who was in a group by the door, was the frequent subject of art world gossip. He seemed to have been born to be laughed at, one of life's natural victims. Not that he needed sympathy. A successful lawyer, immensely fat and comfortably rich, he bought his way into the art scene by patronizing young painters and the fashionable dealers. He was unattractive, deeply shy and socially gauche—but with evident determination not to be put down by his faults.

Gerry's latest gaffe had even made the national press. Always eager to do favors for as many people as possible, Gerry had got into the habit of using agents to buy pictures for him. Recently he had wanted a painting by Wyndham Lewis that was coming up at Sotheby's as part of the estate of one of the original Bloomsbury Group. He had commissioned one of his agents to get it for him at any price. But a couple of days before the sale, he commissioned another agent, forgetting the first, also to get the painting at any price. As a result, they bid against one another, amazed at the sums they were having to offer. Gerry was also amazed. He was actually present at the sale, hoping to keep the price down by buying anonymously. In fact, before one of the agents had the sense to drop out, the picture reached twenty-five times the previous record price for this artist. It was still not a sensational sum in absolute terms—but it made a good story.

Andrew nodded good-bye to Sally Marchant, to the others in the group, and made for the door. He gravely thanked Pearl for asking him, and she seemed genuinely touched by his sincerity.

But Gerry reached out and caught his sleeve. "Andrew, you're not going?" he said accusingly. "You haven't even said hello to me yet."

"Gerry, I'm sorry." He really could not face Gerry now. The way his eyes were saying all the time "Like me, *please* like me." "I'm sorry. I feel bad. I really feel ill. I don't know what it is."

"Champagne, I expect," said Gerry, "on an empty stomach. Can't drink the stuff myself. I am sorry, my dear fellow. I won't keep you. You should get out in the fresh air."

"Yes."

"But not before you introduce us to this extraordinarily pretty girl. Hello, my dear, my name is Melvin German. Call me Gerry. Everyone else does."

Andrew had been pleasantly surprised himself when he had first seen Gail. In New York he had scarcely noticed her, she seemed so young, but now she was a stunning woman with her dark pale beauty, her blue-black curly hair, and the air of vitality under the ivory skin and within the slender limbs.

"This is Gail Peters," he said. "She's visiting from California."

"Welcome," said Gerry. "I hope Andrew is showing you our city—as it really is, not just as the tourists see it."

"I'm sorry, Gerry . . ." Andrew began.

"Yes, of course. You were going. But if you can just hold on a moment, I do particularly want you to meet . . ."

"Gerry, please . . ."

"Andrew, I really think you should make the effort."

Something in his voice made Andrew allow himself to be persuaded.

"This, Ashton, is the young man I was telling you about, Andrew Tait. Andrew, Ashton Lennox. Miss Peters. Perhaps you two know one another already, both being from the West Coast."

Ashton Lennox scarcely even smiled, but Gail said, "It's quite a large country."

Gerry seemed hurt. "I just thought ..." he said. "Andrew, Mr. Ashton Lennox here is looking for one or two things—I told him you might be able to help him."

"Gladly," said Andrew. He felt a surge of excitement. He knew who Lennox was. That physically insignificant man, silent and unsmiling, short and balding —was one of the richest collectors in the world. His museum in California was only five years old but already famous.

"Perhaps you'd come to see me, Mr. Tait. Call my assistant to arrange a time. I'm staying at Claridge's." His look was direct and his manner simple. But he added in a deadpan voice, "And bring the young lady."

Andrew was about to answer when Gail said, in an amused tone, "Why, thank you, Mr. Lennox. I'd love to come."

"And before you go, Andrew," Gerry said, "just one more thing. I insist you must have dinner with me next week. I have something I particularly want to talk to you about."

Andrew quickly agreed. He was feeling ill again. Anything to get out of that atmosphere.

"You heard of my latest folly, I suppose?" Gerry asked, wringing his plump, manicured hands.

"Yes, I did," said Andrew as he moved away. "Sorry. Bad luck. I meant to phone you, but . . ."

"Not at all. Not at all," Gerry interrupted, almost cheerfully. "The price of fame."

# 2

Wɪᴛʜ Mᴀx Mᴀʀsᴋᴇ, Andrew told Gail, he reckoned
he had found that rare combination—a really original
artist and a promotable personality.

Max was perfect. He was a really sharp boy. He
had that uncanny instinct for doing the right, *unex-
pected* thing, at the right time. After a dazzling
career at art school, he had given up painting for two
years. With paint on canvas, he told everyone, there
was nothing more to be said. He worked in kinetics,
experimented with sound pictures, with environments.
The rumor was that he was on to extraordinary work.
His reputation grew on air.

But the more it grew, the more difficult it was for
him to put it to the test by actually showing. The
block seemed final. He doubted he would ever be
able to break it.

Meanwhile, he had an easy life. He taught in
Chelsea a couple of days a week. He went to openings, to the right discotheques, was cheerfully promis-
cuous with a lot of girls on the London scene. London

was like that in the sixties. There was always a party at someone's place, a weekend at someone's house, a holiday at someone's *château.* . . .

But Andrew persuaded him to have a show.

"We'll have to hire a gallery," Andrew told him. "I'm not just quite ready to branch out on my own— not for a year or two."

"That's all right, man. That's really okay. It's really better. I don't want to feel, you know, the pressures. I may never need another show. I mean, this gallery art, it's really full of shit, man."

"Yeah," said Andrew. "Sure."

Nevertheless he put a price of five hundred pounds on Max's pieces. And he guessed Max wouldn't find it too difficult to accept his fifty percent.

"Sure, man. Screw the pigs."

Andrew hired one of the three or four galleries in London that will mount a show at the artist's expense. Normally the critics ignore these "vanity" shows. But Andrew spent three months canvassing support. His position at the Gallery of Modern Art was the best lever he could have. Not only was he known to every critic in London, but a good many of them could see some possible need of Andrew's help—a job, a protégé, the loan of a painting for an exhibition—that meant they should not offend him. Still, it took a lot of Andrew's time.

The night before the opening, Max rang Andrew.

"Andrew. I have to see you, man."

"What is it? You sound ill."

"No, man. I'm not sick. I'm okay. But I have to see you."

"Okay. Come over. I'm here for another hour."

"No. I'd rather you come here. Can you do that?"

With some impatience, Andrew took a cab to Max's

studio in Notting Hill. It was raining after a hot day, and there was a steaming, tropical smell in the streets. Max opened the door. He was wearing a thin cotton African robe, and he was shivering.

"My God. You look bad," said Andrew.

Max's girl was smoking, lying on the mattress that was just about the only furniture in the room, with a pillow behind her back against the wall. Her legs were under a thin cotton spread. As far as Andrew could see, she was naked.

"Hi," she said to him, without smiling.

Max slid back in the bed beside her and pulled the cover to his chin.

A bottle of wine stood on the floor beside the bed. Andrew went to the kitchen for a glass. The sink was full of dirty dishes, with ashes and crushed butts on the plates and in the glasses. He rinsed a glass under the tap.

In the other room he squatted by the bed and held out the glass. The girl poured him wine. She took care not to cover her breasts. Her eyes were telling him she didn't go for that bourgeois modesty shit, but she didn't say anything. Her breasts were firm and full, curving upward. The nipples were red. Were they sore, Andrew wondered, or did she rouge them?

"What's the matter with Max?" he asked her.

She shrugged. Her breasts rose and fell.

Andrew stood up and turned away. "Max," he said, going to the window and looking out on the slate roofs glistening in the wet, "Max, what's the matter?"

Max struggled up. "You got a cigarette, man?"

"What's the matter? You on a bad trip?"

"I can't make it, man. I can't make the show. It's all wrong. It's full of shit."

"What do you mean?"

"I mean, call it off. I can't make it. I don't want it."

"But, Max . . ."

"Sorry, man." He lay back pulling on the cigarette and pushing a jet of smoke towards the ceiling.

"You can't do this."

"It's my work, man."

"It's nerves. You're nervous. It's natural."

"Man, I'm not nervous. I'm not the type."

"Everyone's the type. It shows different ways. You're nervous, believe me."

"Cancel it, man. That's what I say."

"No, Max." He was losing patience—dragged out in the rain to this dump just for Max to indulge his first-night nerves. He had the girl, if he needed comfort. She seemed sympathetic. Under the cover her hand was caressing Max.

"You can't cancel it now. Don't be so damn stupid. You know you can't cancel it. The whole thing's set up. I've worked for three months to set this thing up. I'm not going to stop it now."

"I said cancel it, man."

"Oh for Christ's sake, Max. Grow up. If you cancel it now you're finished. It'll take you ten years to make it up. Is that what you want? I don't believe it."

The girl had pushed the cover back from Max. She hung over him, stroking his legs, moving up under his robe. Her back was to Andrew, bare now as far as the cleavage of her buttocks. Her breasts hung over Max's face. He did not move.

Andrew put down the glass. "Forget it," he said. "Try to forget it till tomorrow. Think of something else. Get pissed. Get stoned. Let the lady help you."

The girl lowered her head to Max's stomach. His eyes closed.

"Forget it," Andrew said again as he went to the door.

Next day Max turned up at the opening. Neither of them mentioned the previous evening.

The show was a success. Andrew talked himself dry. He set up interviews in papers. He got Max on TV. He wrote letters, sent out prints of the paintings. And Max cooperated, as Andrew guessed he would. He lectured at the Institute of Contemporary Arts. He modeled some very tight clothes for *Men in Vogue*. On TV he came over as charming, sexy, and very persuasive on the new directions in modern art.

"The way I see it, there are things you just can't do anymore. That's why I didn't paint. Three years I didn't paint. It's too late for painting."

"But surely, plenty of painters do still—paint?"

Max shrugged and smiled. He was too nice a guy—wasn't he?—to knock his fellow artists.

"But you, nevertheless, would call these—er, works of yours, they are works of art?"

"Works of art? Not creative art, not anymore. There's no place anymore for that sort of pretention. This is—well, I guess it's demonstrative. You could call it 'demonstrative art.' Nature. The eighteenth century idea. What did the man say? 'Nature I loved, and next to Nature art.' We have to go back to Nature, man. You know, we're killing ourselves with pollution, and we have to get back to nature. You know, it's sexual—loving it and getting into it."

"But your work does make use of mechanical aids, doesn't it? You use technology?"

Max's "demonstrative art" was simple: on the walls of the gallery hung rows of blank white shapes. Suspended from the ceiling, one for each canvas, were

spotlights, masked to project a beam the exact size of
the canvases. They threw colored patterns, soft-edged
blobs, delicately tinted, grouped at random, often
crowding to the edges.

"It's beautiful," Max said. "Beautiful!" as if aston-
ished at his own creation.

"But wouldn't you call these works of art?" insisted
his interviewer, who had himself earlier described
them as "sensuous, coolly erotic."

"Oh man, you're full of crap."

Andrew was watching the TV interview on the
monitor in the hospitality suite. He laughed out loud.
Max was really cool. Putting down the interviewer,
when his own work was not much more than a hoax.
Those delicate "sensuous" patterns were blown-up
projections of bacteriological cultures.

Two weeks after the show closed, Andrew had a
call from Bob Wetherby. He sensed danger as soon as
he heard Bob's cheerful tone. He chatted on about
the latest prices, the state of the trade, the rumors of
closing galleries, the thefts and the forgeries. . . .

Then he said, too casually, "Seen Max lately, Andrew?"

"Max?"

"Max Marske? Have you . . ."

"Not for a couple of weeks, I suppose. Why?"

"Oh. Oh dear. I thought he would have talked to
you."

Andrew said nothing. He knew what was coming.

"He did say he would talk to you himself. I made
him promise that. Andrew, I find this embarrassing. I
would never have done this, but Max was adamant,
that if it was not me it would be someone else. I am
sure you understand my position. Oh, I do wish he
had spoken to you. I am most disappointed in him."

"You'll learn."

"After all you have done for him. Quite a lot . . ."

"Okay Bob. Don't overdo it." Andrew put the phone down on him.

As they drove across London to Chelsea, Gail watched him telling this story against himself. He seemed to enjoy doing so. He seemed somehow satisfied that he had come out of it so badly.

" 'Embarrassing.' Like hell it was." He broke off. "I'm sorry. This must be boring for you. As I say, it just isn't my evening. I get very down when I have too much of those people."

"Why did you go through all that with Max Marske, though?"

"I wonder. I really wonder."

"No, but . . ."

"Yes—I suppose I thought . . . if you don't have money of your own, you have to start somewhere."

"Does Bob Wetherby have money?"

"No. But he was smart enough to marry a girl who had. Plenty."

"Well, you haven't lost the chance."

Andrew laughed. "No. I guess not."

Andrew parked in a square around the corner from the restaurant.

"Where are we?" asked Gail.

"Fulham Road."

"Is that Chelsea?"

"Good enough."

The restaurant was small, Italian, with a tiled floor and lights low over the tables. The proprietor greeted Andrew warmly. They discussed the Chelsea team's performance in last Saturday's football league game. He offered Andrew the use of his season tickets in two weeks' time.

Their table was in a corner. They ordered drinks.

Gail looked around. "Is this the real London? ... Why does everyone talk about seeing the *real* London?"

"Lot of nonsense. Just one of those things people say. Unless you're a Cockney or a Pakistani, there is only one London. We all live in it—the same shops, the same restaurants. Yes, there are a lot of tourists in the Portobello Road on Saturday—but there are a lot of British, too. Same in Piccadilly, Bond Street. We don't go to the Tower, or St. Paul's, or Madame Tussaud's—but I guess you don't go up the Empire State Building, or the Statue of Liberty."

"Not very often. And this restaurant—this is real London? There don't seem many Americans here, as far as I can see."

"It's fairly new—that's why, I guess. Just one of those Italian places—tiled floor, pink cloths; they're all the same. Maybe they're *real* London—but everyone knows that. So are hamburger joints."

Their Camparis arrived. Gail raised her glass to Andrew. "I hope you're feeling better, are you?"

"Yes, thanks. It wasn't serious. Not even physical, I guess. I just can't take any more of that sort of chat after a while. It was a bad evening. It's much better here. I had the feeling I was not very popular in that place."

"I don't know. You came out with two invitations—three, really, if you count that little man, Lennox."

"You were included in on that. You made quite an impression. And before you dismiss him as 'that little man,' you should know he's by a long way the richest man in that room—and you can include your father in that."

"That's terrible," she said with a laugh in her voice.

"Actually, I *am* surprised you hadn't heard of him."

"Where does his money come from?"

"Oil originally, I think. But now he's diversified. ...
Canned food. TV Films. Timber. Real estate. News-
papers. ..."

"Daddy wouldn't know him."

"That sounds very English of you."

"Oh, we can be snobs too, just as well as you
British. The rules are different, that's all."

"It's not too attractive, British or American."

"It was a joke, Andrew. Surely ..."

"Sorry."

"You're very sensitive on the subject of privilege."

"Of course I am," he said with sudden feeling.
"When you see those people at that party. They're everyone of them privileged in one way or another. ..."

"You were at that party."

"I know. I'm not saying that it's possible to get rid
of privilege ..."

"Some people would."

"You don't have to tell *me* that." He looked away
into the corner of the room. "But you can't. It's a fact
of life. Whatever people say. What you can expect is
that people should use their privilege *responsibly*. But
*those* people?" he said viciously. "They never think of
anyone but themselves."

"Is it possible," Gail said quietly, "that you are in
the wrong profession?"

Andrew grinned. "Well, I had thought of that too. I
don't think so. Though not everyone would agree
with me—and I don't just mean Sally Marchant." Another look into the distance. Gail guessed there was
someone there who had raised the question with him

before. "I happen to think painting is important. It has to come somewhere after bread, I admit, but way before circuses. I work in the art world because of that, because it is often exhilarating ... and because it doesn't *have* to belong to those awful people."

"I think I detect a crusader inside that discreetly elegant exterior—you aim to change the whole ambience."

Andrew reached across the small table and put his hand on her arm. "You're a very sassy little girl."

She sensed he was putting her back into the "your parents are friends of mine" place. She didn't particularly want to stay there. She had warmed to him in the course of the evening. Very close under his cynical exterior was this sensitive and attractive personality. He seemed afraid to let it show. He was probably right—he wouldn't survive long in that world if he did. But the tension surfaced in this nausea.... She wished she could help him. He seemed to trust her. Probably because she was not really part of the world—and she was young. But he continued to treat her cautiously. He was aware of it himself. Obviously, she was the daughter of a client, and he was going to treat her with a certain respect. But he liked her, he found her disturbingly attractive—and he wasn't able to let it show. Even the waiters were more relaxed than he, frankly enjoying serving such an attractive girl.

He had not told Gail the truth—the depression that had taken hold of him at the Wetherby party was no better. If anything, it was blacker now.

It was only eleven when he dropped her off outside the house on Eaton Square. As she thanked him, he reached across and put his hand on her arm. "How would you like to come to a football match?"

She placed her hand momentarily on his. "Thanks.
I'd like to . . . but would I understand what was going
on?"

"Oh, it's simple. It's a simple game. Not like American football. You'll soon pick it up."

He waited at the curb until she had gone into the
house. She didn't turn on the step to wave—he was
glad of that. And he guessed he was glad she was going to the match with him.

He started the car and drove into the King's Road
and along to Sloane Square. He parked near the station, went in, and found an empty booth.

Martha answered almost immediately.

"Hello," Andrew said. "It's me."

"Hello," she said flatly.

"Martha, are you alone?"

"Yes."

"Can I come and see you?"

"Oh Andrew. What good will it do?"

"None at all, I don't suppose," he said bitterly.

"It's always the same."

"Yes."

There was a long pause. Then Martha said, "Is it
bad?"

"Yes."

"Worse?"

"No, just the usual." How could you compare one
depression with another? Every time the despair was
total, a bitter and hopeless self-disgust.

"Oh, Andrew." Martha sounded hopeless too, but
with an edge of impatience to her voice. "I wish there
was something I could do, but you know . . ."

"You mean, I can't come to see you?"

"Well, it . . ."
"You don't want to see me?"
"If you put it that way."
Andrew replaced the receiver.

# 3

"HAVE YOU SEEN WETHERBY since that opening of his?" Gerry asked from the head of the table. In the basement of his overdesigned house, looking over the Regent's Canal in Little Venice, they were waited on by his discreet manservant. The question was addressed to him, but Andrew left it for someone else to answer.

"Haven't seen him for ages," said the girl beside him. She had striking red-gold hair and a hint of wildness in her green eyes. Her name was Rosemary, and it seemed she was a painter and she had a husband somewhere. This evening, though, she was alone. She had been making it clear to Andrew already that the husband should not be considered a deterrent.

"He looks miserable," said Gerry. *"Miserable."*

A voice at Andrew's ear whispered, "More salad, sir?" It made him start. The man wore soft shoes, creeping about the dark, candlelit room in a really sinister manner. Andrew waved him away.

"You know why?" Gerry went on. "He's waiting for Kroll to die, and he's not sure he can hold out much longer."

"But I thought Kroll was his artist," Rosemary said.

"He is," said Gerry.

"Well, surely he doesn't want him to *die*. He can't paint pictures if he's dead."

"Ah," said Gerry. "Exactly, my dear Rosemary. That's exactly the point. While he's alive he's producing paintings. Wetherby doesn't want that at all."

"But Gerry," said Rosemary, "Bob Wetherby is Kroll's agent. He makes money out of selling his work."

"Not the way Wetherby does it, darling."

Rosemary shrugged, as if it were a guessing game and she was giving up.

The couple for whom Gerry was giving the dinner party—a gaunt, white-haired tax lawyer from Miami and his tiny, elegant wife—both looked blank.

"The way Wetherby sees it," Gerry went on, "he might be able to make *money* now, but if he holds off he could make a *fortune* later."

Under the table Rosemary's knee had connected with Andrew's.

"He's been letting out just enough of Kroll's work to build a reputation. If nothing else, after all, they have a certain scarcity value. And in the meantime, poor Kroll is starving. After he's actually dead and there aren't going to be any more paintings, Wetherby will have a limited *oeuvre*—and then he can really get to work. But Kroll is turning out to be inconveniently tough." He laughed. "Wetherby looks so down in the mouth, I begin to wonder if he won't be the first to go."

Rosemary leaned her elbows nonchalantly on the

table. But underneath, her knee pressed urgently against Andrew's. "I think it's awful," she said.

"My dear," said Gerry, "it's a fact of life. It could be worse."

Rosemary turned to Andrew. She opened her eyes wide, and he watched the pupils visibly contract.

"They're bastards," she said, as if she spoke from experience. "Those dealers are real bastards."

"Not all of them," said Andrew, shifting his knee, but not breaking contact.

Gerry laughed. "My dear Rose, you'll have to be careful what you say. Andrew has ambitions in that direction."

"You mean as a dealer?"

"Well," said Andrew, beginning to feel uneasy. "One day. One day perhaps, I'll . . ."

"Don't you believe him, my love," Gerry interrupted. "He's laying his plans already. He'd start tomorrow if he could. Looking for artists. I warn you—he's not to be trusted. Don't let him get his hands on you."

"Oh, I don't know," Rosemary said with a smile. "I don't know that I shouldn't be prepared to make an exception in this case."

They all laughed and Andrew felt easier. The back of Rosemary's hand was brushing his thigh. He guessed she was twenty-nine, but she could have been that for several years.

"Well, I must say, I thought you would defend Wetherby." Gerry was somewhat petulant. "I thought you were a friend of his."

"Oh no," Andrew said quickly. "Not really," he added, more casually. "I bought one of his artists last year, but I don't think either of us would say we were close friends."

Rosemary left Andrew alone during dessert. He

concentrated on the strawberries and cream. He had decided he would take Rosemary home. She seemed the sort of woman who would have had the forethought to come in a taxi, not her own car. The first sun of summer had brought out the freckles on her breasts, as she was obviously aware. His eyes refused to stay on the bowl in front of him.

The manservant left coffee on a tray upstairs in the drawing room. Gerry put a Stevie Wonder record on the stereo.

The room had gray silk curtains, two marble fireplaces, and thick fur rugs, but it was dominated by paintings. Spotlights hung from the ceiling were masked to throw rectangles of light exactly the size of the frames. There was no other light in the room.

Andrew knew the paintings well. Four of them were entered on the card index he kept of twentieth century paintings.

"I shall be mother," said Rosemary, lifting the silver coffeepot from the tray.

"My dear," said Gerry, "you never told us."

"Oh no," she said. "Not yet." She looked at Andrew. "I haven't decided yet who's to be the father."

"Well, I do hope you'll let the lucky man know in good time." Gerry picked up an inlaid cigarette box from the tray and held it by the lid with a gesture that failed to be graceful. "Now, my friends," he said, with too obvious emphasis, "allow me to offer you some marijuana."

"Oh, they're already made," Rosemary exclaimed, peering into the box. "That's what I call the perfect host." She clasped Gerry affectionately around the shoulders. "I always hate that fiddling about. I never do it properly. Gerry, you're marvelous. The perfect host, who rolls the joints before you come."

The lawyer and his wife said they'd stay with alcohol, thanks. Brandy and liqueurs of every sort were set out on the long carved sideboard. The other guests, a young couple who both worked at Sotheby's, smilingly accepted Gerry's invitation.

Gerry, in a green velvet jacket, squatted like a frog at the edge of the sofa. He looked highly pleased with himself. "Andrew, you light up," he said. He held out the box.

The five of them smoked, passing the joint solemnly from one to the other. "Clockwise, clockwise," Gerry insisted. "It's like port; you pass it clockwise."

Rosemary turned on like a tap, at the first drag it seemed, as if she'd only been waiting for an excuse to drop her inhibitions.

In a few moments she had moved to the other end of the room, dancing by herself, barefoot, preoccupied. Andrew watched, while he concentrated on holding the smoke deep down in his lungs. He felt calmly detached from Rosemary's movements and the insistent beat of the music, and then he realized that the detachment was the start of his own high. With a great and calm pleasure he felt his body ease, felt himself entering the very fabric of the music. He had the strange sensation that he was floating somewhere in a wide dark space that was actually the area between two grooves of the record.

The joint came back to Andrew from Gerry, on his left. He was just about to take another drag when Rosemary leaned over his shoulder and gently took it from between his fingers. "*Excuse* me," she said, in a slow, deep voice.

Soon Andrew found himself dancing at that end of the room with Rosemary. He tried to remember walking there but could not. Time became detached. The

Sotheby's couple also danced at one time. They leaned against one another, almost motionless. They seemed very married. After a while they simply disappeared. It could have been that they went upstairs. It could have been that they went home. It hardly seemed to matter.

Gerry sat on the sofa, smiling vacantly to himself. The lawyer and his wife watched with glazed eyes. "Are you *sure* you won't join us?" Gerry said suddenly. "It's *very* good marijuana, you know. The very best, I do assure you." But they made their excuses and left.

"What a *beautiful* fur," Rosemary said, stroking the wife's mink as they passed. "It's so sexy. Isn't it? Andrew, feel it. Isn't it sexy?"

Andrew stretched out his hand, but it seemed to travel so slowly that they had gone before he reached the fur.

Andrew and Rosemary danced more and more intimately. Gerry was watching them with a strange expression. It seemed like it was time to go. Andrew and Rosemary had no need to say anything. All *that* was understood. With his arm round Rosemary's waist, Andrew faced Gerry. "Gerry," he said, "it was *great*. A great evening."

"You're not going?" Gerry said sharply.

"Yes. Well . . ."

"*You're* not going," he repeated, looking directly at Andrew. "I want to talk to you. I haven't talked to you yet." He was beginning to sound hysterical. "I have something I particularly want to talk to you about."

Andrew and Rosemary exchanged a hopeless look. She withdrew from his arm and began to dance again, quietly, with her head lowered, as if concentrating on the music.

"Don't I make myself clear?" Gerry went on. "I want to talk to you. *Alone.* I have a business proposition I want to discuss with you."

"But Gerry ... Tonight? ... Neither of us is really in a state ..."

"Speak for yourself. It's up to you. I asked you here to discuss a business proposition. If you don't wish to hear it ..."

Andrew's head cleared instantly. He did not want to make an enemy of Gerry. Gerry was pathetic, but he had a lot of friends. And, anyway, he was the sort of person you did not want to offend; he seemed too easily vulnerable.

"Well ..." Andrew began.

"I thought you were ambitious. You seemed very eager to follow up with Lennox when I introduced you. Indecently eager. It was me who introduced you, remember. I think you should remember that, Andrew."

Andrew heard the door of the house slam. He looked around. Rosemary had disappeared.

He heard himself say, "She's gone." He wanted to run after her, but his body did not respond. He stood in front of Gerry and repeated feebly, "She's gone."

Gerry recovered his composure immediately. "*Now,*" he said in a satisfied tone. "Now we can talk."

Andrew still had not moved.

"What's the matter, Andrew? You on a bum trip?"

"No.... I ..."

"I know what you need. I know exactly what you need." He moved with surprising speed to the sideboard and fished behind the rows of records. He held something in his clenched hand and stood behind Andrew. "Here. This will clear your head."

"What is it?"

"Poppers, dear boy. That's all. A popper is what you need. Clear your head."

"No," said Andrew. "I don't want a popper."

"Why not?"

"I don't like poppers."

"What's wrong with poppers?"

"They smell."

"Only afterwards. Only afterwards."

"No, really, Gerry, I'd rather not."

But Gerry lifted his hand and clasped it over Andrew's nose. The capsule was broken, and the sharp smell of amyl nitrate flooded into Andrew's head. "Come on, Andrew," Gerry was saying in a soothing voice. "Let her go. Relax. You don't need her. We don't need her. Stay here and relax with your friend Gerry."

Andrew struggled out of Gerry's grasp. His mind was crystal clear. That was natural adrenaline, he thought to himself. As long as I have that, I don't need poppers.

The depression hit him as he drove across London. The streets were almost deserted. It had been raining. The tires hissed on the shiny roads. He realized he was driving too fast, tearing at top speed away from that unhealthy, unhappy house and its pathetic owner.

He put his foot down to the floor, screaming the tires around Hyde Park Corner. He was lonely. He needed to be with someone. He thought of Rosemary—but he had no idea where she lived.

And did he really want Rosemary and her silly conversation? Wasn't it more complicated than that? Could anyone so dumb be any sort of painter?

He wished he could talk to Martha. She had always understood—even as she attacked him for making the compromise. She couldn't accept that. In the end those basic disagreements forced them to part. The truth was, the chief reason he had gone to New York was to get away from that intolerable relationship. And now she refused to see him. Perhaps she was right. Yet in his present state of depression he would have welcomed the human contact even of those bitter, protracted arguments, the nights of desperate, exhausting talk.

"Don't you see?" she would ask hopelessly, shaking her head so that her dark hair swung against her cheek. Her eyes looked out at him with a bright and desperate sincerity. "Don't you see? You say you disapprove of them, but actually you want to be like them yourself. You're envious—don't you see that? You want to step into their shoes."

He supposed he fought so bitterly with Martha because what she said was so nearly what he believed himself. She never let him get away with untidy thinking. They had met when she was at the London School of Economics and he was studying Art History at the Courtauld Institute. They were perfect together—except that they disagreed over the basic rules of life.

Martha loved painting too, probably more even than Andrew. But the manipulation of art for money she found disgusting.

"Painters should be properly paid," she said. "Art should be available for everyone to see what they want."

"You sound like Karl Marx," Andrew said.

"Is that so shameful?" she flashed. "What *you* want is to be a parasite. A dealer. A bloodsucker. We do not need dealers."

"Just a minute. Just a minute. I'm not planning to make a killing."

"You're aiming to support the system," she scoffed. "That's enough."

Andrew had thought he had found the answer, the way to spend his life among beautiful objects, without the advantage of wealth or connections. By hard work and scholarship he would earn a place among the most beautiful paintings in the world. It was an innocent view, perhaps. At least he had believed it was. Martha killed that innocence. The irony was that her parents were rich. He used to visit their great gray stone house in Yorkshire, where the halls were hung with priceless masterpieces—many of them known to Andrew from illustrations in books.

Andrew's reaction to this involvement was a driving ambition. Having made the choice, the decision that finally made Martha close the door on him, he *had* to succeed. It was the way he would prove to himself that he was right.

He had told Gail, "You can't get rid of privilege." Martha was privileged. In one sense, everyone who isn't starving to death is privileged. Gail was privileged, and she knew it. She didn't agonize over it. Maybe that was why he liked her.

# 4

AT THE AGE OF TWENTY-FOUR, Corinna Proudfoot
found herself the most stable element in a troubled
family. Her mother had called her "Fidget" when she
was a girl. The name had stuck. But actually, among
the tensions and stormy currents of Boys Hall, Corinna remained an island of calm and serenity.

Corinna's mother was an extravagant woman—in
both senses of the word—her father (Lord de Boys)
impotent, sexually and socially. Her brother Giles
(the elder of her two brothers), overwhelmed by the
responsibility of his inheritance, agonized over every
decision that affected the estates. Tim (the younger
brother) was less effectual still—he simply drifted
through life, making no decisions at all. And all of
them, increasingly, found in Corinna the common
sense and confidence they lacked themselves.

Her status gave her a particular sense of detachment. There had never been any secret about her pa-
ternity. She was born only three months after David
Proudfoot came back from the war. And it was com-

mon knowledge that he had left his manhood in the Italian peninsula. But he agreed to accept Corinna as his own.

Yet her legal father could not change her appearance. Her coloring, her black hair and dark eyes, her smooth, not quite-olive, skin, were features from a medieval Florentine portrait, not the coloring of the famous English rose. There were times—particularly as she walked and rode alone through the woods and fields that she loved so much—when she had a desperate need to know her real father, to see him and find out what sort of man he was. But she knew that if she asked her mother, she would not be told the truth.

When she was twenty-one, her parents gave Corinna a cottage about a mile and a half from Boys Hall. She could live there, they said, in freedom and privacy. In the days before machine milking and butter factories, when the dairy herd had required five times the present number of cowmen, it had been the head dairyman's house. The roof was thatched and the walls whitewashed. Two white lilacs grew by the front door. To the rear stood an orchard of old apple trees. Among the outhouses were stables where Corinna kept her two hunters. Beyond was a ten-acre field where they were turned out to graze.

Corinna had no pretensions to elegance. She had furnished the cottage simply, with a few pieces from the house and secondhand furniture picked up at local sales. She was happy there. She helped Giles with the estate. She groomed and exercised her horses. She ate at least one meal a day at the Hall. For the remainder of the time she was content in the cottage.

The other members of the family got into the habit of calling on her. Even Giles's fiancée, Polly, liked to

visit Corinna at the cottage. As the future mistress of
Boys Hall, she had had a frosty welcome from the
current lady. Delphine objected strongly to the engagement. "She is quite unsuitable," she declared
categorically, within Polly's hearing. "Her father is a
farmer." That was perfectly true. But he was farmer
of more acres than the Boys estate had covered for a
hundred and fifty years. He ran a highly mechanized
system, and it made him vast profits. "He visits people
in a *helicopter*," scoffed Lady de Boys. "How extraordinarily vulgar."

"You mustn't mind Mother," Corinna had told
Polly.

Tim Proudfoot had repeated the invitation from his
mother he'd made at the Wetherby opening, and Andrew went to the Hall for the weekend. It was perfect
summer weather—one of those spells that seemed intended to compensate for the usual British weather.

The party around the pool had been discussing the
future of Boys Hall. For weeks Lord de Boys had lain
in the East Wing, hanging on to life by a thread. The
problem of the future preoccupied them all. Apparently Lord de Boys had stubbornly refused to
make arrangements to avoid death duties, and probably the only hope of the family staying in the house
was to allow the estate to be administered by the
Ministry responsible for Historic Properties.

Lady Delphine was enraged at the thought.
"Never," she said vehemently, "never shall I allow
myself to become an ancient monument."

"It seems to me," Andrew said gallantly, "extremely
unlikely that anyone is ever likely to mistake you for
such a thing."

This was his second visit to Boys Hall. He was fascinated by Delphine. She was so confident, so arro-

gant. In her black bikini, she lay in the deck chair
and raised her hands gracefully over her head. At Andrew's compliment, she smiled briefly. Her eyes flickered over his body.

"The house, of course I meant. Imagine. One becomes an employee of the Ministry of Works. What
an appalling prospect. Could anything be less glamorous? I couldn't bear it. Why should I allow all those
people to gape at what I have had to fight for years
to achieve? Let them go and make their own collections. They haven't the guts to do it themselves, that's
the trouble. And I don't see why I should be forced to
share what I have done with them."

Andrew rose from his deck chair. The canvas sling
seat was decorated—somewhat suggestively, he
thought, as he glanced back—with a male nude. Delphine had commissioned seats for her pool chairs
from a dozen different artists. Andrew had been lying
on the David Hockney.

He walked now to the diving board, aware of Delphine's eyes on him. He felt naked, and somewhat
embarrassed. Delphine was certainly no ancient monument. Her tanned body was as slender as a girl's.
But her beauty seemed artificial, too carefully
preserved, compared to Corinna's.

Since he had arrived, Corinna had shown no more
than polite interest in Andrew, and she lay back now
in her chair with her eyes closed. He wished he could
make her realize he did not appreciate her mother's
attentions.

"If we were an ancient monument, the Ministry of
Works would *encourage* them to come and *gape* at
my things."

Andrew stood at the end of the diving board, and

the gesture Delphine made seemed to include him in "her things." He dived.

The pool had been built five years ago. That was when Delphine had at last achieved her great ambition and built the modern annex, joining the East Wing and the West wing on the south side of house, an uncompromising structure of steel and tinted glass erected between towers of red Elizabethan brick. It was an undoubted success: the materials, instead of clashing, complemented one another. Already it was one of the architectural landmarks of Britain.

Inside, the walls were painted stark white, and there hung paintings of the New York School—Jackson Pollock, Rothko, Albers. Delphine traveled every year to New York, direct from the South of France. She was well known on the New York scene. All the painters she bought were represented by carefully chosen examples. "People think I am playing," she said to Andrew once. "But I work. I like doing everything well—collecting well is also hard work."

The pool itself was the last word in luxury. All year it was heated to a temperature of 78°. In cold weather a transparent polythene cover, operated electrically, slid silently into place, covering the pool and the terrace.

"It's a great pool," said Andrew, as he toweled himself down.

"Yes," she said, "I love it. It was *fearfully* expensive."

"I'll bet."

"But it was worth every penny. My father died, you know, and left me some money. It paid for the annex and this pool. I never had any money before, and I haven't any now. I haven't a bean left—not a bean.

But I have this. And do you know why I have done it? I have done it for Boys Hall." There was a strange look in her eyes. "Boys Hall is alive. You see, that's what I mean. It must never be an ancient monument. Ancient monuments are dead." The tendons stood out on her neck. "Nobody knows how much this has cost me," she said. "I will defend it with my life."

In front of the pool on the upper lawn the head gardener, Barnard, was working with a fine rake and a bucket of earth. He was making repairs to Delphine's latest purchase. During a recent visit to New York she had met a young Los Angeles artist and had agreed to pay his expenses to come over and create an "earthwork" at Boys Hall. He had stayed three months. For two weeks he had walked about the grounds and waited for inspiration. For three weeks he measured out a design and laid out complicated guidelines with white tape. And then he decided the ground was too wet to be worked. He mooned about the house, unconcerned. Giles was quite irritated. "I suppose he was all right," he told Andrew later. "Not much to say for himself. You know these young Americans—damn casual. His hair was pretty long." At the end of six weeks he had tied thick layers of felt around the tires of a tractor and driven it to the center of the lawn. Then he hitched the plough behind it and, very carefully, driving slowly but steadily on his own guidelines, ploughed a clean double spiral, fifty yards across, in the smooth green turf.

Delphine had been delighted. She declared it to be a *great* success. She wanted all the right people to know that she was "doing interesting things." She always entertained freely but that spring half the art world came for the weekend—chiefly to admire her "earthwork."

Then Polly's father, thinking he would do least damage where the ground was already dug—he thought it was to be a new flower bed, he said afterwards—landed his helicopter smack in the middle of it. It didn't do anything to improve his relations with Delphine.

"What did I tell you?" she shouted at Giles. "The girl is quite unsuitable. Her father is a philistine. An oaf." She was hysterical with rage. "I forbid him to bring that damn machine here ever again."

Andrew felt that he had allowed Delphine to monopolize him. It was getting a little obvious. He could tell from the expression on Corinna's face that she was miles away. And it did seem almost indecent to be sitting here beside that luxurious pool, talking of painting and artists, when Lord de Boys's life was ebbing away somewhere within the house. But that was not Andrew's fault. . . . Delphine should have been with her husband. She did not seem in the least concerned about him. But even then—how could Andrew judge? Perhaps Lord de Boys preferred to be alone? Perhaps he had asked her to stay outside in the sun with her guests.

Corinna opened her eyes. "I'm going to see Father," she said quietly, not to anyone in particular. They all seemed preoccupied that afternoon. The air was hazy with heat; it was like a pall lying over the whole countryside. Even the doves had ceased cooing. It was somehow sinister, almost frightening, the immense heavy silence.

Tim picked up his towel. "And I'm going to see how they're getting on down at the cricket ground," he said.

"I'll come with you," said Andrew, "if that's okay."

"Sure," said Tim easily. "Fine."

Sally Marchant sank back in her chair. Andrew guessed she had been going to suggest going with Tim, but decided against it when Andrew said he'd go along. He had done his best to befriend her, but her dislike was almost a chemical reaction. They talked politely enough, but she was not even able to hide the effort it was costing her.

"If you're going up, Fidget," said Delphine, "tell Father I shall come up as usual when Carol goes." She smiled sweetly at Andrew. "We are reading Proust together. We read for two hours every afternoon before dinner. I am so enjoying it."

Andrew felt himself flush. He was ashamed to have misjudged Delphine.

He was also somewhat ashamed of other thoughts that had been running through his mind. The de Boys family, it was clear, were going to be in financial trouble when Lord de Boys died. He had refused to take any steps to avoid breaking up of the estates. Whatever the terms of his will, the taxes would now be crippling. The family would be driven into the arms of the Ministry of Works—it was difficult to see any alternative. But for Delphine that fate would be worse than any death. She would do anything to avoid it—and Andrew had been trying out in his head possible operations in which he himself would be involved.

The de Boys had unique and almost priceless paintings. Ashton Lennox had almost limitless funds. The de Boys would need money. Ashton Lennox needed major paintings. . . .

There was one painting in particular Andrew knew Lennox would pay almost anything for. Lennox loved painting, and he also loved women. Given the choice

of paintings by an artist he wanted represented in his
collection, he always chose the nude. What would he
not give for Rembrandt's *Nude Diana?*

It was one of the great paintings of all time. Andrew had gone back to see it the day before. He had
spent half an hour in front of her—he found himself
thinking of her as a person, the personality of the
painting was so strong. Standing in front of that
painting, he knew he was in the presence of
greatness. It was so simple and yet so subtly complicated. The goddess lay back on the grass bank. A
greenish light fell on her from above, filtered through
the trees around the pool. She wore pearl earrings
and a gold bracelet on her upper arm. Otherwise she
was quite naked. By modern standards she was a
somewhat lumpy figure. She was certainly not depicted as an unattainable spiritual being. She had lived,
and her body showed the consequences of it. Her skin
was yellowish—Rembrandt put that deep golden varnish over all his paintings. Her thighs and her stomach, swelling in deep folds even as she lay on her
back, were soft with fat. The pubic hair was dark and
wiry. She did not conform to the modern ideal of an
antiseptic beanpole. Obviously Rembrandt did not
want his women to be plastic dolls. He saw them as
they are, and appreciated them like that. Diana was a
real woman. But for all that, there was an air of authority about her. She was human, but also definitely
superhuman, a goddess whose deity lay in the
celebration of her human body, not in the ascetic ritu-
als of self-denial. A masterpiece.

Corinna walked without hurrying to Lord de Boys's
room. She was thinking of Andrew. All afternoon by
the pool she had been surreptitiously watching him.

It was amazing the way Delphine drew men to her. To Corinna her tactics seemed too blatant. She felt protective to Andrew. She understood the insecurities that made him so easy to impress.

Corinna was smiling as she tapped gently at the door of Lord De Boys's room and went in without waiting for an answer.

"Hello, Father."

His face brightened as she bent over to kiss his brow. The skin of his face was thin as parchment, etched with deep lines of suffering. His body was fleshless, like two sticks laid in the bed under the blanket.

Corinna dismissed the nurse. "I will be here until Carol comes," she said.

When they were alone, she smiled conspiratorially, as if their being alone was a forbidden pleasure. She began to tell him about the simple events of the day—her horse had stumbled in a rabbit hole but seemed unharmed; the preparations for the annual cricket match in the grounds (she had spent all yesterday afternoon in the cottage baking cakes).

Lord de Boys especially liked to hear about the cricket match. Now a tradition, it had been started by him shortly after the war, twenty-five years ago. Before he was ill he used to supervise every detail himself. He would have the gardeners moving covers on and off the pitch for weeks beforehand. And on the day of the match he would be out at 6:00 in the morning to check that the ground was in good condition.

Lord de Boys reached weakly for Corinna's hand. "Corinna," he said huskily.

"Don't talk, Father. It isn't necessary."

"Yes, I want to talk to you." He spoke slowly, painfully, with heartbreaking effort. "I don't want you to say anything to Mother. But I'm soon—I'm going soon."

Corinna pressed his hand. Tears welled in her eyes.

"Yes. It won't be long now. I knew you would understand that I wished to say this to you. I don't want to say good-bye to anyone else."

"Father. Please. You don't have to say these things. I understand."

"No, I want to tell you. I must tell you how happy I have been that you have been my daughter."

"Yes, Father. Yes."

"For me, you have truly been my daughter. You have made me happy."

The words came so slowly Corinna wondered if he would finish the sentences. His voice was rasping in his throat.

"Father. Please. Don't strain yourself."

"I have made my will. I have made a new will. . . ."

"Father. Please. Don't tell me. I don't want to know. I shall go away if you don't stop. You must rest. I shall go and leave you alone. There will be time enough for all that. I don't want to hear it now."

"If you're going down to the cricket ground," Delphine said to Tim and Andrew as they came out of the changing room, "do have a word with Barnard and ask him to be sure and clean off the Henry Moore."

"Righto, Mother," said Tim, suppressing a smile.

"I do wish peacocks could be house-trained. They do make such a mess. But they look so well."

"They make a damned awful noise in the morning," commented Tim.

Delphine ignored him.

"She's magnificent," said Andrew as they crossed the lawn.

"For a weekend, yes, I suppose she is. To live with, she's a pain, I assure you."

Andrew laughed.

"Oh, don't think I dislike her. I'm very fond of the old girl. But there only ever is, or will be, one person in her life—herself. As long as you keep that in mind, she makes a good mother."

"Not your father?"

"Yes, I suppose she does care for Father. In a way. But she cares for herself more."

Tim spoke without rancor. His voice, his movements, his sentiments were all of a piece—the casual English type. But Andrew was beginning to understand that Tim had a tough core underneath that relaxed exterior.

Andrew had never directly broached the subject of going into partnership with Tim. He had dropped hints in plenty—and Sally had picked them up. But Tim was too vague to catch on. Andrew had been waiting for the opportunity to put it to him directly, without Sally to influence him. Now seemed the perfect time. And, apart from anything else, a partnership with Tim would make the de Boys paintings accessible. . . . When he thought how important it could be, Andrew felt a knot of apprehension in his stomach. And when he spoke he was nervous and hesitant.

"Why—er, don't you branch out on your own?"

Tim turned to him. "What do you mean?"

"Oh, I don't know." It was unbearably hot. Andrew could feel the sweat running down the small of his back. "You're pretty interested in painting. Why don't you open a gallery?"

Tim looked at him oddly. "You know, Andrew, that's amazing. That's exactly what I should like to do."

"Well, why don't you? It's a good time. Art is even considered a safe investment. Compared to everything else, it keeps its value. The trade unions are putting their pension funds in art. Not to mention the Arabs. Why don't you do it? If"—he hesitated—"I don't know what you're planning, but if you need any help ... you know, I'd be glad to be involved in a thing like this."

"Thanks. Thanks. I shall take you up on that, you can be sure."

"I mean it. I hope you do."

"Well, perhaps we should have a talk about it, Andrew. Several times I've meant to, but you know ..." He didn't finish the sentence. With a nervous gesture he repeatedly smoothed his hand across his balding head. Andrew noticed that the leather strap of his watch was frayed. "You have a lot of connections in that world. Maybe you *could* help. On the financial side." He smiled weakly. "Can't do a thing till we get some cash together."

"You mean ..."

"Got to find someone to finance us, eh? You must know any number of fellas want to invest in this sort of thing."

Andrew was beginning to suspect something was wrong. "I don't think I do, Tim," he said slowly. "I thought ..."

"You don't have a bit of money yourself that would set us up?"

Andrew laughed. "No, Tim. That I can't help you with. I'm afraid I don't have any money at all."

"Neither do I. It's a bugger, isn't it?"

"Couldn't your mother . . . ?" Andrew began.

"She hasn't a cent. Spent every penny she ever had—not that she'd part with it if she had any. I asked her once. Of course she liked the idea of having a finger in the gallery. You know what she's like. She tried to persuade Father to put up the money. But he wouldn't. He was sorry and all that. But he says enough Boys's money has been spent on art in the last twenty years. I can't say I blame him."

"Couldn't he sell something?"

"Yes. He could. But he doesn't want to. That's all there is to it."

They walked in silence across the stringy turf, on the humpbacked bridge over the neck of the lake, to the lower lawn where the cricket match was to take place.

Andrew could not believe that there was not some way in which Tim, with all the security and all the connections the family had, could raise the money he needed. That was the trouble with these people, he thought. They had never had to fight. They gave up too easily.

"It's no good," said Tim, as if it were no more important than missing a TV program. "There just isn't the money to be had. Sally's got nothing much of her own either. Her parents are living on capital."

"Oh," said Andrew. He was deeply disappointed. He had misjudged the problem with Tim. Somehow he had imagined that the difficulty would be to galvanize him to make some sort of decision. He had not imagined that money would be any real difficulty. Looking around him now at the rich acres of Boys Hall, the well-kept lawns, the gardeners trimming the drive hedges, the fat cattle and the glossy horses grazing in the park ... it seemed ridiculous that anyone connected with such riches could say he had no money.

On the lower lawn the mower had been out over the grass for the last time. At the center the creases were marked out in perfect white lines, and a great oval boundary line had been drawn around the outside of the pitch. Beside the summerhouse a refreshment tent had been erected under the elm trees.

As they stood at the edge of the drive looking over at the ground, a girl on a bicycle approached from the direction of the lodge. She was neatly dressed in sandals and a short cotton dress. Her hair was fair, and her pretty face had an open, cheerful look.

"Afternoon, Carol."

"Afternoon, Mr. Timothy." She smiled cheerfully at him. "Afternoon, sir," she added to Andrew.

"Good afternoon," he answered.

"Pretty girl," Tim said as she cycled on.

"Who is she?"

"Carol. Carol from the lodge. She's going to do her turn with Father."

"She lives here?"

"Oh yes. Her parents have been here for years. Mrs. Baxter's done the cooking for ages. We used to play with Carol." He smiled wryly. "My first fuck, Carol was."

Andrew smiled. "You could have done worse."

"Sure. She's a nice girl. Giles too. I think he was *her* first as a matter of fact. Giles and Carol had a bit of a thing, you know, at one time. They fixed up one of the rooms in Corinna's cottage—there was no one living there then. They used to sneak out there in the afternoons. But her mother found out." He laughed at the memories of those good old times.

Andrew laughed too. But he was amazed by this conversation. The head of the family lay in the East Wing, at death's door, and the family seemed quite unconcerned. They sat around casually and talked about cricket, and art, and fucking the servants. He would never understand the British aristocracy.

Dinner that evening was equally amazing. Conversation was of friends in London—their engagements, their villas in Tuscany, their ventures into mobile discotheques and Chelsea boutiques. They spoke of the various dances to be held locally in the summer. Polly's parents gave one every year.

"How brave," Delphine commented, with a scarcely veiled sneer.

It was not as if they were unaware that Lord de Boys was gravely ill. They discussed the estate at some length. He had made a new will only two weeks ago. Alberto, the Italian butler, had been called to witness it. Alberto was actually at that moment pouring the burgundy for Giles to taste, but they spoke about him as if he were not there.

The meal consisted of thin soup, followed by a pike caught in the lake by one of the gardeners. The fish was actually too small to feed them all. But, boiled plainly, without herbs or sauce, its earthy flavor was so unpleasant that Andrew was glad to have such a small portion.

The poor food seemed only to emphasize the superb Adam decoration of the dining room and the priceless paintings hung on the pale green paneled walls. It was in rooms like this, Andrew thought, that British food had become notorious. He found himself wondering that Gail Peters would have made of it. Was this the *real* England?

Later, when the men came into the drawing room, Corinna was sitting in a corner apart from the others.

Andrew went to her. "May I sit by you?" he asked.

"I hoped you would."

"That's a beautiful chess set."

"Yes, isn't it? It's Chinese, I think."

"And jade."

"Yes."

"It's beautiful."

"Well, yes, I've always liked it. But to tell the truth I wasn't just admiring it. I was hoping *someone* would ask me to play."

They played for two hours, almost without speaking. The TV set was on at the other side of the room, but they shut it out of their minds. Corinna played coolly, picking up the pieces after long intervals of concentration, and moving them gracefully. Andrew realized quite soon that she was going to beat him. But it did not matter. He was playing well enough. It was not important to win. There was not that sort of competition between them. He began to see the details of her appearance—the soft down on her arms, the flat end of her long fingers and the rounded, unpolished nails. She looked so gravely and calmly at the board while she considered her move, scarcely even blinking. The parting in her hair was a deep black shadow. Her hair was so fine and smooth, falling over her forehead as she leaned over. He wanted to reach out and touch it.

"Check," she said finally, without a smile.

"Yes. You have me. You win."

"Yes. I'm afraid so." She stood up. "Thank you," she said simply. "I enjoyed it. And now, if you don't mind, I'm going home."

"I'll take you," Andrew said.

"No. Thank you. I have my car here. I shall be perfectly safe." Her eyes were telling him not to be offended. "I'm very tired. I shall see you tomorrow. Thanks for the game."

Next day the cricket match started at 11:00 in the morning. At that time there were already two hundred spectators present. The Lord Lieutenant of the County made a speech. He referred to Lord de Boys "tragically overtaken by ill health in the prime of his life." Andrew stole a glance at Delphine. She was looking straight ahead into the trees on the far side of the field.

In front of the summerhouse a number of seats had been put out inside a rope enclosure—for guests, friends, and relations of the teams. Corinna had come to the house before they finished breakfast, and she and Andrew had come down to the cricket match together.

"Are you a cricketer?" she asked.

"I learned at school. I wasn't much good at it."

"You're lucky they didn't ask you to play here. There's usually someone who doesn't turn up."

"If I'd known it was going to be as grand as this I'd have worn the old school tie."

Corinna laughed.

At lunchtime the Regimental Band of the local yeomanry played selections from *My Fair Lady* outside the refreshment tent. Inside, the two teams sat down to lunch with the de Boys family. Every year Lord de Boys's mother, Lady Amelia, insisted that it was her duty to be there—mainly because Delphine insisted that it was quite unnecessary. Lady Amelia's duty, however, was also to her racehorses. She did have to keep an eye on the racing results. She had two runners that afternoon. After some trouble with the aerial, her portable TV was set up beside her at the head of the table. She scarcely spoke to the team captain beside her for the entire meal. While her horse was actually running, the table was reduced to silence. It finished seventh out of eight.

After lunch cars arrived by the hundreds. The cows had been moved from the field behind the lodge, and the gardeners organized parking there. People were everywhere. It was like a fairground without the sideshows. Dogs barked at the ducks on the lake. Occasionally one would run on the pitch after the ball. A line formed at the refreshment tent. The litter baskets were filling with plastic cups and ice cream cartons.

Even in the shade of the elms it was unbearably hot. Giles had been batting for two hours. He played a defensive game, content to save his wicket without adding much to the score. It was not very interesting to watch.

"How is your father today?" Andrew asked Corinna.

"About the same," she said evenly.

"Doesn't it upset you that your father—that Lord de Boys is so ill? You all seem so—well, so calm about it."

"You can speak of him as my father. Most people do." She looked at him directly, and he could see the anger spark in her eyes. "Of course we are upset. Because we don't show our emotions for everyone to see, it doesn't mean that we feel nothing."

"That's a very English attitude."

"Perhaps. What's wrong with that? You're English too, surely?"

Andrew cursed himself. He and Corinna had spent the day in one another's company. A sense of intimacy had grown between them. They were both aware of it. Andrew had begun to feel he could be natural with her, he could relax some of that defensive dishonesty that he had built around himself.

Corinna stared ahead, with a stony expression on her face. But after a minute she turned to him and said, in an almost tender voice. "Andrew. Look. He is ill. He is extremely ill. He's not going to recover—there's no point in pretending to myself that he is. Nobody knows better than I how ill he is. But you must understand, surely, that the only possible thing to do is to go on as if it were just a temporary setback. It's the only way to cope with it. It isn't just that it's easier for us. I don't suppose it is, in fact. But it is easier for him. He knows we are pretending. But we know he knows. There's no deception in it, really. Do you think Mother wouldn't rather spend every minute of the day with him? Why do you think she's reading Proust with him? There are twenty-four volumes of that book." There were tears in her eyes. "They'll never finish it. Father knows it. And Mother knows it. But they both pretend they're looking forward to going right through it together. It would take them two years."

"I'm sorry," said Andrew. "I'm sorry. It was stupid of me."

"Yes," said Corinna, with a soft smile, warm but sad. "It was. But don't worry. I understand."

Barnard's grandson was in charge of the scoreboard, rearranging the tin figures on the hooks at the end of each over. As Giles eventually reached his fifty, the spectators applauded thinly.

Andrew said to Corinna, "Would you do something for me?"

She looked at him, waiting to hear what it was. Questions like that, her expression said, do not need an answer.

"Would you like to make me a cup of tea?"

"Yes. I'd like to."

They drove to Corinna's cottage in Andrew's old MG, with the hood down. The roads were dusty, shimmering in the heat. They passed great expanses of ripening wheat. There was not even a breath of wind. The fields stood like golden reservoirs contained by high green hedges. The only movement came from the larks that hung over the fields, rising and falling as if on threads, pouring their throbbing song into the sky.

Andrew drove steadily, controling his first inclination to put his foot down and make for the cottage like a madman. The air poured into the car like warm water.

Andrew drew up at the gate of the cottage and turned off the engine. Neither of them moved. The silence was almost unnatural, like a physical presence. It was broken suddenly by the sound of a horse whinnying from the stable.

Corinna turned to Andrew and smiled.

"I know just how he feels," said Andrew. He took Corinna's arms and drew her to him. He kissed her slowly and gently.

The cottage door was not locked. Inside, by contrast it seemed cool. The sunlight threw squares of brightness on the walls and carpets, spotlighting random objects—a patchwork cushion, a picture, brass candlesticks.

Corinna went ahead, and Andrew followed, up the narrow stairs to the bedroom, with its low ceiling and chintz curtains. Then she turned and waited for him to come to her.

They kissed again, tenderly, their lips gently drawn together.

But suddenly Corinna was urgent. She pressed herself to him, parting his lips with hers, gripped his tongue with her teeth.

"Oh Andrew. Andrew. Quick. God. Quick." She began pulling off her clothes, as if the feel of them on her body would drive her mad. "Take off your things."

Now Andrew was urgent, too. He kicked off his shoes, flung off his clothes.

They stood facing one another, naked. Her eyes were smiling into his. Then she stepped forward and grasped him.

With a sigh she said, "Oh, I wanted to see that."

"It's . . ." Andrew began.

"Ever since yesterday. I've been . . . Yesterday. By the pool. Ever since . . ."

"You were watching me? I didn't realize you were interested. I didn't know you were even watching."

"Of course I was watching."

She lowered her head and touched him with her lips.

But Andrew raised her head. He put his arm around her and took her to the bed. He threw back the covers roughly. "Lie down," he said. "I want to see you too."

He leaned over her, admiring the smooth skin of her breasts, the nipples like dark buds, the brownish aureole, a shade darker than the olive skin. It's good to take it slowly, he thought, when there's no doubt you're going to get there in the end.

He lowered his mouth gently, touching with his tongue.

But Corinna pulled him down on her. "No," she breathed urgently in his ear. "No, Andrew. Quick. I want you now. Now."

Andrew felt her come with him, felt the tension drain away from them both. They lay together, without moving. The touch of their bodies smoothed all the misunderstandings of mood and gesture and intonation, the edgy dialogue of the last twenty-four hours.

Corinna sighed under him. In his ear she breathed, "Oh, that was good."

"For me, too."

They turned on their sides, still clasped together, still joined.

"I'm sorry about last night," Corinna said. "I was afraid you'd think I—I didn't want to."

"Well, I certainly wondered."

"I wanted time to think. That's all. I wanted to be by myself for a while, to have a chance to think. That's necessary sometimes, isn't it?"

"Yes. All right."

"And today, I knew I needed to be with you. I'm so glad you're here. Being alone is fine—most of the time I prefer it. But every now and then you need someone."

"Well, I'm glad I was here."

"Oh, don't get me wrong. It's not just anyone that you need. You need someone you like, who understands. . . . I didn't mean that. Don't be offended."

Andrew was still hard inside her. He pushed his hips against her. "Do I seem offended?"

"No. Not that I'm fool enough to judge by *that*."

She gave him an answering pressure. "*That* has no conscience, isn't that what they say?"

Slowly Andrew began to move.

"Does it make any difference that he's not your real father?"

"No. I've always thought of him as my father. I love him as if he were my father. Except . . ." Her voice was uncertain. "I don't know. These last weeks I've begun to realize that it's not quite the same. I've sort of allowed him to take the place of my real father. I never knew my father. And Father—Lord de Boys—was there, so I didn't have to think about it. But now I realize it wasn't really the same thing. I think I do need my real father."

Andrew stroked her back soothingly, drawing her gently to him, moving his hips.

"I think that's natural. We all need to know our parents. It helps us to understand what we are ourselves."

"The funny thing is, I've always felt more like Father's—Lord de Boys's—daughter than I have Mother's. I'm not really like her at all, that I can see. I look a bit like her, but . . ."

"She's one of those people. Exceptional. Exceptions to everything. Even their children are not like them."

Corinna herself was moving against him now, drawing breath deep into her lungs and letting it out in long sighs.

"The only thing we have in common is fancying you."

"She doesn't fancy me."

"Oh Andrew. Don't be silly. You know perfectly well she does."

"You said she only liked dark men."

"At night all cats are gray."

They were moving together now, talking wildly.

"But in the afternoon, I'm glad to say, the difference is obvious."

Outside the swallows were chattering at their nest under the eaves.

Andrew's mouth found Corinna's. The sheets were cool and smooth to their skin. Andrew let himself float away. It seemed he was rising out of his body, yet he was aware of nothing else but its physical sensations. Moving together, the rhythm grew faster, more urgent.

On the table beside the bed the phone began to ring.

Andrew stopped.

"No. No." Corinna said desperately. "Leave it. Don't answer it. Oh Andrew. Andrew."

The shrill ring of the phone continued. Whoever was calling was really persistent. Corinna and Andrew clung together, shutting their ears to the harsh sound, concentrating on their bodies.

Andrew could feel his climax approach, the irresistible, rising tide within him. He felt that Corinna was with him. The sound of the phone was there. Or perhaps it wasn't. All that existed for them was their bodies, the aching, deep private joy of their communion ...

For a while they were silent, floating still, slowly descending, ballooning by slow degrees to ground level.

"Who was that on the phone?"

"I don't know. It could have been anyone. It doesn't matter. If I'd been out with the horses I shouldn't have heard it."

"But you weren't out with the horses."

"No. But that doesn't mean I have to answer the phone."

Andrew drew away from her.

"What's the matter?"

"You're so sure of yourself, aren't you? All of you, you're so sure of yourselves."

"What do you mean, all of you?"

"All you people. Your family. All the people like you."

"Oh, I see." Her voice was cold. "No. I don't think it's us particularly. There's surely nothing wrong with being sure of yourself. It's a matter of knowing yourself for what you are. You don't have to be 'people like us' to be sure of yourself in that way."

Andrew leaned from the bed and found cigarettes and matches from his trousers' pocket on the floor.

"Cigarette?"

"No thanks."

He felt Corinna was watching him.

"It bothers you, doesn't it?" she said.

"What?"

"It bothers you that there are people like us. People that have things that you haven't. Without working for them."

"It doesn't bother me. It's a fact."

"Oh Andrew."

"What does bother me is when I see opportunities just not being used." He was fighting to control his irritation. It was true, it did bother him. The whole world was wide open to these people, and they couldn't even organize edible food. "When you are born with opportunities like that, you have a duty to take advantage of them. You *ought* to make some constructive use of them."

"And do you think I'm making 'constructive use?'"

"I don't know. I don't really . . ."

"Oh Andrew. Don't hedge. You don't, obviously."

Andrew drew on his cigarette through clenched jaws. Why did he have to treat Corinna like this? He couldn't even pay her the compliment of telling her the truth. And she was so frank and open with him. Even sexually she was frank, frank about wanting him. "Oh that was good," she had said, frankly acknowledging her own pleasure. But of course it was easy for these people. They were privileged. They could tell the truth. It didn't matter what they said. The rest of us, he thought bitterly, are vulnerable. The rest of us have to be careful, even with the truth.

The silence was broken by the sound of a car approaching the cottage. It stopped outside. Andrew looked at Corinna. She was staring at the ceiling, as if she had not heard it.

A car door slammed.

"Corinna!" The voice was Delphine's. She called urgently, angrily. "Corinna!"

Corinna did not move. Nor did Andrew. Some force held him down on the bed, some instinct that told him he was not part of the drama that was about to unfold in front of him.

"Corinna!" Delphine beat on the front door with her fists. "Corinna! Where are you? You must be here. The car is here. Someone must be here."

Now Andrew heard her in the room below them. "Corinna!" A note of anxiety had entered her voice. "Corinna! I have to see you. Where are you?"

The bedroom door burst open. Delphine gasped. "Oh! Oh! Corinna!"

Suddenly her voice was controlled. With deep, cold fury she said, "Corinna, you must come. Father is dead."

Delphine stood at the door. Her face was flushed. Her eyes ran over the two bodies. Andrew did not move to cover himself.

Delphine waited in her car outside the cottage until they came down.

They dressed in silence. There was nothing to say. Corinna had wanted her mother to see her in bed with Andrew. She recognized that, and was ashamed—as if Lord de Boys's dying were not painful enough, she had to add this sexual taunt, like a cheap whore. She had known when the phone rang what it was. She had deliberately ignored it. He was not *her* father, she had told herself. He could die with his own family, without the benefit of her attendance. When her real father died, would they gather at his bedside? Perhaps he was already dead. Perhaps he had died alone somewhere, without the comfort of the woman he loved, without the child of their union.

As they stood ready at the door of the bedroom, Corinna kissed Andrew solemnly. "Thank you," she said. "I enjoyed it."

Andrew held her arms and kissed her lightly. "That's what you said after our game of chess."

"Yes," she said. "I enjoyed that too."

When they appeared at the door Delphine drove off. Andrew followed. It was difficult to keep up with her. She was driving flat out, taking corners on the wrong side of the road, not even hesitating at crossroads, recklessly overtaking. Whenever they drew up close behind her, Corinna could see that she was hardly looking at the road, but turning her head from side to side, repeatedly adjusting the rearview mirror. She should not have been allowed to drive. Corinna cursed herself for not thinking of this. Del-

phine was in a state of shock. She was beside herself—
was it grief or anger?

By some miracle they reached the Hall without an
accident. As they turned in to the drive Corinna
looked across the lake to the house. She almost
gasped. The fact that for twenty-four hours she had
been refusing to acknowledge, hiding it in her heart
like a guilty secret, was there displayed for the world
to see: the de Boys standard was at half-mast.

# 5

EVEN IF HE HAD WANTED TO, Andrew could not have avoided Mel German. Andrew's job took him to the gallery openings and the parties of the art world—and at those events Gerry was practically a part of the furniture. But there were no more invitations to dinner at Gerry's house.

One evening Andrew took Gail to a candlelit reception at the Tate Gallery. It was a fine early fall night and, as they arrived, the glow of the setting sun still colored the sky. They paused on the steps and looked over the Thames. Mist was beginning to rise and the river barges seemed to be suspended just above the water.

"It's beautiful," Gail said.

"Yes," Andrew agreed. "Who needs painting?"

They laughed and went in.

Inside, the high rooms were already crowded. The candlelight, Andrew noticed, perfectly suited Gail's ivory skin and added a black intensity to her dark hair.

They spoke briefly to a number of people—the men all dressed formally in black ties. After a while they found themselves in a corner with Gerry. Gerry had evidently been working at getting his money's worth of champagne. But alcohol did not seem to give him a lift. He looked lonely and desperately unhappy. Andrew felt sorry for him.

Though not as sorry as Gerry was for himself. "Nobody wants to talk to me," he said miserably.

"We're talking to you," said Andrew.

Gerry touched his elbow. "Yes, dear boy. Of course, I do appreciate it. Thank you." He seemed perfectly serious. "Gail, my dear," he said as if he had just noticed her, "you look ravishing. What a handsome couple! But you know what I mean," he went on. "They don't even seem to want to laugh at me anymore."

"Who do you mean? Why did they laugh at you?"

"Oh, you know. Everybody. I know they were laughing at me. I didn't mind them laughing at me. As long as they don't ignore me. They can laugh at me as much as they like. It's the price I have to pay for them to take any notice of me at all."

"Oh Gerry. Don't be ridiculous."

"No. It's true. If there's one thing the law teaches you, it's to see things as they are and not to allow your judgment to be clouded by emotion. These people have tolerated me for two reasons. One was money. But I have only a very limited amount of that, as you know. And anyway, money alone is not enough. There are plenty of successful men about with more money than sense. But as well as a little money, I give them someone to laugh at. They like laughing at other people. I am vulgar, and ugly, and pathetic. . . ."

"Gerry. For God's sake. Don't do this to yourself."

He'd always suspected Gerry enjoyed the humiliation he got from some of these people. He actually looked for it. And now he was desperate that no one despised him any more.

Gerry took Andrew's elbow. "You're so kind to me, Andrew. You've always been kind to me. I'm very conscious of that." He drew Andrew and Gail further into the corner and turned his back to the crowded, noisy room. "As a matter of fact," he said, lowering his voice, "I was going to telephone you. Have you seen Lennox yet?"

"No. We're going tomorrow."

"I'm really looking forward to it," Gail said. "I think I liked Mr. Lennox."

"I've no doubt whatever that he took a shine to you too, my dear."

"In a funny way, he sort of reminded me of my father. He's different, but he reminded me of Dad a lot."

"I shouldn't tell him that if I were you." Gerry's voice became serious as he turned to Andrew. "How much do you know about Mr. Lennox, Andrew?"

"I know he's one of the fifty richest men in the United States. I know about his museum. . . ."

"Yes. He is extremely rich. Amazing. His name wasn't always Lennox. His father, I believe it was, was a Polish immigrant. You know how they are over there. There seems to be no *loyalty* to a family name." He sighed. "In one generation from rags to riches. It does actually happen. As I say, he is extremely rich. Fortunately, however," he added with a sly look at Andrew, "there are some things that money can't buy."

"But what can I do for him?"

"My dear boy, can't you guess? You know these multi-millionaires. You've lived in New York—where I understand the streets are paved with them. As soon as they realize they're rich, what's the first thing they want?"

"Good taste. Retrospectively."

"Well, culture, at least. I'm not sure that even they imagine they can acquire good taste. But culture they believe is attainable. They feel insecure about it, of course. They only understand the judgments of computers. Everything has to be put to them in terms of monetary value, so that the computer can read it. They manage it somehow. Even women are pretty well assessable. But with culture, they need someone to translate it for them into computer terms."

"Forget the philosophy, Gerry. What are you getting at?"

"Calm yourself, dear boy. I merely recommended to Mr. Lennox that you might be prepared to advise him in connection with acquisitions for his museum."

"That's nice of you, Gerry."

"Not at all. Not at all. As I told our friend Lennox, I only wished I could afford to make use of your services myself."

"Gerry, you old fraud. You know damn well you don't need me. . . ."

Gerry eased his collar with his finger. "My goodness, it's hot in here, isn't it?" Sweat was running off his forehead. In his black tie and dinner jacket, with his gross stomach bursting the starched white shirt, he looked, Andrew thought, like a penguin trapped in a Turkish bath.

"Go to see him, dear boy, at any rate. You never know."

Ashton Lennox's suite at Claridge's was colorless. The decor had not changed for forty years, and now it was fashionable again. Even the sprays of orchids in the vases were unobtrusive shades of cream and brown.

Andrew decided he agreed with Gail—he liked Lennox. Lennox was short and balding—not a very impressive figure. As they talked about painting, he was laconic, but he was direct. He tried to put himself over as some kind of red-necked philistine, but he really cared about painting. He was moved by the history of painting. "This actual paint was worked on this canvas three hundred years ago in a castle in Florence, while this princess, in this ermine, posed by this window"—that was the idea that really turned him on. It was a genuine, deeply felt response, and he was evidently somewhat embarrassed by it. He kept insisting that the prices were all that interested him. But Andrew could see that it was not true. His assistant, McIntyre—a stocky Scotsman of about forty, with graying hair and frown lines set permanently in his forehead—poured them drinks at the sideboard.

Then, without further introduction, McIntyre produced a list of paintings in alphabetical order.

Andrew glanced through it. Two hundred and thirty-four paintings were listed.

"You have all these?" Andrew asked.

"Yes," said Lennox. "Quite a shopping list, eh?"

"It's very impressive. What are the asterisks?"

McIntyre answered. "On those," he said, with great dignity, "the authenticity is not wholly satisfactory."

"In other words," said Lennox with a straight face, "there's some folk say they're fakes."

Meanwhile McIntyre had set up a portable screen and plugged in a projector. They gave Gail and Andrew a tour on slides of the museum in Santa Barbara, all fifty-two rooms, and close-ups of all the major paintings. McIntyre gave a running commentary, with facts about each of the paintings, which he had obviously repeated many times before. It was almost as bad as movies of a vacation.

But apart from the commentary, Andrew *was* impressed. Many of the paintings he recognized. They had been on the market over the past three or four years. Two Gainsboroughs and a Van Dyck came from a sale at Christie's less than a year before. Almost all the big names in painting were represented. They must have added up to a cool fortune of several million dollars.

In some cases Andrew too would have had grave doubts about the authenticity. The Raphael was almost certainly a student copy. The Titian looked like a fake—though it was difficult to tell with Titian. But no matter—it was still a very impressive show.

"How long have you been collecting, Mr. Lennox?" he asked.

"Five years," said Lennox, allowing a slight hint of pride to enter his voice. "What do you think?"

"I think it's a remarkable achievement," said Andrew. "Remarkable."

"And would you say the collection was—weak any place?"

"The Italian Renaissance. But that's inevitable. They're in short supply. There are almost no genuine Renaissance pieces that will ever come on the market again."

"Yes?" Lennox spoke to Andrew, but he looked at Gail as he talked. Now and then he gave her a brief, conspiratorial smile.

"The moderns. There's very little post-Impressionist. Perhaps that's a matter of taste?"

"It is, as you say, a matter of taste. I don't hold with that abstract junk."

"If you don't mind my saying so, you may well find you grow to appreciate it in time. Painting is like music. Many people think they'll never grow to like the progressive stuff. But after a while they find they get to like it. . . ."

"Maybe," said Lennox laconically. "Anything else?"

"The Dutch," Andrew said. "The Van Dyck is beautiful. It's a great painting. But the Rembrandt—that's a very minor Rembrandt. If I had to guess I'd say it was painted by a student. Rembrandt often signed student work if he liked it. Honestly, I don't think he should have signed this one."

"Good." Lennox said simply.

"Good? Why?"

"Because it's a fake. McIntyre here says it's not, but I'm telling you it is."

McIntyre opened his mouth to object but thought better of it.

"So you see," said Lennox, as if it were a simple matter, "what we need is a genuine Rembrandt. The real McCoy. A few other little things as well of course, but Rembrandt's right there at the top of the list. Think you can do that for us?"

"Well," said Andrew cautiously, "as a matter of fact, I think I might."

Lennox's expression showed nothing. He could have made his millions playing poker. "Good," he said. He held out his hand. "Mr. Tait, you are working for us."

They shook hands.

"You have my word on it. You can work out the details with McIntyre later."

"Okay."

"I want the Lennox Museum put right there on the

map of the art world. A big red spot. A capital. Not just a hick town. . . . How much is my Rembrandt going to cost me, Mr. Tait?"

"Two million dollars. Two and a half. Maybe three." He avoided looking at Gail. "I know where it is. I just have to get it for you."

"Okay. Whenever you're ready."

Before he left, Andrew had arranged with McIntyre to have a duplicate of the "shopping list," and he was going back before Lennox left Europe with suggestions for filling in the gaps in the collection. He also had a commission to round up a dozen paintings for Lennox to take home as gifts for his family.

"You know," said Lennox, "good minor stuff, say a couple of thousand dollars apiece." Andrew agreed to work for seven and a half percent. Gerry had warned him he would have to offer himself at bargain rates.

Outside Claridge's the doorman had a row of cabs at his disposal. He made to open the door of the first in line as Andrew and Gail walked out. But Andrew waved him away.

"Let's walk a little," he said to Gail. "It's a beautiful day."

They walked up through Grosvenor Square, past the American Embassy to Park Lane and crossed into Hyde Park.

The afternoon sun on the fall colors of the trees gave a golden light to the whole park.

"It's beautiful," Gail said. "The grass is so green."

"Rain," said Andrew. "You just happen to have chosen the annual three weeks of English sunshine."

Gail laughed. "Phooey," she said. "You British just like to say that."

"Were you bored by Lennox?"

"Not at all. Absolutely not. I had a marvelous time."

"He hardly spoke to you."

"Oh, I understand that type," she said. "He didn't have to talk to me." She smiled. "But he appreciated me."

"Do I hear a note of criticism aimed in this direction?"

"Oh no." She put her arm through his as they walked by the lake. "I didn't mean that. Not at all."

But it was true that Andrew was preoccupied. The Rembrandt business had really set his heart beating. Here at last was the break he had been waiting for. There was only one good Rembrandt in Europe that there was any hope of prying loose. And that was a great Rembrandt, Lennox would really love it. That was important, the real art of dealing—matching the painting to the buyer. For a good work, one his collection needs, a collector will pay a high price. For something he really falls for, he will ignore his financial advisers and go mad. *The Nude Diana* was absolutely Lennox's painting. Andrew knew it was. Now he had to prize it loose from Boys Hall.

# 6

IT WAS A BUSY TIME for Andrew at the gallery.
They were getting together two separate traveling exhibitions of British artists, which were to tour in the
winter. As usual, everyone was behind schedule. The
artists did not deliver their work on time. The framers
were late. The packing cases took two weeks longer
to make than planned. The printers failed to keep
their date.

Andrew himself had written the catalogue introduction for the show of British Surrealist Art—the first
serious study of the British branch of the Surrealist
movement ever undertaken. After touring ten cities,
the show was to end up at the Gallery of Modern Art
during the following summer.

His job was going well, but it no longer gave him
any satisfaction. He had been doing it so long it was
becoming a routine. At thirty, there were not many
years left of being a bright young man. Finding a
backer for a gallery of his own seemed as remote as
ever. Even for reliable enterprises the financial atmo-

sphere was very cool—and contemporary British painting could hardly be promoted as a gilt-edged investment.

Quite frequently he spent the weekend with Corinna at her cottage. Often the whole weekend would pass without his seeing anyone from Boys Hall. Corinna protected her privacy fiercely. She grew vegetables and fruit in her garden, and her two horses demanded much of her time.

She and Andrew were quietly comfortable together. They avoided tricky subjects. They each knew the limitations of the other's commitment.

Corinna never came to London. She didn't see any reason to. Andrew took Gail to watch Chelsea in the first football match of the season, against Tottenham Hotspurs ("the Spurs"). At first she couldn't understand how the players could keep their hands off the ball. But it was easy to get the hang of it, and she was soon able to understand what was going on. The crowd was wildly enthusiastic, and she actually found herself cheering on "her" side.

She saw Andrew once or twice a week. He never asked her to come to his apartment. He was usually away on weekends. She didn't ask where. But one evening, when they had been to a movie and were waiting in a Greek restaurant for their order to arrive, he filled her glass from the bottle of wine and said, "I think I might owe you an explanation."

"Oh? Why?"

"I don't know—I suppose I feel I ought to make myself clear."

"In what way?"

"Well. We see one another quite often. . . ."

He seemed embarrassed. "Are you trying to tell me something?" Gail asked. "That you're—gay?"

He laughed down his nose. "No. No—is that what you thought?"

"I wondered. It doesn't matter."

"No. It's just, well, I guess I'm not any good at more than one relationship at a time. I'm not even sure I'm too good at just the one."

"You don't have to make explanations. . . . Really, I enjoy seeing you. It's simple. I don't have to come out with you. I do because I like to."

"No. Well, I just wanted to make myself clear."

Gail put her hand over his. "I'm pretty good at being a friend," she said. "I like friendship."

Corinna asked Andrew to the cottage one weekend—to protect her, she said. On the Sunday afternoon Lord de Boys's will was to be read. The family lawyer was coming from London.

"It's the traditional way," she answered, when Andrew asked why such formality was necessary. "An awful lot depends on it."

"I can believe that," Andrew said.

"Polly and Sally are stalking about up there at the house with tragic expressions."

"But they won't be present when the will is read?"

"Good heavens, no. Strictly family."

After breakfast on Saturday morning they had saddled Corinna's horses and ridden for two hours through the woods and fields of the estate. They had not seen a single person. The hay had been carted, and the wheat was dark gold. The countryside was peaceful. It was that waiting period, the lull before the activity of harvest.

When they got back they watered the horses and rubbed them down. Then they went upstairs to bathe. Corinna was due at the Hall for lunch at 12:30.

"When it comes to money, people can turn really nasty," Corinna said as she sat on the edge of the bed. "Believe me, I trusted Father. While he was alive, I was one of the family. But now—well, it might just be convenient to remember that I'm not really 'family' after all."

"Your mother will look after you."

"I wish I could be sure.... Give my boot a tug, would you?"

"But surely . . . ?" Andrew gripped the heel and toe of her slender black leather boot and drew it off.

"She has her own problems."

"Maybe she's doing a bit of a Lady Macbeth herself."

Corinna laughed. "Something like that," she said lightly.

Andrew drew off the other boot.

"Anyway, it isn't really fair to ask you to protect me from my own family."

"I don't mind."

"And it's certainly not the only reason I asked you here."

"Oh?" he said, looking up with a smile. "And how else, pray, might I be of service?" He had put down her boots and was squatting on his haunches at her feet.

"Take off your clothes, and I'll show you."

Andrew laughed and stood up. "Shameless. Quite shameless. I shall need protection. *I* shall ask *your* family for protection. . . ."

"I wanted to when we were in the woods, but you didn't seem . . ."

"I was too busy making sure I didn't fall off that horse. She can't have been exercised for weeks."

"She's used to me, that's all. No one else rides her."

She smiled. "Perhaps if you had fallen off, it might have occurred to you."

"I don't have your imagination. That's my trouble."

They made love lightheartedly. Andrew lay on his back. Corinna sat astride him. They made a joke of it. She directed him into her, gripping him with her knees—riding him with the same smooth graceful rhythm she had ridden her horse two hours before.

While she showered and dressed to go off to the Hall, Andrew lay and smoked a cigarette. . . . He wondered why he had allowed Corinna to take the initiative. She had wanted him to make love to her earlier in the morning out in the woods—and he had not even thought of it. It was not usually like that. He could not understand it. He really cared about Corinna. Yet he could not resist congratulating himself that she had asked him down to be with her on the very weekend that the future of the Boys inheritance would be settled.

He tried to put the thought out of his mind. But he could feel the depression settling in. He was glad Corinna had to go to the Hall and leave him alone to fight it.


Conversation over lunch was stilted. No one dared ask the questions they all wanted to know. The lawyer did not help. Nothing seemed to interest him. An owlish old man, he seemed embarrassed by the situation. By the end of the meal all of them were convinced that the will contained provisions that would put everyone of them out on the street.

Delphine suggested they ask for coffee to be served in the library.

The lawyer, seated at the leather-topped desk, accepted brandy and a cigar. He seemed quite an expert. He held the cigar under his nose and smelled it carefully. He produced his own silver cigar cutter and delicately trimmed the end. Before he finally lit it he warmed the tip with half a dozen matches.

Lady Amelia sat in a deep leather armchair and watched him with ill-concealed impatience.

Eventually, releasing a cloud of smoke and a heavy sigh of satisfaction, the lawyer cleared his throat. "This is a sad occasion for us all," he began. "I will be as brief as possible. The document before me on this desk is the last will and testament of the late Lord David de Boys. In a moment I shall acquaint you with its contents." He cleared his throat and drew deeply at the cigar. "It is quite short. As I am sure all of you know, the lands and estates of the mansion of Boys Hall were not within the gift of the late Lord de Boys. Being entailed, they passed automatically on Lord de Boys's death to the elder extant son and heir, Giles." He nodded briefly in Giles's direction.

Lady Amelia snorted. "Why doesn't he get on with it?" she stage-whispered to Corinna.

The lawyer cleared his throat. " 'I, David Herbert Richard Suivant Proudfoot, fourteenth Baron de Boys, hereby revoke all former wills and testamentary dispositions made by me and declare this to be my last will . . .' "

Corinna glanced right and left at the semicircle of expectant faces. Anxiety, tension, even fear showed in every one. You might have thought they were criminals awaiting sentence, not a devoted family expecting a share of paternal benefits. And in a way, she thought, they *were* awaiting sentence—a sentence to a type of life, harsh or easy according to the whim of Lord de Boys.

Delphine's hands were clasped in her lap. Her knuckles showed white. Her name did not occur in the first part of the will. There were a number of small bequests, to Lord de Boys's batman, who had worked at the Hall after the war; to Carol Baxter and two or three other of the Hall estate servants.

The next section dealt with Lady Amelia. It was Lord de Boys's earnest wish that she be allowed to remain at the Mill House for the remainder of her life should she so desire. All the paintings by Canaletto at present hanging in the Mill House became her property absolutely.

Delphine's face was like stone.

"'To my son Timothy, I bequeath any such six paintings that he may select from those I die possessed of, to dispose of as he may wish.'"

Giles and Timothy exchanged a quick glance. But Giles turned away almost immediately, as the lawyer read out his name. To him Lord de Boys left all the contents of Boys Hall and the entire residue of his estate, expressing the wish that he preserve it as far as possible without decrease for posterity and successive generations of the Proudfoot family. At the same time he entrusted to Giles the care of Lord de Boys's wife and Giles's mother, Lady de Boys, knowing that he could rely on Giles to make proper provision for her comfort and livelihood from the income of the estates. He further expressed the desire that Delphine, who had done so much to create Boys Hall in its modern form, should be permitted to remain in residence therein for the remainder of her natural life.

"These are all the material clauses. The remainder are concerned only with the formalities of administration and estate duty."

Then, almost before any of them realized what he

was doing, he rose from his chair, quickly shook hands with them each in turn, and left the room.

Delphine was the first to collect herself. Without a word she stood up and walked regally from the room.

The whole family filed out of the library in silence, avoiding one another's eyes. Polly and Sally were waiting in the saloon. They were pale and tense, but dignified, both of them. Like the wives of condemned men, Corinna thought. Everyone moved as if in a carefully rehearsed mime, finding their partners and separating to different parts of the house.

Giles and Polly went up to his study in the East Wing. Polly went to the window and stood looking out over the park.

"Well?" she said.

Giles briefly ran through the provisions of the will. As he went on Polly's face began to assume a satisfied expression. She frowned momentarily at the bequest of paintings to Timothy. But she did not care much about paintings herself, and half a dozen fewer paintings from the hundreds in the house would hardly leave noticeable spaces on the walls.

When Giles came to the final clause a triumphant smile came to her lips.

"The entire residue? What does that mean?"

"Everything else, presumably. All Father possessed when he died."

"But what about your mother? Does she have money of her own? She says she hasn't a bean. Or did he provide for her while he was alive?"

Giles went to the bookshelves. One section of the shelves opened out, being in fact a door with rows of leather spines glued to it. In the cupboard behind were drinks and glasses.

"Would you like a drink?" he asked.

"No, thank you," said Polly.

"Well, I think I shall. Are you sure?"

"Yes, quite sure."

Giles poured himself a generous scotch. He drank the first mouthful with exaggerated pleasure. "Ah. That's better," he said.

"You haven't answered my question." Polly was beginning to suspect that something was wrong.

"What question?"

"You know. What about your mother?"

"Oh yes, well . . ."

"You're looking very sheepish, Giles," Polly said sharply. "What is it?"

"Well. Father wants—Father *wanted* Mother to go on living here, in the Hall, that is . . ."

"No."

"Well, I'm sorry, old girl . . ."

"Never."

"Well, I'm afraid that's what the will said."

"But you said he left everything to you—the entire residue, you said. The house is yours already. How can the will give your mother the right to the house when it's already yours?"

"Well, it doesn't give her the right, that's true. It's Father's wish. He particularly wished that she continue to live in this house, which she has done so much to create."

"To create? To create? She practically ruined it. Your mother is the worst thing that's happened to this house for five hundred years."

"It hasn't been here that long."

"Oh, you know what I mean. The swimming pool. It's the most vulgar thing I've ever seen. That new wing of hers. It looks like a cheap plastic box. You should hear what people say about the things she's done here. . . . She's the laughingstock of the county. Of the *country*. She's spent a fortune on rubbish. Absolute rubbish. Imagine paying someone to plough up the lawn. Heaven knows how much she paid him—paid to have the grounds ruined."

She was beside herself with fury. Her eyes were blazing, and angry patches of red had appeared on her cheeks.

Giles sipped at his whisky and watched her with a strangely calm expression.

Polly turned to the window and pointed out into the garden. "Look at them. *Look* at them."

On the lawn below the window, two of Delphine's sculptures were visible—one rising from the ground like giant sections of plumbing, made of polished shining steel; the other consisted of iron girders leaning against one another, apparently casually, painted raspberry and almond green.

"You know, I am ashamed. When people ask me what they are and I have to tell them they are sculptures, part of your mother's priceless collection of modern art, I am ashamed, I tell you."

"But why?" said Giles quietly. "Why should you be ashamed?"

"Well!" she said, as if the answer was too obvious to need expressing.

"Why should you feel ashamed? They're nothing to do with you."

Polly looked at him incredulously. "But surely you don't intend—you never intended to keep them? Don't tell me you like them, I know you don't. You told me a hundred times . . ."

"No. I don't like them. I don't understand them.

But I certainly was not intending to remove them. I don't understand French poetry either, but I should not want it destroyed."

"But . . ." Polly looked at him as if she were seeing him for the first time, as if at that moment she had realized that all she knew about him was based on totally false assumptions.

"Polly," he said, "I intend to carry out my father's wishes. Mother will remain in this house for the rest of her life."

"But no one else can ever be mistress of this house while she is here."

"Perhaps not," said Giles with a lethal calm. "Is that all you want, Polly, to be mistress of this house?"

"Of course not. Of course not, Giles."

"You have a simple choice."

"I want to be your wife."

"To live here with me on those terms . . . ?"

"I love you, Giles."

"Or not live here at all. And if I ever hear a single word of disrespect from you towards my mother—at any time, either to her face or behind her back, you will go."

Her tone changed suddenly. Her anger returned. "You wouldn't dare."

"I assure you."

She stepped back and looked him up and down. "My God! What sort of a mother's boy are you? You don't have to take any notice of the will. It's not legally binding; you said so yourself. You're frightened of her, that's what it is, you're frightened of her. Tied to your mother's apron strings. It's taken this to make me realize it. That's something, I suppose. Do you think I'd want to marry a man like that? A mother's boy, that's what you are."

"I don't think you really mean that, Polly." Giles's voice was icy.

Polly ran to him. "Oh no. No. I didn't mean it. Oh Giles, I didn't mean it. Forgive me." She clung to him, sobbing. "I didn't mean it. I was so upset. Forgive me. It's been so terrible, Giles. It's been such a terrible strain."

Giles held her in his arms. Polly buried her head in his shoulder. But Giles was looking over her head at the sculpture out in the grounds. As he watched, a peacock on its favorite perch proudly opened the giant fan of its tail. A hundred eyes stared at Giles, unblinking.

Alberto rang the first gong for dinner as usual at 7:30.

Corinna and Andrew were alone in the drawing room. They had arrived ten minutes before. No one else had come down yet.

In the car on the way over Corinna had told Andrew about the will. She would not speak about it earlier. She had come back from the Hall, pale and evidently distressed. "Let's go to bed," was all she would say. "What, again?" Andrew had laughed. "No," she had answered. "I don't want sex, I just want to be with you. To be close." Even so, as she clung to him, her hand found and grasped him. Andrew had tenderly made love to her. The third time that day already, he thought, and only five in the afternoon.

In the car she had tried to tell him how she felt. That was not easy, since she was not at all sure herself.

"I'm certainly not upset," she said. But she was not sure if even that was true. "I don't need money," she answered Andrew's unspoken question. "The cottage is mine. I have a small income from Granny—from Amelia. I don't need much. Giles gives me feed for the horses."

"But the will didn't say anything. He didn't mention you?"

"No. That's it. That's what hurts. He didn't have to give me anything, but at least ..." Her voice broke, and she turned away from Andrew. The road was narrow and the hedges sped by close to her face. "He could have acknowledged my existence. Left me some little thing—a ring or something. I don't understand. I loved him. I loved him as if he were my father. And now ..."

She left the sentence unfinished. For the rest of the journey she was silent. She found a handkerchief in her bag and now and then pressed it to her eyes.

The second dinner gong sounded at 7:45. Dinner would be ready at 8:00. Corinna and Andrew were still alone.

"Where is everyone?" Andrew asked.

"They're all afraid. They're afraid if they're alone with anyone, the others will think they're cooking something up."

"Christ," said Andrew. "It's worse than politics."

"Yes."

They lapsed into silence. Andrew looked at the morning's *Times.* Corinna held the *Telegraph* in front of her, but her eyes did not focus on it.

On the stroke of the hour the rest of the family appeared. Delphine was at her most impressive. She wore a long, narrowly fitting gown of black velvet. Her hair was drawn back and coiled meticulously on top of her head. It was the first time Andrew had seen her without at least one piece of her famous jewelry. She wore no more than her wedding and engagement rings. Giles and Polly followed down the stairs. Timothy and Sally were at their heels.

Delphine did not even sit down. "Let us go in to dinner," she said.

Then at the door of the dining room, she stopped. "Giles," she said. "I hope you don't mind. I told Alberto to rearrange the table."

Only at one end of the table was a place laid. "You are now the head of the family. You shall sit at the top."

"Oh Mother," said Giles. "I don't want it to be like that."

"I'm sorry, Giles," Delphine said firmly, "but I think you should understand the responsibility of your position."

She took Polly's arm. "Now, my dear," she said, "you come and sit over here."

Polly followed her obediently. She understood the significance of Delphine's placing perfectly well. Delphine herself was to sit on one side of Giles, Corinna on the other. They were family. They belonged there. Polly, at the other end of the table, between Timothy and Andrew, was a *guest*. Well, she thought, that's pretty well what she was: like a guest, she was there on sufferance of the host. Even when she and Giles were married, she'd still be a guest, as long as Delphine was on the scene. But she was smiling. She'd pasted a noncommittal smile on her face before she stepped out of Giles's study, and she knew she damn well had to keep it there.

Alberto served the soup and poured the first glasses of wine.

As soon as he left the room, Delphine said, "I think we should talk about the subject that is in all our minds, don't you?" She was addressing Giles. "I'm quite sure we don't have any secrets from the guests we have asked to be with us at this sad time."

She gave Andrew a hard, antagonistic glance. But she had other fish to fry.

Giles mumbled, "Yes, yes. Of course."

"I'm sure you are all relieved to know the contents of Father's will. Of course he had discussed it with me. But it didn't seem right for me to tell you what he intended."

In fact, Corinna had said, the will had knocked Delphine sideways. That made sense, Andrew thought. She was now totally dependent on her son. She would hate that. But she had made a rapid recovery. She had not wasted the last few hours. She had it all worked out, and she dominated the table. Andrew wondered if it could be generations of inbreeding that rendered the Proudfoot males so ineffectual, so easily dominated by new female blood. Perhaps it was a genetic fault. These tough females, like Delphine and Lady Amelia, married into the family, but they did not pass on their own qualities to their offspring.

"Of course, you must all have known that Father would provide for us, but still, it is a relief to be *sure.*" She smiled at Polly. "We can all go on living here, just as we always have, which, of course, is exactly what Father wanted." Her manner was grave but charming. She looked around the table. No one was eating. "Giles," she said, "don't you think you should press the bell for Alberto?"

Giles blushed. "Oh yes," he said. "Sorry, I knew I shouldn't have sat here." He pressed the button under the carpet at his feet.

Alberto took away the soup plates and served roast lamb, carved wafer-thin and swimming in gravy.

When he had gone, Delphine turned to Timothy. "Timmy darling," she said, "I don't know how you feel about things ..."

Timothy shrugged. Andrew watched him closely. He could see that Sally's knee was pressed against Timothy's under the table.

"... but I must admit that Father and I did not agree about what he wanted to do for you. As you know, I did try to persuade him to finance you in a—a venture of your own while he was still, while he was still with us. I really did think that would be best."

Timothy was watching her warily. Andrew felt the excitement begin to knot his stomach.

"To tell you the truth, darling, I think Father misunderstood me. After all, he did expressly ask Giles to preserve our inheritance, 'without decrease' I think was the lawyer's expression."

"Yes," said Timothy.

"I think he felt so unhappy that he couldn't do what I had asked for you. I honestly don't think he wanted to split things up. He wanted to help you, of course, darling. I'm not saying he didn't want to help you. ..."

"If you're talking about the paintings ..."

"Yes, I am, darling. That's what we're all concerned with, surely. We none of us would want to see a single one of the things we all treasure so having to leave the Hall. Once things go out, they never come back, do they? And our things are irreplaceable, that's the point. Once they're gone, they're lost for ever. Of course, if you want to borrow paintings for your flat, or a house, well, I'm sure Giles ..."

"Well, actually, Mother"—Timothy's voice was deceptively casual—"we've already decided on our paintings."

"We?" said Delphine sharply.

"Sally and I. We decided this afternoon."

Delphine looked at Sally as if only her influence might cause Timothy to defy her.

"Look, I say," said Giles, "it would be the most damned awful shame . . ."

But Delphine came straight to the point. "And which have you decided to *take?*"

"Well, actually, we haven't decided exactly which. What we have decided is to have only one really big painting. We decided that would make less of a hole than half a dozen medium-range things. We don't want to take them either. We don't want to take Proudfoot things." He was talking to Giles, not his mother. "Obviously we could take the six biggest of the lot—the Raphael, the Rembrandt, and so on. I suppose we could have lived in luxury for the rest of our lives. But we worked it out the other way. We started with how much we thought we'd need, and tried to think how we could get that and do the least damage."

"How much you would need for *what?*" said Delphine.

"To open a gallery, Mother," Timothy said patiently.

Andrew felt his heart jump. It was almost a physical sensation. His eyes were smarting with excitement.

"But those paintings are our *inheritance*," said Giles. "I mean, Timmy, Father asked us to do all we can to preserve that. Isn't that what we all want?"

"He gave me the pictures to sell, Giles. He knew I had to have money. The will says to 'to dispose of', doesn't it?"

"But Timmy, you *can't*." Giles looked helplessly at his mother. "You can't just sell our paintings."

Andrew had been pretending to concentrate on his food. Now he put down his knife and fork and said. "Giles. How do you intend to pay the duty on what you have inherited?"

"I fail to see what concern that might be of yours, young man."

"Mother!" said Corinna. "Really!"

Andrew looked steadily up the table at Giles, waiting for an answer. He was cool now. In anticipation he was always nervous. When the engagement finally came, he was cold as steel.

"I . . ." stammered Giles.

"You'll have to sell paintings, surely? The contents of the house are worth millions. The paintings alone. You'll have to pay duty on that. And Lord de Boys must have known that. He must have expected that you would have to sell quite a number of paintings. Otherwise he would have made them over to you in his lifetime. Or at least made some other provision."

Delphine was trembling with rage. "How do you come to know the contents of my husband's will?" she asked.

"Because I told him, Mother," Corinna said quietly.

"It's not a secret, Delphine," Andrew said. He could see from her expression that she regretted insisting he call her by her first name. "Anyone can get a copy of the will from Somerset House."

"Exactly," said Timothy. "Thank you, Andrew. It's not fair to treat us as some sort of—well, traitors, when you're going to do exactly the same yourself."

"But Giles has no alternative," Delphine said. "He will be assessed on the whole of Father's estate."

"I believe he could refuse the gift," said Andrew.

"Oh really!" Delphine snorted.

"And the more valuable the paintings we take, the less duty Giles will have to pay."

"Timothy, be serious. How can you joke about this?"

"I am serious. I've never been more serious. We've given it a great deal of thought."

"One afternoon!"

"You can do a great deal of thinking in one afternoon, Mother, if you have to."

"And what did you decide, then? Which of our paintings are you going to take from us?"

"Well, it was a matter really between the Raphael and the Rembrandt."

"Oh no!"

"But I don't think we'll need as much as the Raphael."

"Oh no! No!"

"Is Raphael worth more than Rembrandt?" Polly asked. She had not spoken during the whole meal, and she was beginning to feel she had to say something.

"Yes," snapped Delphine with a really vicious smile.

"It's quite complicated," Timothy went on, "because of course we shall have to pay duty ourselves on whatever the paintings fetch. The Raphael would fetch two million at least. Above one million pounds, the estate duty is 85 percent anyway. By the time we've paid the auctioneer's commission we should be out of pocket."

Andrew was beginning to think he had underestimated Timothy. He was shrewd and clearheaded. And thinking straight in that company needed a really cool nerve.

"We! We! We!" Delphine almost shouted at him. "Who is 'we?' This is your responsibility, Timothy. You can't avoid responsibility by trying to share it. You are responsible. You will bear the responsibility for what you are doing for the rest of your life."

Something terrible seemed to be happening to Delphine. Andrew watched with horror. Defiance of her authority seemed to be destroying her. Her face was collapsing.

"And what," she said hoarsely, "what did you decide?"

"We decided that the Rembrandt would be best. The *Diana*."

"Oh no! Oh no!" She held her chin high. Her face was a tragic mask. Tears ran from her eyes, streaming down her cheeks. "Timmy," she almost whispered. "Timmy, darling. *Please*. Please, for my sake. Not the *Diana*. That painting—that painting I love best in the whole house. Anything but that. Please. Take anything but that."

"But Mother"—Tim spoke evenly, but his jaw was clenched—"it will be painful whatever we take. What would you rather? The *Madonna?*"

"Yes. Anything." She was trembling with emotion. "Take the *Madonna*. But not the Rembrandt. Not the *Diana*."

"No." Giles's voice was firm. "Not the *Madonna*. That painting must never leave the house. That is the Proudfoot Raphael."

"Timmy. Please. I beg you. Not the *Diana*."

"Giles." Corinna's voice was quiet but firm. "We are all upset. This is surely not the time to decide." She stood up. "If you'll excuse me, I think I shall go home."

Corinna and Andrew talked long into the night. But Andrew did not tell her of the things he was hoping for himself. For one thing he believed in the power of secrecy. Shared plans never succeed. And he wasn't sure she would understand. He had the feeling that it would sound far cruder in words than it did in his head.

Two great chances had opened before him at once. If only he could pull off the double—persuade Timothy to sell the Rembrandt to Lennox, and then to invest the proceeds in a gallery with Andrew as partner. No wonder he was not able to sleep. He lay in the dark and listened to the unfamiliar country noises: an owl hunting, a fox barking in the wood, sparrows fidgeting in the eaves. Corinna slept peacefully beside him. It was an effort to make himself lie still.

Soon after breakfast next morning, Timothy phoned. He wanted to come to see Andrew.

"Do you want me to be out?" Corinna asked Timothy.

"Well . . . well, no, it doesn't matter."

"That's all right. I've loads to do in the stables. Would Sally like to exercise the horses with me?"

"Well, I think she'd like to be there."

"Oh all right."

"It sounds awfully mysterious," Corinna said to Andrew. "I hope they're not plotting something. I told you it would be like this."

"You did. And to tell the truth, I didn't really believe you."

But his mind was filled with his own plans. And plots, he thought, is only the word for plans you disapprove of. He lit a cigarette. His hand was shaking.

Tim and Sally, on the other hand, were brisk and

self-possessed. Andrew had never seen them like this. They really were together. They both wore superbly tailored tweed suits, not quite his and hers. Andrew poured them the coffee Corinna had left, but they did not waste time with polite talk.

"We wanted to thank you for your support last night," Timothy said.

"Oh. Well. That's all right. I only said what I thought."

"Nasty business," said Tim.

"Your mother seemed extremely upset."

"I shouldn't worry too much about that," Tim said drily. "She has a low threshold of emotion. I've seen it too often to be much affected. And usually when she is not getting her own way."

Sally left the talking to Timothy. She was watching Andrew. Knowing her dislike, he found her scrutiny disconcerting.

"How much should we get for the Rembrandt?"

"One million, eight hundred thousand pounds."

"You're very precise."

"That's my job," Andrew replied. He smiled. "And I am also accurate." He could also be briskly confident.

"Yes. That's what we thought," Sally said. "More or less."

"Sally's incredible," Timothy said proudly. "She always knows exactly what a picture will fetch."

"She works in the right place. But of course, a lot depends—on what else is about. And who."

"Yes," they both said together.

There was an awkward silence. Andrew offered them more coffee. They both refused. So he waited for them to tell him why they had come to see him.

"Well," said Timothy, "I expect you're wondering

why we came to see you. Well, the fact is, we thought we ought to tell you what we plan to do."

Andrew felt his throat tighten. "Oh yes?" he said. He hoped he sounded casual. "I gathered last night you *are* going to get into the gallery game. That's marvelous. Can you tell me about it?"

"Yes, well, that's roughly it. We shall go and stay at the castle for a while, while the formalities are sorted out. Sally has some holiday due."

"The castle?"

"Sally's parents' place. Then we shall put the *Diana* up at Christie's."

Timothy's tone seemed to indicate that staying at the castle and selling a Rembrandt are everyday matters.

"The thing is," Timothy went on, "we thought— well, Sally thought—" he glanced in her direction but she was looking out of the window. Andrew held his breath. "We thought it was only fair . . . well, we thought perhaps you were interested in some sort of partnership with us . . ."

Andrew opened his mouth to speak, but Timothy continued.

". . . but, well, it would be super, of course. I'm sure you'd be a terrific help—but, well, we decided in the end we'd rather like to try and make a go of it on our own. I'm sure you'll understand."

Andrew could taste the disappointment like bile at the back of his throat. "Yes, of course," he managed to say. "Of course I understand. I think I should probably want to do the same myself, if I were in your place."

He smiled as he said it. But the bitterness was choking him. It was Sally who had set this up. He guessed that. "Sally thought it was only fair. . . ."

If she thought it was so damn fair, why was she so busy avoiding his eye and looking out at the apple trees in the orchard? She must have seen them a hundred times before. She was getting a kick out of it. She'd got Timothy to come to the cottage just so she could watch him rub Andrew's nose in it.

He didn't intend to give her the satisfaction of seeing his disappointment.

Perhaps it was not the best time to raise the idea of Lennox buying the *Diana*, but it was the only time he had. He could see that they could hardly wait to get the picture off the wall and up to Christie's in St. James's. And it was not going to be easy to persuade them. Now that the cards were on the table, Sally was watching him as if he had crawled out of a crack in the wall.

Andrew had two arguments in his favor. First, that by selling to Lennox, they avoided the auctioneer's commission.

"But when you get above ten thousand, the commission's only ten percent," Timothy said.

"Ten percent of two million is twenty thousand."

"And eighty-five percent of it goes to the Estate Duty Office."

"So does eighty-five percent of the rest of whatever you get. You'll need to keep every penny you can."

"But it's important to Sally. Don't you see, Andrew? Christie's will be pleased she brought it in."

"She'll be leaving anyway, surely?"

"Oh no. Not for a year at least. Not till the gallery is on its feet."

But he could see that his second argument got home to Timothy: selling to Lennox would be discreet. A sale at Christie's would get maximum press coverage. Famous Rembrandts are not sold ev-

ery week. The TV cameras would record every detail.
The gossip columnists would be up at Boys Hall getting the reactions of the family. Particularly Delphine, the famous collector. And that was a reaction
Andrew was sure Timothy and Sally would rather
avoid.

"Yes. But we could suffer it if necessary. And I
somehow think Mother would take care not to make
too much of a fool of herself in print."

"But that's not the real point. A sale to Lennox
could be discreet, yes. But much more important—the
actual price could be secret. I'm sure Lennox would
cooperate. We could fix an 'official' price and arrange
some sort of additional payment on the side. There
are ways and means. The Estate Duty Office need
never know."

"I see," said Timothy thoughtfully.

"You're really going to have to think about that estate duty. If you're not careful, you'll find yourself
without even enough left to set yourself up. Eighty-
five percent away from anything doesn't leave much
to put in the bank."

"Well, yes. We had realized that it isn't going to be
easy."

Sally crossed the room and stood by Timothy. She
faced Andrew squarely.

"I don't think you understand," she said. "I'm sorry,
Andrew, but the fact is that Timothy and I would just
rather not do business with you."

"I see."

"I never liked you, as I think you know."

"You've made it quite clear."

"I've always tried to be polite. After all, you were a
friend of Timothy's."

"Oh, you've always been exceedingly polite. And you don't have to spoil it now. I get the message."

Andrew turned on his heel and walked from the room. There was no point in staying. She really hated him. Argument about it was not going to do any good.

He crossed the yard to the stables. The black mare he had ridden the day before was in her stall. Corinna was out on the bay gelding, her other horse. Why did they have to cut the balls off everything, he thought?

He was almost blind with rage and frustration, but he worked frantically. The mare's tack hung where he had left it. He lifted the saddle from the post and laid it on the mare. She began to shift her feet uneasily. Andrew reached under her belly for the girth. He speedily fastened the buckle, tight enough for him just to be able to slip his hand sideways under it. Then with a sudden sharp movement he tightened it another two holes. The mare lay back her ears, sliding away from him.

"Stand still," Andrew hissed at her.

He slid the bridle over her muzzle and pressed the bit between her teeth. He handled her roughly. She was kicking back her head to get away from him. He smacked her nose sharply. "Cut that out. You can cut that out," he said.

By the time he had mounted her and taken her out into the yard she was nervous and excited, skittering sideways, pulling at the bit. "Whoa. Whoa," he said roughly, bringing her around in a tight circle. "Quiet, damn you. Whoa."

Sally and Tim appeared at the door of the cottage. They looked at him in amazement. "Does Fidget know that you . . . ?" Sally began.

But Andrew turned the mare towards the house and dug his heels in her side. She bounded forward, a great leap up from her haunches, her hooves clattering on the stone yard.

Sally and Tim stepped back. "My God!" Sally turned to Timothy. "Stop him, Tim. You must stop him."

Andrew ground his heels into the mare's ribs, urging her on across the fields at full gallop. The sides of her neck were soon showing dark sweat marks. As they entered the woods he tried to rein her in, but she ignored him. He sawed the bit roughly in her mouth, ducking his head under the branches of the trees.

He and Corinna had come this way the day before. The woods were intersected by long grass rides. Pheasants used them as a feeding ground. They were quite tame. Lord de Boys's ban on shooting had provided them with an easy life. They flew squawking into the undergrowth as Andrew galloped by.

He was sweating himself now. The mare was strong. He could feel her under him, angry and fighting. She tossed her head against the bit, and flecks of white foam flew back in Andrew's face.

Then in the distance he saw Corinna. She was riding towards him, trotting easily. Andrew began to pull in the mare. She resisted. He jerked at her mouth. "Come on," he said through clenched teeth. He was pulling at her now with all his strengh. The reins had raised blisters between his fingers, and then broken them open. The mare's head was drawn back, the skin of her neck creased. Andrew's fingers stung as he fought with her. "Whoa there," he shouted angrily. "Whoa."

"What's the matter?" Corinna asked as he drew up

to her. Coins of sunlight were dancing on her face through the branches of the trees. She shaded her eyes and looked anxiously at the mare. "What's the matter?" she repeated anxiously.

"Nothing," said Andrew shortly. The mare would not stand still. She circled Corinna, shaking her head, picking up her hooves in high, dancing steps.

"What is it?"

"I thought I'd take the hint," he said.

"What do you mean?"

"Get off. Get off that horse and I'll show you."

"But . . ."

"Get off, I said."

Corinna dismounted. She held her horse by the reins just behind the bit. Andrew threw his leg over the mare and jumped from the stirrup. "Let go," he said. "Let him go." He had left the mare's reins lying on her neck. She shook her head. As soon as she realized she was free, she galloped away along the ride.

"She's bolted," Corinna said.

"Let him go," Andrew said.

Corinna looked at him blankly.

"Did you hear me? Let him go."

Slowly Corinna took her hand from the reins. The horse stood still beside her.

Andrew shouted. "Go on then, you stupid creature. What's the matter with you? What are you waiting for, you stupid fucking creature?"

He stepped forward and slapped it as hard as he could with the flat of his hand on the haunch. It jumped and laid back its ears. Then it turned and galloped away after the mare.

Andrew turned to Corinna. "Right," he said.

"Andrew. Andrew, what is it? What's the matter?"

"Shut up," he said viciously. He was pushing her to

the ground, pulling at her shirt. "I'm going to fuck you, Corinna. Corinna *Proudfoot*." He spat the name at her. "That's what you wanted, isn't it?"

Andrew buried his face in Corinna's breasts. His shoulders heaved. He was sobbing, deep dry sobs gagging at the back of his throat. "Oh God!" he said. "Oh my God!"

Corinna held his head in her arms. "What is it, Andrew?" she said tenderly. "What happened? Tell me what happened."

But only when they were walking back along the ride to find the horses did he answer her. He told her everything then—this hopes, his schemes, the elaborate structures he had built up in anticipation of the partnership with Timothy. And the sale of the Rembrandt.

"It's a beautiful painting," he said. "It's such a beautiful painting."

"But you were going to sell it?"

"Yes, of course." Andrew looked at her with innocent eyes. "It's good it should be sold. It circulates a little. The same people look at it all the time, and after a while they forget to look at it any more." He gave her an odd smile. "And there is another point, of course. I am a dealer, you see. Whatever else I might do to make a living, that's what I am, a dealer. And the point of being a dealer is, everything that goes through your hands, in a sort of a way, you own it. That's why you're a dealer. Thousands of things, thousands of paintings go through your hands. You can't afford to keep any of them. But they're yours. And they stay yours. If I'd been in on the sale of the *Diana*, it would have been mine. Do you see? Whenever I saw it, or talked about it, I'd have thought about it as 'my' Rembrandt. That's what being a dealer is about." Suddenly his expression changed. "And she screwed it." His voice was filled with hatred. "That supercilious bloody bitch . . ."

"Perhaps it's for the best."

"For the best? Christ! What do you mean? God moves in a mysterious way his wonders to perform?"

"No. Of course not. I just mean that it's better to find out now than have it all go wrong when you're really involved. And anyway, it's more satisfying to build up something yourself, surely?"

"Oh, don't give me that!"

"What's the matter?"

"Christ. You people, you have it so easy. You can afford to take up these beautiful moral positions. It's 'more satisfying' to do it by yourself. That's just a lot of propaganda put out by you people to keep the natives happy."

"Oh Andrew. Please. I do understand."

"Understand? God help us! I don't want to be understood. My God, you people are so damn patronizing. You don't even begin to know what it's all about."

Ahead of them the ride opened into a hayfield. The second crop of the summer was already a rich pale green. A shimmering haze hung over it. They could see the horses were out there, quietly grazing.

But in his mind Andrew saw a different version of the scene. At the edge of the blue sky, black clouds were gathering, threatening the whole sunlit landscape with gloom and bitter despair. He shuddered.

"What's the matter?"

"Nothing," he said sharply.

Andrew took Gail with him to see the Velasquez sold at Christie's.

Every Friday in the season there is a sale of paintings at Christie's. But on this day the air of excitement rose from something more than the usual anticipation. Today was the big one. Today was the day when records were to be broken. The TV cameras were installed. In the actual sale room all the seats were reserved for dealers and buyers and friends of the house. An amazing collection of paintings had been assembled from various owners. But the star of the show was undoubtedly the Velasquez *Portrait of a Nobleman*. Probably the last important Velasquez to come on the market for many years, it stood a chance of surpassing the amazing price of $5¾ million paid for the Velasquez portrait of Juan de Pareja in 1970. The media had built up the sale into a great event. Everyone in London was quoting the odds as if it were a horse race.

Half an hour before the sale started, the rooms were already packed. The desk had run out of catalogues a quarter of an hour before. Taxis were lining up at the King Street entrance, with its imposing classical doorway, and the doorman could not keep up with the number of arrivals. Inside, the stairs were crowded with gossiping dealers, art critics, socialites, and tourists speaking half a dozen languages—Spanish, French, German, English, Italian—as if it were some international cocktail party.

Sally Marchant's mother was also coming to this sale. She had put in "a little picture that no one ever looks at." In fact it was worth several thousand pounds, and Sally knew her mother was thinking of the expense of her marriage to Tim Proudfoot. It would be a matter of pride to her parents that they "do things properly" for her.

Sally had spoken to Quentin Gold, the art director she worked for, and they had decided that this sale would be the best for her mother's picture. Because of the Velasquez everyone would be there.

Quentin Gold had stayed in the office as long as he could, in order to meet Lady Marchant, but she had not yet arrived, and he had to go for a final briefing before taking his place on the rostrum in one of the overflow rooms.

Before he left their office Sally had told him about the Proudfoot Rembrandt. She decided this was the opportune moment. At first he'd seemed politely interested, no more. And she understood why. He had heard it a thousand times, as they all had—the vague mention of sending this or that painting to auction.

But Sally had anticipated that. She had already had Tim sign the letter of authority for Christie's to handle it. When he saw that, Quentin became very excited.

"My dear girl," he said, putting his arm around her shoulder. "That's fantastic. How *clever* of you."

"Well, Quentin, it wasn't exactly clever. It does belong to my fiancé."

"Cleverer yet," he exclaimed, chuckling excitedly. Sally could see he was impatient to get away and tell the other directors. She could hardly blame him. The sale of that one painting would bring Christie's about £ 200,000.

When her mother arrived, Sally took her straight to their seats in the main sale room. They had to fight their way through the crowds that blocked the doorway and stood, jammed solid, at the back of the room.

"My goodness. Is it always like this?" her mother asked in amazement.

"Oh no. This is because of the Velasquez—there." She pointed to where the portrait, in a carved gilt frame, hung behind the auctioneer's rostrum.

"Oh" said Lady Marchant in her down-to-earth manner. "It doesn't look to me to be very different from any other picture."

In front of the rostrum the heads of a dozen microphones were poised like snakes at the edge of the desk. The arc lights already made the room unbearably hot. Two sets of TV cameras were mounted at the rear of the room, one for the closed circuit to the other rooms, the other for news film of the sale.

The auctioneer took his place at two minutes to the hour. At 11:00 precisely he struck the desk with the ivory hammer. He was brisk, almost impatient. "Let us begin the sale, ladies and gentlemen," he said firmly, when the conversations did not stop.

And when he did start he raced through the lots at an amazing pace.

"Number one. Anyone to start it? Fifteen? Fifteen thousand guineas. Twenty. Thirty. Thirty thousand guineas. Two places … Thirty-five … Forty…. The bid is in the front. Forty thousand guineas … "

Lady Marchant whispered to Sally. "I don't see anyone bidding at all."

"No. He knows them all. He just looks at them. If they want to drop out, they just shake their heads."

"… Fifty-five thousand guineas." As assistant with a phone in his hand nodded to him. "Sixty thousand. In the other room sixty-two thousand. Sixty-four thousand. Sixty-four thousand. The bid's in the middle. Any more? Sixty-four thousand guineas. Any more?

Sixty-four thousand guineas." *Crack* with the hammer. "Agnew."

There was a buzz of conversation. But the auctioneer hurried on. "Number Two," he said. An assistant indicated the painting on the wall. The TV camera transmitted its image to the screens in the other rooms. It was brisk and businesslike. Great paintings were disposed of like cattle. And fortunes that could have supported thousands for life were spent in seconds on a few square feet of canvas and paint.

The sale held plenty of surprises. And not all at the vastness of the prices. Sometimes the buzz as a painting was knocked down had a different sound.

"That was bought in," Sally said to her mother. "It didn't reach its price."

"But someone bought it—Frost, didn't he say?"

"Oh, that's only us buying it back. It's a false name. It looks better than withdrawing lots because they don't reach the reserve."

"Bad luck for the owner," said her mother.

"Yes. It's all right for us, though," Sally whispered. "We still charge a commission. On the last real bid. Only two and a half percent. But we don't lose."

"Would you please mind not continuing your conversations?" the auctioneer rebuked them like a schoolmaster. "We must get on with the sale."

The Velasquez was the last lot of the morning. The auctioneer went into it without preamble. "Number twenty-seven. Three hundred thousand guineas offered. Twenty. Fifty. Eighty. Four hundred thousand guineas. Where are you? I can't see you."

Now the excitement was intense. The bidding rose at breakneck speed. There were murmurs as it reached one million guineas. But at that price there was not even a pause. The bids still rocketed upwards.

"... One million five hundred thousand guineas. Against you, sir ... One million six hundred thousand guineas. One million six hundred thousand guineas. For you, sir."

For a few tricky moments bidding slowed. But the auctioneer skillfully led it on. His face showed no emotion. He kept up his schoolmasterly manner. At the price of two million guineas, there was a gasp, and a scattering of applause. He silenced it with a frown.

"Two million one hundred thousand guineas. Any more? Against you, sir. Two million one hundred thousand guineas. Two million one hundred thousand guineas."

The room was silent. Everyone held his breath. It had now reached the previous record price of any painting anywhere in the world.

The auctioneer seemed unimpressed. "Against you, sir," he said calmly. He was looking around the room for further bids. He glanced at the assistants on the phone to the other rooms. No one moved.

Then with a glance at the back of the room, he said, "Two million, two hundred thousand guineas."

There was a gasp from the spectators. Many of them turned to see if they could identify the bidder.

"Two million two hundred and fifty thousand guineas. Two million three hundred thousand guineas."

Once over the hump of the previous record, bidding quickened again. After a brief battle between an American dealer and Colnaghi, the Bond Street gallery, the American secured the picture at a price of two million four hundred and fifty thousand guineas.

The whole audience broke into applause and excited conversation. The auctioneer looked at them disapprovingly but made no attempt to quiet the din. The time was 12:30. He had averaged four minutes for the sale of each picture.

The room began to clear immediately. Andrew and Gail had been watching on TV in one of the other rooms. They had not had time to see the Velasquez before the sale. They decided to go in now and look at it. Andrew waited for the crowd to thin a little and then fought his way against the tide into the main auction room.

He would not have expected Sally to be pleased to see him, but since she was directly in his path, she could hardly avoid him. She introduced him briefly to her mother. "A friend of Tim's. They were at Cambridge at the same time." Andrew introduced Gail.

"Fantastic price," said Andrew. "I hope they give you all a bonus."

"Yes," said Sally, as if she had not heard him.

Andrew glanced towards the Velasquez. A TV commentator, microphone in hand, stood before it, talking to the cameras.

"So another record has been broken," he was saying. "Another of the last few great paintings that remain in private hands suffers the indignity of public auction. Two million five hundred seventy-two thousand five hundred pounds—the highest figure paid for a painting ever, anywhere in the world. A king's ransom. But how long will such a record stand? Not for long, I would venture to suggest. We may see even this phenomenal price overtaken in the very near future, in fact. And in this very room. Only five minutes ago I was informed by the director of paintings here at Christie's that they have been entrusted with the sale of another world-famous painting—*The Nude Di-*

*ana* by Rembrandt, which has been the property of
the Proudfoot family for generations. The painting
comes on the market following the recent death of
Lord de Boys. And though they would never be so
rash as to commit themselves to a figure, I believe the
people at Christie's here think they stand a good
chance of breaking the record once again with that
picture. We shall see. And you can be sure we shall
be here with our cameras once again to witness the
event. . . ."

Sally's face was ashen.

"What's the matter?" said Andrew.

"Nothing," Sally said abruptly. "Excuse me. We
must go, Mother. Excuse me." She pushed past Andrew.

Gail and Andrew stood briefly before the Velasquez. "Can anything be worth so much money?"
Gail said.

On the stairs as they left young men from rival galleries greeted one another with a sort of languid
friendship. They talked as if they might have been
buying for their own collections.

"Did you buy the Canaletto?"

"No. The Greuze."

"Your father here?"

"No."

Andrew tried to push his way down the stairs. In
front of them another similar exchange was taking
place.

"Did you buy anything?"

"No. On the Van Dyck we were also-rans."

"Nice picture."

"Yes."

These casually superior young men made Andrew
see red. Their laconic conversation assumed a whole

world of privilege. These younger sons of the aristocracy used to be able to play about with pictures, because there was so much money from land that they didn't have to earn a living. Now money was tight, but pictures were big business—and these people had the connections to take advantage of both.

When they finally fought their way out into the street, Andrew drew deep breaths of air, as if he had been suffocating in there.

# 7

ANDREW TOLD GAIL about the weekend at Boys Hall. He felt he had to talk to someone about it. She was sympathetic. But he felt no better—it seemed that sympathy was no help.

"And now," Gail said, "my friend Lennox will simply buy the *Diana* at Christie's?"

"No. It's not that simple. I don't think they'd let it out of the country. It's a very important picture. There'd be a lot of fuss."

"How could they stop it?"

"It would need an export license. I doubt if they'd give it one. Rembrandt is very poorly represented in British museums."

But he really did not want to talk about it. That weekend at Boys Hall snapped something in Andrew's head. He could not wait around any longer.

He gave notice at the gallery. He had been left money, he told them, by relatives in South Africa. In time he would be opening his own gallery. He'd show old stuff and new together. He did not intend to specialize. But right now he planned to tour Europe and accumulate some stock.

He traded in his MG for a station wagon. At the end of September he took it on the ferry from Harwich to the Hook of Holland.

For three weeks he worked his way south, from Amsterdam, through Belgium, then east into Germany, then west to Strasbourg, then east again to Austria. In every town he visited galleries and antique shops. Most often he found what he wanted in small towns. He preferred to buy from the old-fashioned dealers, old men who hung on to a crowded shop, in a back street, scarcely making a living. But there weren't many of this type left.

And he bought very little. By the time he drove into Venice and parked in one of the two great garages at the Piazzale Roma, he had six large seventeenth-century paintings in the back of the wagon. He had not given much for them. The artists were unknown. The canvases were badly executed, and on most the surface was damaged. They were practically worthless. And they were exactly what he needed.

Well away from St. Mark's Square and the Doge's Palace, a different Venice exists, unseen by tourists, a warren of narrow alleys and dark courtyards that the sun never reaches, where the canals are wide enough only for a single gondola.

In October in Venice there are days of rain and mist and sudden cold that drive the tourists to take shelter in the cafes and the pigeons to huddle under the portico of the hundred churches that are the pride of the city.

On one of these mornings, in that hidden quarter of

the city, in his cluttered and filthy room, an old man
was preparing to go out. Over his threadbare jacket
he put on a dark, shapeless coat. Once it had been
part of the gray uniform of the Italian Army. Now it
was almost unrecognizable. The hem was frayed.
There were dark, shiny patches of grease on the cuffs
and around the pockets. He put a broad-brimmed
black hat on his head and left the room.

The old man double-locked the door with keys
heavy enough for a dungeon. He glanced quickly to
left and right. The courtyard was empty. Furtively he
hurried across and disappeared into the dark alley on
the other side.

The *vaporetto* was packed with clerks and office
workers and shop assistants on their way to work. The
heat of their crowded bodies raised steam from their
clothes. The old man closed his eyes with an expression of distaste.

The boat puttered up the Grand Canal, under the
sharp angle of the Ponte di Rialto. At each stop passengers jostled off and on, folding and unfolding um-
brellas with lethal urgency. At the Ca' d'Oro, the
House of Gold, the old man stepped ashore. The
richly carved stone facade had once been heavily
gilded and lavishly painted with red and ultramarine,
but it stands now somewhat forlorn, a giant gray
uneaten wedding cake.

The old man did not even raise his head to glance
at it. He hurried down the Calle del Ca' d'Oro, into
the market in the Strada Nuova. Ignoring the stalls of
brightly colored fruit and vegetables and the multi-
tudinous varieties of fish from the Adriatic, he turned
left, then right into the Calle delle Rachetta, crossing
two bridges, without pausing until he stood over-
looking the water on the Fontamente Nuova. He

seemed relieved to have left the crowds and to be alone again. As he looked out over the Lagoon, a gondola, intricately carved, painted black and heavily gilded, hung with black velvet, slid silently out from under the bridge. The old man took off his hat and held it against his breast. The rain plastered the white hair to his head. Behind the hearse followed a full funeral procession slowly making its way over to the cemetery of San Michele.

The old man watched the funeral until it disappeared into the rain out on the water. He put his hat back on his dripping head and walked to his right along the waterfront. He turned to the right along another *calle*. Ahead stood the church of Santa Maria Assunta. The old man went in.

Inside, in the gloom, it seems at first that the walls are draped with green and white silk, hung with thick tassels. But it turns out that the drapery is executed entirely in colored marble. The elaborately painted ceiling is framed in gold and white. On the altar stands a tabernacle of brilliant lapis lazuli. Marble statues of saints and angels look down from every corner of the church.

But the old man did not look at them. Instead he turned to one side, knocked on a heavy wooden door, and opened it without waiting for an answer.

The verger looked up. He had his breakfast spread on a sheet of newspaper in front of him—coffee and a thick slice of *polènta*. "Ah," he said. "*Buon giorno, Professore*."

"*Buon giorno*," mumbled the old man gruffly.

Against the wall under the window stood an old, paint-spotted easel, a very old mahogany box, and a large canvas wrapped in an old sheet. One at a time

the old man took them out of the verger's room. The
verger did not offer to help.

The old man left the canvas until last. He took it
across to the small chapel off to the left of the aisle
and placed it on the easel. He took off the sheet. The
painting was partially completed: a marble temple, lit
by a flickering fire and by a beam of light that shone
down from the dark night sky: soldiers with torches:
their helmets also catching the light.

The old man studied it carefully. Then he looked
up to where, above the altar hung the complete
painting—Titian's *Martyrdom of St. Lawrence.*

On the old man's painting the figure of the saint
was still only sketched in. He opened the wooden box
and lifted out his palette. He took one of the jars he
used for paint, unscrewed the top, and dipped in a
brush.

For the first time that day, his face took on a con-
tented expression.


At noon the old man reversed the morning's operation exactly. He packed away his equipment in the
verger's room. He retraced his steps to the jetty at the
Ca' d'Oro. He took the slow *vaporetto* along the
Grand Canal, under the Ponte di Pialto. The *vaporetto* was almost as crowded as it had been in the
morning. Afternoon naps are the unwritten law of
Italy—and one that every Italian obeys.

Andrew had been waiting half an hour outside the
old man's door. A woman had come out from next
door, when he had knocked earlier that morning.

"*Non e qui, il Professore.*" He is not here, she said.

"He will be back?" Andrew asked.

She had shrugged and opened her palms. "Perhaps.

Sometimes he goes away. For weeks sometimes he is not here."

"He was here this morning?"

"*Si.* If he has not gone away he will be home at midday. For *la colazione,* you know. Though I don't know what he can eat. Sometimes I ask myself if he eats at all. He is so thin. I tried to give him food, many times, long ago. But he never would take it. He allows no one into his room. He has the oven in there, but . . ." She threw up her hands, as if she did not have to explain what a man was like with a stove.

She came close and bent her head to talk into his ear. "They say in there it is filthy." She was pressing against him. "Sometimes there is such a smell-phoui!" She held her nose dramatically. "When he is *making* something," She rolled her eyes to heaven and crossed herself. "The Lord knows what he is using. It's not paint that would smell like that. It can't be food either. Not food for *humans* at any rate. Signor, you know, they say . . ." she had begun, but whatever it was she could not bring herself to tell Andrew what it was that people said.

So Andrew had come back at noon and stood in the rain for half an hour. He had even bought himself an umbrella. It was ridiculous—in London he refused to carry one. And in Venice, the first thing he did was to go out and buy one—the real thing. *Made in England!*

The old man hurried through the rain to his door, digging in the pockets of his coat for his keys.

"*Scusi,*" Andrew said. "*Professore?*"

The old man looked at him. A heavy beard hid the lower half of his face. His dark eyes were bleary and bloodshot. He did not answer.

Andrew stepped forward. "*Professore Ruggero?*" he said.

"No," said the old man. "You made a mistake." He began to unlock the door. But his neighbor must have been watching from behind her lace curtains. She came bustling out with her scarf over her head. "Ah, *Professore*. The gentleman has found you." Then to Andrew. "You have found Professore Ruggero then?"

"Yes, thanks," Andrew said.

"You'd better come in," said the old man in an irritated voice.

He led Andrew down a dark passage to another locked door. Behind it was a room large enough to be a warehouse. Dozens of canvases on the floor. Others leaned against the two vast tables, covered with pots and jars and jumbled rubbish, that stood in the middle of the room. Another stood on an easel in front of the high window. At the far end of the room was a gallery that looked as if it might be some sort of bedroom, reached by a ladder from the ground floor.

The old man shook his hat and went to the end of the room to take off his coat. Andrew walked to the window. He found he was looking straight out on to a canal, just above water level.

"It's a fine studio," Andrew said.

"What do you want?" asked Franco.

"What do you do here?"

"What do you mean?"

"What do you do? What kind of painting?"

"I make copies. Sometimes for an order. Someone wants a 'real' painting, but they can't afford to buy an actual Botticelli. I can paint them a new copy. Americans usually. Sometimes I make a copy myself, hoping to sell it later."

He looked tired Andrew thought. And old—unshaven and bent, in his shabby clothes. Yet it was evident he was no more than fifty or so.

"Yes?"

"Also I do restoration work."

"Ah."

"After the floods. There is a lot of restoration work. . . . But you did not really come here not knowing what work I do."

"No . . . I had heard about you, of course." Andrew was beginning to look through the paintings. "And it pays well—the copying and the restoration?"

"Do I look rich?"

"No. But appearances can be deceptive." He was only giving Franco part of his attention. He seemed to be looking for something.

"What do you want?" Franco asked. There was fear in his voice now.

Andrew looked up. He held the painting he had been looking at steady with the palm of his hand. "Why did you let me in, Ruggero? Why didn't you send me away?"

"I . . . I . . . Sometimes people come whom I have to see. I can't send them away. I thought you were one of these people."

Andrew was going through the canvases again. "I think you were right," he said. "They tell me . . . Ah!" he exclaimed suddenly. "Ah. Now these are *very* interesting."

There was a hunted look in Franco's eyes. "I knew," he whispered half to himself. "I knew."

"They told me no one could 'copy' a Rembrandt like you. You know what you are called? They call you the Rembrandt master."

"I won't do it," Franco burst out. "I won't do it."

Andrew ignored him. "But what is this? What are these sketches? These details—these are details of *The Nude Diana?*"

Franco looked away and did not answer.

"When did you see it? They're perfect. This is the Proudfoot Rembrandt. When did you see it?"

"I never saw it," France stammered. "I never saw it. I made these sketches from a reproduction."

Andrew was studying the canvas closely. "It's incredible," he said.

"But I will not do what you want."

"How do you know what I want?"

"Because you all want the same. All the people like you, you want the same."

"Are there many people like me who come here?"

"No. Not many. But every few years someone comes. And you all want the same. But I will not do it. I tell you. This time I will not do it."

"I don't see that you have very much alternative, Signor," Andrew said. "You no longer have the choice."

"I will not do it. I *will* not do it any more."

The old man was now near to tears. But Andrew himself was trembling. His heart was beating like a drum in his chest. He forced himself to speak calmly.

"I am sorry, Signor. You will do it. The first time, when you copied the *Diana* for Delphine Proudfoot, was the last time you ever had the choice. I myself know definitely of three paintings that fetched a great deal of money, and were hung as genuine old masters—two of them in museums. Two Titian and a Velasquez. And they started here, in this room, as blank canvases—or at least, as different paintings. I congratulate you, Signor. They are magnificent paintings. They are masterpieces. But they were not painted by old masters."

Franco sank on to the stool at the table and buried his head in his hands.

"No," he said.

"You'll be well paid."

Franco looked up. "Of course," he said in a bitterly resigned voice. "You have to pay me well to make me a criminal. But I won't do it."

"Signor," Andrew replied through clenched teeth, "You are wasting the time of both of us. You will do it. I'm afraid you have to."

After Andrew had gone, Franco remained at the table, staring into space. He knew Andrew was right. He would have to do it. He did not have the choice.

His eyes filled with tears as he recalled how happily it had all started. Even in England, in those days it seemed that the sun was always shining. A prisoner, in a foreign country, and he was so happy! And now, in "sunny Italy," his own country, there was nothing but gloom. . . .

When he knew Delphine was pregnant, he had begged her to let him stay at the Hall. He wanted to marry her, of course. But he would have done anything—servant, gardener, anything—just to be near her. She would not hear of it. She insisted he must go back to Italy with the rest of the prisoners. He pleaded with her. He had not realized she could be so unreasonable.

In the end she had agreed he could stay, hidden away in a cottage miles from the Hall. And only on condition that he paint for her a replica of the Proudfoot *Diana*.

He did it willingly, to be near her, and to see his child. But he wished he had not agreed. She scarcely came near him, except to see how the work was progressing. She let him see the child twice only. And as soon as the painting was done, she packed him off to Venice with scarcely a word of regret. Even the old

dog that had come to keep him company, she had
had shot by the gamekeeper.

And here he was now, living a lonely, furtive life,
hating the work that should be giving him so much
pleasure, old before his time. She had sworn so often
that she loved him, but all her actions had been cruel
and selfish. She loved her paintings. She loved herself.
But she had never loved him. He had long ago realized that.


Andrew had given Franco three months to make
him a new "Rembrandt." He knew exactly what he
wanted. It had to be a nude. Lord Duveen, the great
Edwardian dealer, had made the point long ago: take
two masters, he had said, one of an ugly old man and
the other of a beautiful girl. They are both old masters—but the second is also a painting of an attractive
woman.

An unknown Rembrandt nude would be a rare but
possible discovery. There were three known nudes of
his already, and several women bathing, wearing
loose shifts or raising their skirts and showing their
legs. Even so, Rembrandt had only once flaunted con-
vention to the extent of painting a woman without a
few tactful draperies. That was the Proudfoot Rembrandt, the famous *Nude Diana*. A total nude would
command the highest price. It would also provide a
convincing reason why the painting had never been
seen. Rembrandt had probably painted it secretly, at
that time in the mid-1650s when he made other nude
studies of Hendrickje, his common-law wife. Always
desperate for money, he had perhaps sold the
painting on the understanding that it not be publicly
displayed.... The story of the "discovery" was already forming in Andrew's mind....

Before Andrew left Venice he and Franco paid a
visit to the car park on the Piazzale Roma. At dusk
one evening they took a *sandalo*, a Venetian rowing-
boat, to the nearest jetty, and told the boatman to
wait. They took the paintings from the back of the
station wagon and leaned them all around it. Franco
studied them closely. He took out a magnifying glass
and peered at the surface. He clicked his tongue. "Impossible," he said. "In this light it is impossible."

He made a dozen circuits of the car, at snail's pace.
Andrew was losing patience. The fee for the *sandalo*
was mounting all the time. . . .

Eventually Franco selected two of the paintings.
He and Andrew replaced the others in the back of the
wagon. Andrew told Franco to meet him on the jetty
and not to come near until he had loaded the pictures
onto the boat. He was too noticeable, with his wild
appearance, in his ragged coat and high black hat.

When he joined Andrew in the boat, Franco could
not keep his hands off the paintings. He touched their
surface, stroking them gently with his fingertips, as if
he could read some message from them in braille.

As soon as they were safely in his room he said to
Andrew, "Now you must go. I have work to do. You
must go."

Despite his reluctance to undertake it, he was excited at the prospect of the work. Andrew was glad to
leave him to get on with it. "All right!" he said. "I'll
go. But remember, Franco, it has to be perfect. You
understand? *Perfect.*"

"Go away," Franco growled at him.

Andrew left.

The chaos in Franco's room was deceptive. Under
the dust and litter, the sketches and scraps of paper
and jars and broken brushes and stained rags, Franco

knew where everything was. One table was set up like an alchemist's laboratory, with crucibles, pestles and mortars, jars containing lumps and resin and substances like colored clay. One corner of the room, by the sink, was arranged as a photographic bench. On the shelf above, microphotographs of brushwork, or of the granular pattern of paint, lay in jumbled confusion. Nearby, the door of a great pizza oven stood open. It appeared that Franco used the inside for storing his canvas.

Franco knew where everything was. And in that room was everything he needed. He set to work to make his Rembrandt.

Both the paintings he had taken from Andrew were genuine seventeenth-century Dutch works, in their original frames. They were of no artistic merit whatever.

The two paintings were very similar. They were both very dark—almost black. Both were landscapes—one of farm buildings, the other of cows in a country lane. They were both almost the same size. And most important, nothing had been done to either of them since they left the artists' studios. Only time and neglect had altered their materials. And that was exactly what Franco needed.

He examined the surfaces with his fingers. He looked at them through a strong magnifying glass. He had to decide which to use. And his decision would rest on the quality of the crackle—the crazing of the paint that takes place in all oil paintings as the paint dries. It is this, and the hardness of the old paint, that are so difficult to reproduce artificially. Compared to these, a convincing style is easy. There is no scientific test for the character of a painting.

Oil paint takes years to dry thoroughly. It may

cease to be tacky after a few days, but the complete drying can take fifty years. As it dries it cracks, not just on the surface, but through all the layers of paint from the varnish down to the first coat of ground color. The pattern of the crackle is set where the paint has least freedom of movement—at the canvas. Artificially aged paint, dried in an oven, will crack *back* from the surface. An expert will spot this in ten minutes.

Franco made his choice. He set the other painting aside safely, in case of disasters. He prayed God he would not need it.

First of all he removed the canvas from the frame. No need for particular care over that. Anyone seeking to authenticate it would have been sure to take it out to see if the back held any clues.

But taking the canvas from the stretcher had to be very carefully handled. The nails would have to be used again. They had to go back in the exact same holes. Behind them were squares of leather, to save the canvas from tears. These were dry and brittle with age. It was a delicate task to lift them away. The edges of the canvas, naturally worn and discolored with age, must be left intact. The canvas shrinks in from the edge and is held in place by the nails, so that over the years the edges develop a scalloped effect. A straight edge to the canvas would immediately make an expert wary. Was it a "fishy" painting?

Franco put the nails carefully aside. Then, using the same holes, he nailed the canvas to a sheet of plywood. Now he was faced with a task of almost surgical delicacy—to remove the top layers of paint but to leave the last intact, with its pattern of crackle unspoiled. And an operation of such delicacy had to be carried out on paint so old and so dry that it was virtually insoluble. If the paint is soluble, it has been recently applied.

For years Franco had experimented, but there seemed to be only one method that worked. It was slow and laborious, but it worked.

Franco laid the board with the canvas attached, on the table. Then, with soft soap and a smooth pumice stone, he began to rub gently at the surface of the paint. It had to be done with infinite care. He touched the surface with his fingers, feeling every gradation of the paint. Continually he had to clean off the surface and inspect it, to make sure there was no part of it coming away too quickly, laying open the last, precious layer to danger. He worked at it slowly, as if caressing it, with gentle, circular motions, for fear of tearing scabs of paint and taking too much away. The concentration brought sweat to his brow. . . .

Every day for three weeks he spent bent patiently over the table. His shoulders, his arms, his fingers ached from the continuous motion. But finally he had what he needed—the original gray ground, now clean and even. And if you looked at it closely you could see the irregular hairline web of crackle, safely preserved.

At the beginning of January Andrew was back in Venice.

He banged at Franco's door for ten minutes before he would come out.

"It's not ready," he said as soon as he saw Andrew. "Another week. Come in another week, and it will be ready."

But Andrew pushed past him. "I'll stay," he said. "Maybe I can help you with the finishing touches."

Franco shrugged. "Help? How can you help? You would only hinder."

"Then I'll stay and hinder," Andrew said.

Inside the room he saw no sign of the painting he expected. "Where is it?" he asked.

Franco could see what Andrew was thinking. A flicker of amusement appeared in his eyes. "It's in there," he said, nodding to the closed door of the pizza oven.

"In the oven?"

"Yes."

Andrew crossed the room.

"Don't touch. Leave it. It must stay another two hours."

"It's warm. You're cooking it? This is for the *craquelure?*"

"Ah. You know, of course. So you see, you will not see it until tomorrow."

"Is this the last time in the oven?"

"No. There's one more—the varnish."

"Has it worked? Has the crackle come through? How many layers have you put on?"

Franco raised his hand to silence him. "You will see. You must be patient. It's a slow process. Slow. One mistake, just one tiny mistake, and the whole painting is ruined."

"Of course I am impatient. But tell me—does it work? Has the crackle come through?"

"Yes. It's coming."

"What is the smell in here? Not the paint. A sweet smell. Scent?"

"What?" Franco seemed startled by Andrew's question. "What do you say?"

"The smell. What is the smell in here? Lavender— that's it."

"Ah." Again a flicker of amusement appeared in his eyes. "You like the smell of lavender?"

"Come on, Franco. I know it isn't aftershave."

Franco's face cracked into a wry smile. "No. It is—what shall I say? A trade secret." He was proud of his craftsmanship, but the habit of secrecy had become ingrained in his character after years of these clandestine activities. He hesitated. Then, with a gesture of resignation, he went to one of the tables. "I will show you. Look."

Andrew stood beside him. Franco picked up one of the dozens of jars that lay half-buried in the clutter. "I will give you a lecture, eh?"

"All right."

"You know what is our chief problem—we paint a canvas today, and it must seem tomorrow that it has been drying for three, four hundred years. Those old paints you cannot dissolve, not with alcohol, not with anything at all practically. They are like rock. So we have to find something that will harden the paint like that for us. It must also dry very quickly. And it must not reveal itself when the painting is—what shall I say—tested. It's not easy to find something like that."

"Others have done it?"

"How do you know?" Franco said sharply. "Those that have not been discovered you do not know about. And those that have been discovered—have been discovered."

"You have not been discovered."

"That is because I have found the technique. But it was not easy."

Andrew was beginning to suspect that Franco was in a sense disappointed by his success. He seemed to want to be found out. Andrew supposed he could see why Franco was an artist. In secret he painted masterpieces, and no one acknowledged him. The more successful he was, the less the chance of acknowledgment. There must have been a temptation, even if it were only subconscious, to make just one small error that might betray him. A chill ran up Andrew's spine. "Go on," he said.

"But I thought of plastic. Plastic is a liquid. And when it is cooked, it changes. It is hard. Nothing will dissolve it. People are complaining that they can't get rid of plastic. Pollution." He held up the jar. "Phenolformaldehyde. Phenol is carbolic acid—that is from carbon, which is the base of plastic, as you know. . . . You see, I as quite a chemist. It hardens so quickly, I add it only just before I apply the paint."

"But that's not the smell of lavender."

"No. Of course. But I cannot apply the paint without some oil. What is the color—dust, most of it. And this"—he touched the jar again—"this is like water. You can't paint with that. But the oil of lavender *evaporates*. And with a little heating it evaporates even quicker. So we are left with a solid compound, which analysis will show contains pigment, and perhaps a little natural oil . . . nothing suspicious. And it is hard—hard as rock."

"I hope it's as good as it sounds."

"Why not? It has taken me years to make this solution."

"Sure," said Andrew. He was beginning to move around the table.

Andrew picked up a paintbrush. The hairs were crudely bound to the shaft with twine. "You make your own brushes?"

"Of course. The brushes Rembrandt used were made from badger hair. They don't make such paintbrushes now. But there are shaving brushes. It is necessary to get these things correct. Perhaps we leave a hair 'by mistake' in the paint. Maybe an expert will pick it out. Ah, he will say—so clever—'A *badger* hair. That is correct.'"

"And the colors you make yourself?"

"You are checking on me? You will not find I make mistakes."

"No. I'm not checking. I am not expecting you to have made mistakes."

"Yes, I make them myself, of course." He moved along the table, touching the jars and bowls of strange mixtures. "This is cinnabar, for the red." A jar containing rocky lumps of reddish ore. "White lead—not zinc, because we did not have that until eighteen hundred and so. Also it's good for covering the old work. The X-rays don't like it. It's good you wanted a nude. A lot of white. . . . But one must take care. Rembrandt did not use so much." He moved to an old marble pestle and mortar. "And not too much blue for the nude either. Lapis lazuli is very expensive. Even for so little I spent a fortune."

"And you grind it by hand?"

"Rembrandt ground it by hand. . . !"

"Yes but . . ."

". . . and if it is ground by machine, the grains are even, you understand? In the pestle they are not even. With a powerful microscope these differences can be seen."

"Okay, Franco. Okay."

"You are satisfied?"

"Yes, I am satisfied. Technically I am quite satisfied. But I still want to see the painting."

"You know what that is like. We decided before you left how it should be. I made a sketch for it."

But Andrew could tell from Franco's manner that

he was anxious to show him the painting. Obviously
he was proud of it. That was a good sign. Unless he
was playing some elaborate joke, and he couldn't wait
to get to the punch line. . . .

"Come tomorrow. I shall varnish her tomorrow.
Come tomorrow and you shall see her."

Andrew knew he would not sleep that night. He ate
dinner alone in his hotel. The dining room was almost
deserted. Afterwards he took a gondola to Harry's Bar
on the Calle Valresso. But, out of season, it was pa-
tronized by regulars. They looked at him as if he
were intruding. He left after one drink.

Outside, at the San Marco boat station, a gondolier
leered at him. "You like a nice time, Signor? My sis-
ter. Beautiful lady. Fantastic."

"How much?"

"Fifteen thousand. Twenty-five dollars." He held up
his hands, with fingers extended, then again, then one
alone.

"Fifteen," said Andrew.

"Twenty-five, Signor. Very special. Fantastic."

"Fifteen."

"Okay. For you, twenty."

Andrew climbed into the gondola.

The gondola took him through a maze of narrow
canals. And he charged an exorbitant fare for doing
so. Andrew had not the energy to argue. The girl
worked at the top of an old house. The gondolier
rang the bell twice. She looked down. In dumb show
he indicated Andrew, and she beckoned him up.

"Hello, lover," she said when he had climbed the
stairs. There were ninety steps. He counted them on
the way up.

"You speak English?" he asked.

She was quite young—eighteen or nineteen he

guessed, it was hard to tell. Her hair was black, teased into an elaborate pile on top of her head. Her skin was pasty, and she was considerably overweight.

"Oh yes."

"Well, I speak Italian."

The room was dimly lit. She had draped a red scarf over the single lamp beside the bed.

"Oh."

"And I don't want to talk."

She shrugged. "Okay. You pay the money. You put it on the table. How much did he say?"

"Eight thousand—fifteen dollars."

"Liar!" she said without malice. "The price is thirty!"

"We agreed twenty."

"Okay. Twenty. I'll take twenty. Off-season rate."

"But I have lire. That's ten thousand."

"Oh no, you don't. It's twelve thousand. You can put it on the table." She did not seem concerned that he had tried to trick her.

"Wash yourself there," she said. She took off her sweater and skirt, kicking off her shoes, and lay naked on the bed.

Andrew pulled off his clothes. He washed himself at the basin. He didn't want an argument. When he came to the bed, she raised herself on her elbow and inspected him. She squeezed the head and peered into the eye. A medical inspection, Andrew thought. *Twelve thousand lire for a medical inspection.*

But she lay back and looked at the ceiling. By the rosy light her flesh was like a rolling pink landscape. Seeing her there, apparently defenseless, still young, and without hope, condemned for the rest of her life to these joyless encounters, he felt sorry for her. She did not have a chance.

He took her gently. For some reason, he wanted to give her pleasure. He worked at her with long steady strokes. And as he approached the climax, raising himself from his hips, he saw she was biting her lip. But she kept silent.

Next morning Andrew was early at Franco's studio. He had stopped at a bakery by the hotel and bought fresh sugared rolls.

"I've come for breakfast, Franco," he said. "I hope the coffee's brewing."

Franco led him along the passage in silence. He had put the painting on the easel in the window.

Andrew had intended to react coolly. But when he saw it he exclaimed without thinking, "Oh, she's beautiful, Franco. Beautiful."

As they had agreed, she was the twin of the Proudfoot *Diana*. Evidently painted at the same time, here was Hendrickje again, with her plump, cheerful features and her soft, pneumatic body. The background was the same: the same trees, filtering the same green light; the pool throwing up the same dark reflection. But in this picture Hendrickje's pose was more sensuous. One hand was between her legs. Her head was thrown back on the grass. Her hair was disheveled. There was an expression of sublime satisfaction on her face.

Franco came and stood beside Andrew. "She is too pale, of course. But you know his varnish—asphalt, like black treacle."

That morning Andrew watched Franco at work. The varnish was so thick that he had to warm it in his hands before he could apply it. He put it on the canvas with his fingers and the heel of his hand, working it across the picture until the whole surface was covered in a filter of honey brown.

Then he baked it again in the oven for two hours.
When it was cool he took out from one corner of the
room a great cylinder he had constructed from six
oars and the center of a cable drum. He wrapped the
painting around this, face outwards. The edges failed
to meet by two or three inches.

"Now," he said, taking up a jar of black fluid from
the table. "What would you suppose this to be?"

"I don't know."

"Dirt."

"Dirt?"

"Yes. That's what I said. Did you ever see a *clean*
old painting?"

"No. But they can be cleaned. It . . ."

"Not in the crackle. The crackle holds the dirt of
centuries. This is where you have to be so careful.
Not just any dirt will do. Modern dirt can be
*recognized*. They can take dirt from a crevice with
the point of a needle and *analyze* it. Modern dirt has
diesel fumes in it. Did you know that? Pollution. But
here is what is beautiful—in Venice we have not had
diesel fumes so much." He smiled slightly. "It seems
funny, but in a way, here the dirt is clean. And this is
my special *old* dirt. I have a special place. It is an old
church. In a poor district. The canals are too narrow
around there for motor boats. The people are too poor
for central heating. The dirt has lain there, in the
roof, for hundreds of years." He held up the jar. "And
this is it."

He shook the jar. Then with a thick brush he covered the entire surface of the painting on the cylinder
with the thick black slime. Andrew held his breath.
He understood the nerve it required at every stage of
an operation like this.

Franco wiped the canvas clean with a cloth. Then

he unfastened it and laid it on the floor on the plywood to which he had originally attached it.

"See," he said. "Now the cracks close. The excess dirt is squeezed out. There. Now it is almost finished."

His voice was calm, but Andrew could see that his hand was trembling.

"Now it must dry. I shall not put it in the oven again. The crackle is sufficient. It must dry by itself. You can come back in two days, and it will be dry enough to take away."

Two days later Andrew went back to the studio. The painting was on the easel in the frame. It was perfect. He would have sworn it was the work of Rembrandt's own hand. Franco had captured it exactly—the brush strokes, the texture of the paint, the sense of light, the confidence. . . .

"What about fly specks?" Andrew asked.

"I think they would have been removed if the surface had been thoroughly cleaned with alcohol. At least, one could say that, and no one could prove otherwise."

"Good," said Andrew. He held up the stump of a paintbrush, a handle and the empty metal holder from which Franco had pulled the hairs. "This will do."

He walked to the window. He stood in front of the canvas. For several moments he gazed at it. Then, with a sudden fierce movement, he thrust the rough metal edge of the broken brush through the canvas, just at the point where Diana's foot entered the water.

Franco cried out. "No! My God. No! What are you doing?"

Andrew looked at him over the top of the painting.

He smiled. "You will restore it. I will come back for it in a week."

"But why? Why do you do this to my painting?"

"It was too perfect, Franco. That's all. You did it too well."

"But . . ."

"It didn't look right. It was too perfect. In three hundred years nothing has happened to it. Now it has had an accident. It will have been restored. Then it will be really perfect."

*1974*

# 1

CORINNA HAD BEEN SURPRISED to get Andrew's letter. He had told her, as he told everyone, of his South African inheritance. She had not believed him. And she told him so. But he insisted it was the truth. It saddened her that he should have to lie to her. He had sent her postcards—from Bruges, from Brussels, from Munich. He wrote a few words on them that told her nothing. She guessed he was working out some scheme. She wondered what it could be.

At Boys Hall everything seemed exactly as it had been before Lord de Boys died. But, in some way Corinna could not understand, it was not. She found she spent most of her time alone in the cottage or exercising the horses. Her mother was kind to her in her offhand manner, but preoccupied with her paintings and her artists. That was not unusual. Delphine had always been like that. Perhaps it was Polly that made things different. Now that she and Giles were definitely to be married, as soon as a "decent interval" had lapsed after Lord de Boys's death, Polly had become

impossible to talk to. She just made polite remarks,
innocuous and perfectly boring.

Whatever it was, Corinna no longer felt part of a
family.

Corinna told her mother she was going to stay with
a girlfriend in New York.

"Oh, how nice," Delphine said. "Have you got
enough money?"

"Yes, thank you," said Corinna. She doubted Delphine would have noticed if she had said she was going to the moon.

She almost might as well have been. She could not
think why she had agreed to go. Andrew's letter had
not been very pressing. He had written to say he was
going to New York, to take some paintings for Lennox
(so that was what he had been doing); he knew she
had friends there; he felt sure she needed a holiday—
so why didn't she get herself a reservation and travel
over on the same boat? She noticed he carefully did
not offer to make a reservation for her.

But after all, she thought, why not? She had the
money. She did have friends in New York. She was
always saying she would visit them, and she never
had. It was time she went to America. Though she
did not like to discuss it with her mother, she was interested in American painting. She was feeling
restless. No one seemed to need her in England. She
*did* need a holiday. Andrew was perfectly right. . . .

As the *Josephine* slid alongside the quay at Cherbourg, Corinna was leaning over the rails, searching
for Andrew's tall, spare figure in the crowds below.
What if he weren't there? A hundred things could
have held him up. Would she have to sail to New
York alone? She smiled to herself. Even if she did, she
doubted that she would be lonely. Between

Southampton and Cherbourg—four or five hours' sailing—the assistant purser had already made it clear he was prepared to be very attentive.

A stiff breeze was blowing across the docks, carrying the smell of tar and diesel and the unhealthy aroma of the sea. Down by the galley portholes, the gulls flocked and fought for scraps.

There was music on the quay below. A very rough version of "Colonel Bogey," on drums and trumpets, echoed between the terminal sheds and the side of the ship, drowning the noise of the gulls and the shouts of the porters. A team of drum majorettes was marching and countermarching between the feet of two giant cranes. They wore the briefest tunics, gray trimmed with scarlet, and white boots tied with ribbons. Their leader was a monumental blonde. She threw her staff in the air, but she did not seem quite confident she would catch it. As Corinna watched, she realized all the girls were like that—they weren't sure what to do, and they didn't seem to think it mattered. They looked around to check that they had made the right move. They chatted with their neighbors. They looked as if they'd got there only just in time. Their boots were scuffed. They didn't wear makeup. Their complexions were bad. Many of them were overweight.

Corinna did not see Andrew anywhere. But he had plenty of time. The ship did not sail for another hour. She thought she might go down and have a drink. That was the trouble with sea travel—there were so many times when the only thing to do was to go and have a drink. She had already spent several hours in The Pub.

Just as she was about to turn from the rail and go down to the bar, Corinna caught sight of Andrew.

Her attention was drawn by a porter pushing a trolley loaded with a strange package—tall and flat, wrapped in green canvas. She guessed it must be a painting. Behind the porter was Andrew.

"Well come, Monsieur," the stewardess said to Andrew. "Well come aboard. A good voyage."

Mme. Morin was proud of her English. And of course it was necessary to speak it. The British and the Americans liked to try out their high school French on her. But if they really needed anything they had to ask for it in English. And Mme. Morin always made out she understood, even when she didn't.

"If you like," she said, "this you leave to me, to *défaire* the *valises*. You can get to the deck to see the last of the passengers come on the *Josephine*."

Andrew found Mme. Morin irritating. She had a permanently resigned expression, as if life owed her something better than this. And her accent was like one of those professionally foreign actresses, "vairy Franch." "I'll unpack myself, thanks. I can manage that all right," he said.

She looked annoyed. She probably enjoyed going through other people's suitcases, hoping for dirty pictures, or rubberwear.

"Who else shall we have on the trip?" Andrew asked, to humor her. With Corinna on board, it occurred to him, he might need Mme. Morin's cooperation.

"Oh—nobody. Not anyone—you know. It will be very dull, this crossing."

"That's a shame. I thought these ships were meant to be glamorous."

"Not anymore. People these days—they are all in such a hurry. In the old days they believed one should travel in style. Nowadays all they think about is speed. There is no romance any more. Those—how do you say?—Jumbo Jets, they get you to New York two hours before you have left Paris. Where is the romance? It's not natural."

Mme. Morin sighed. She looked around the cabin as if remembering all the glamorous ghosts. Her eyes rested on the package of paintings. "You are a painter?" she asked hopefully.

"No, Madame. I am taking them to New York for a friend."

"I see," she said. She was one of those people who give you the impression that they don't believe you. Andrew wished she would go.

There was a knock at the door. Mme. Morin looked startled. "Who can it be?" she said.

"A friend, I expect," said Andrew. "*Une amie.*"

"Oh."

Andrew guessed it must have seemed fast work, even by the standards of shipboard romances. He opened the door for Corinna. They embraced on the threshold.

After Mme. Morin had gone, they bolted the door.

"Oh, it's good to see you," said Corinna. "It's been such a long time. What have you been doing?" She looked around the cabin. "I saw you come on board with the painting. I'm dying to see it."

"There are three of them," said Andrew. "But there's nothing to see. They're not very exciting. Not worth undoing all the packing."

Corinna drew away from him. "But Andrew," she said, looking into his face, "I want to see them."

"They're not worth unwrapping, I tell you. I want to keep you in suspense."

Corinna released herself from his arms. "And I'm

going to keep *you* in suspense," she said. "Let's go up
on deck and watch the ship leave. It'll be five days
before we see land again."

"But," Andrew protested weakly, "it's been five
months. . . ."

"No," said Corinna firmly. "I want to go up on
deck."

She wondered why Andrew would not show her
the paintings.

As sailing time approached the passengers lined the
rails. Corinna and Andrew found a space next to a
small man in a gray homburg. He touched the top of
his hat in acknowledgment as they took their places.

The majorettes were playing again. They were
formed up opposite the gangplank, listlessly prancing
on the spot.

"My God," said Andrew. "They're coming aboard."

"They are indeed," said their neighbor. He seemed
to find it amusing.

"Who are they?" Andrew asked.

"The New Royal Netherlands Girl Majorettes. They
are going to New York, I understand, to take part in a
competition." He smiled wryly. "I suspect they are
wasting their time."

"I'm damn sure of it," Andrew said.

The *Josephine* was singled up, held now only by
one hawser forward and one astern. Two tugs were in
position under the bows.

On the rail to their right a dozen short-haired
American boys were hanging over the rail, avidly
watching the majorettes. They laughed in sudden unnatural gusts, and then looked round self-consciously.

"Oh dear," said their neighbor. "I wish my boys did
not have to be quite so crude."

"Your boys?"

"Yes," he said, delighted at Andrew's mystified expression. "In a manner of speaking, mine. . . . The name is Jonas Field, incidentally."

"Andrew Tait."

They shook hands. Corinna, on the other side of Andrew, had not been listening to the conversation.

"They're my choir. You don't believe it now, do you? It's really true. I am their chaperone. I bring them every year. Not the same boys, of course—but every year I bring boys from the choir. It's really all a joke, of course. I take them to Chartres, the King's College at Cambridge. Actually the boys don't give a damn about all that stuff. The parents really know it, but they don't let themselves think too much about it. It gets the kids out of their hair for the summer. For the kids it's a free trip. So . . . it's really all a joke."

"A very expensive joke."

"Oh dear. Don't you think it's fair? They are all *very* rich, you know. Oh *my*, they're rich."

The hooter of the *Josephine* blew two deep long blasts to announce the departure of the ship. The Dutch girls were at the foot of the gangway. It was already hooked to a crane, ready to be lifted away once they were aboard.

The blonde majorette raised her staff. Along the rail the movie cameras began to whir. The boys began to call out from the rail. Andrew hoped the girls would not understand what they were telling them to do.

"Your boys seem very—high-spirited," said Andrew.

"I know," said Jonas. "I'm not responsible for their behavior. I wasn't going to get caught like that. I set out with twelve, and I take twelve back. In between they can do what they like."

Half an hour before dinner Andrew knocked at the door of Corinna's cabin.

"Am I forgiven?" he asked when she let him in.

"Do you need forgiving?" she asked. She had changed into a dress of deep dusty pink that he had not seen before. She looked vulnerable, and her dark eyes seemed deep and sad.

"You've certainly been acting as if I did. You've hardly spoken to me."

"I didn't mean to give that impression."

"Kiss and make up?"

"Make up but no kiss."

"What's the matter, Corinna?"

She looked at him seriously. "It's such a long time since I saw you last, Andrew. It's almost like having to get to know you all over again."

"I don't feel that about you."

"Don't you? Well, I don't know. Something's different. One of us has changed. Perhaps it's me."

"Are you trying to tell me you're not interested in me any more?"

Corinna laughed. She took hold of his arm tenderly. "No, Andrew. No. I'm sorry. It must be me. I'm so confused. I've been so confused in the last few months. Since Father ... Lord de Boys ... Oh, I don't know." She broke off and turned away from him.

He took her chin in his hand and turned her head to face him.

"You're crying, Corinna," he said. "What's the matter?"

"It's nothing. I'm sorry. I'm feeling rather emotional, that's all. It's nothing. Let's go and have a drink."

Corinna had thought that when she saw Andrew again she would find her bearings. She realized now that was probably the reason she had decided to come. Her relationship with Andrew had been something separate from the family, and she had expected that if she took it up again, she would find that sense of herself she seemed to have lost at Boys Hall. But of course, the fact that Andrew was quite separate from the family, and indeed was pretty much disliked by some of them, could actually have been the reason she was attracted to him in the first place. . . . Oh, she really was confused. There was no doubt about *that*.

When they went to dinner, the dining room was half-empty. It was shabby and in need of redecoration. There were pillars covered with beechwood veneer, and light flowed from the top of them up on the curved sections of the ceiling.

Corinna and Andrew were seated together at the First Officer's table. When they went in, the seat next to Andrew was empty. But in the seat beside Corinna she was surprised to see the purser who had been so attentive earlier in the day.

He had evidently been waiting for her. He leaped to his feet and held her chair. And he smiled at her knowingly, as if this were something they had arranged between them.

Corinna was pleased to see him, she realized. She was beginning to feel better. She had not thought that she would eat any dinner, but now she decided she might even enjoy it. A little rivalry would do Andrew no harm at all.

"Allow me to introduce myself, Mademoiselle. My name is François Lapierre. I am delighted to find that we are neighbors at table."

"You didn't know?"

He gave her a Gallic shrug and a sleepy smile. "Sometimes one is able to use a little influence . . ."

With Corinna ignoring him on one side and an
empty seat on the other, Andrew turned to the menu.
He was considering the intricacy of cooking pheasant
"*en plumage*," when he was interrupted by a voice
beside him. "Oh, Mr. Tait. You must forgive me."

Andrew turned, "Good heavens!" he said. "Mrs.
Roscoe!" He stood up and held her chair for her as
she sat down.

"Oh, I'm so glad," she said. "I hoped you wouldn't
know I was on board. I wanted to give you a surprise.
Was that awfully silly?"

"Of course not. And you certainly did, Mrs. Roscoe."

"Now look here." she said, laying her hand on Andrew's arm. "You simply can't be so formal on board
ship. There really is not the time. You must call me
Enid . . . and I shall call you Andrew."

"Please."

Andrew was amused. He had met Mrs. Roscoe
three or four times in London. Her husband had been
American, but she was English. She lived in New
York but traveled every year to London, to go to the
theater and to buy some paintings. She bought carefully, middle-of-the-road stuff. She was not an art fa-
natic like Delphine de Boys. She liked painting, she
liked the life that went with collecting, but she was
not going to lose five minutes' sleep if her little
Bonnard got lifted. She'd get something else she liked
with the insurance money.

"I wondered if it might be you when I saw the pas-
senger list. And then I saw you come on board, with a
package that couldn't be anything but a painting. I
had a word with the purser. I arranged for us to sit
together. I hope you don't mind. I knew we should
find a lot to talk about. It is the most marvelous coin-

cidence." She looked around the dining room as if happy coincidences were always turning up for her, and there might be another waiting out there somewhere.

In some indefinable but obvious way, Mrs. Roscoe was a lady. She was direct, but she was not vulgar. She was warm and friendly. She concentrated on you and did not look around, but she wasn't overpowering. Her hair was loosely waved, and there was a hint of fervor in her prominent, clear blue eyes. She was certainly nice, but you did not forget she was a woman.

"And who is that beautiful girl on your other side? Do you know her?"

"Yes," said Andrew. "I know her quite well. It's Corinna—Corinna Proudfoot."

"Oh? Is she connected with the de Boys family, I wonder?"

"Yes," said Andrew. "She's the daughter of the late Lord de Boys—he died a little while ago."

Andrew felt a shadow of irritation cross his mind. Why was it these people, whenever they came across anyone new, always asked, first thing, whether they might be connected with this or that well-known family. That damned English social snobbery!

"Yes, I had heard. Poor girl. She is such a beautiful creature. I really must not monopolize you. I'm sure you want to talk to your friend."

"She seems to be quite busy practicing her French," said Andrew.

Enid Roscoe smiled. "In that case," she said, "you will have to witness my shameful ritual."

She was already lifting a huge purse of black braid on to the table. "My husband used to hate it," she said, "when I started to take my pills."

She took out a small tube and stood it on the table. Then another. Then a small white packet. "Oh dear," she kept saying. "I'm so sorry." But she was enjoying it.

Before she found what she was looking for, she had a dozen or more vials and packets lined up on the cloth in front of her. The rest of the table were openly watching her.

"Ah!" she said at last. "*Here* it is. Felamine. I always take a couple when I think I might eat more than usual." She smiled disarmingly. "Just in case."

"I'm sorry," said Andrew. She looked very healthy—but that could have come out of other bottles.

"Oh no," she said. "I'm not ill. Oh no." She seemed amused at the idea. "That is why I have these. To *prevent* my becoming ill. You see," she held up her drugs one at a time before replacing them in her purse, "cold pills: Copyronil and Redoxon. You haven't got a cold about you, have you now?"

"Not as far as I know."

"Avolium. Vitamin A."

"Mmmm."

"Valium. Well, I have to admit that *is* a little bit of tranquilizer."

Andrew admired her confidence and her ability to laugh at herself.

She repacked her medicine bag. She picked up the menu. But before she settled down to make her choice, she looked around the dining room again. In the corner opposite them Jonas Field sat at the head of a table of his boys. They were shouting and throwing bread at one another. "I do hope they don't redecorate this room," Enid Roscoe said. "It's so genuine. They ruin these ships trying to bring them up to date. Look at the QE2. . . . That style," she added mischievously, "is known as stockbroker's swinging."

Andrew scarcely spoke to Corinna during the entire meal.

But afterwards, when he suggested they go to the discotheque, she politely wished the purser good night and went with Andrew.

In the old days the discotheque had been the ship's night club. Then it had been called The Blue Angel. Now it had been renamed La Cave Napoléon.

It was a small, crowded, noisy box. They did not try to talk. The pulsing strobe lights made Andrew dizzy. Corinna danced dreamily, her eyes closed.

In a pause between numbers, Andrew asked if she would like a drink.

"No thanks," she said. "I think I want to go to bed. I'm tired."

They went together through the warm, humming corridors of the ship to Corinna's cabin. Andrew did not know what to expect. Corinna was so distant. Yet they knew one another too well for him to make a pass at her.

At the door of her cabin, as she searched for the key, she said, "Would you like a drink? I've got some Scotch."

Andrew sat on the bed. Corinna fetched two glasses from the bathroom. She picked up the bottle of Scotch and came and sat beside him.

"Let's talk," she said. "Talking helps."

"I don't talk too well to order," Andrew said.

But having said that, they didn't need so much to talk. They sat together on the bed and kissed, only touching with their mouths.

"If you don't talk," Corinna said, "you might as well go away and do it by yourself."

Andrew took a deep gulp of Scotch. He put his glass on the floor. When he kissed her again, Corinna's mouth was warm and slippery inside, tangy with the taste of Scotch.

"You must talk," she said again, as if it were vitally important.

"You are beautiful," Andrew said.

Corinna smiled wistfully. "You have on too many clothes," she said.

"This isn't turning out to be such a brilliant conversation."

They kicked off their shoes and lay close together on the bed.

"But talking is important."

"We are talking, love, in another language, but we are talking."

"Yes," she said. "All right, I think we are."

Andrew ran the zipper down the back of her dress. She raised her hips for him to slide it off. Against her bra—a strip of white lace—and her cream tights, her skin was brown and smooth as an Indian's.

"That's better," he said, unhooking her bra.

She fumbled with the buckle of his belt. He unfastened it for her.

Their mouths were frantic now. Andrew's hand ran over her back. His tongue probed her mouth, her ears, under the arms. Her hand was on him, stroking, tenderly grasping. . . .

Afterwards they lay together. "I'm not going to talk for a minute," said Andrew, "because there's nothing to say. I'm with you. I'm not going away."

"All right," she said tenderly. "All right."

For five minutes they lay together, making small

movements to savor the fading sensation. Then Corinna kissed him deeply on the mouth and turned on her back.

"Cigarette?" Andrew asked.

"Yes, thanks."

He lit two together and passed one to her. She drew deeply.

Then she said calmly, "I'm sorry I was such a bitch. . . ."

"You weren't a bitch."

"Well, it was a good imitation."

He stroked her breast lightly with his palm. "It didn't fool me." He took her nipple tenderly between thumb and forefinger. "I knew something must be the matter. Can you tell me what it was?"

"I don't know. That's the trouble. I really don't know what it is, I just know I feel—well, I feel I don't really know who I am any more. I suppose that's what it is. I used to be so sure. I used to be sorry for people who didn't know absolutely what they were."

Andrew's hand moved down her stomach, brushing her hair, now stroking her thighs.

"I used to be sorry for you, you know. I used to think you really didn't know what you wanted, where you were going."

"I guess you were right."

"No I wasn't. You might not be sure where you are going. But you know where you come from. You know your family, your parents. . . . I don't have a family like that. My mother—well, you know my mother. And my father—I don't even know if my father is alive or dead."

Andrew withdrew his hand suddenly. He drew sharply on his cigarette.

"Having a family doesn't make the slightest difference," he said. "You can have mine any day you like. I don't want them. They're no good to me. I wish I didn't have them at all."

"That's easy enough to say when you *have* got them. It's only because you have had them that you have the strength to say you could do without."

"You don't know what you're talking about," Andrew said stiffly.

Corinna turned and put her arm across him. "Oh Andrew. I don't want to argue. I just know how it feels to be me. And I feel lost. Maybe it's this ship. It's unreal. Like a dream. It's like being nowhere. It's not like real life at all."

Andrew slid out from under her arm. "I don't know," he said. "I think we both need some rest. You'll feel better when you've had a good night's sleep." He had pulled on his shorts and was getting together the rest of his clothes.

But after he had gone Corinna lay awake. She had never felt so lonely in her life. Andrew must have known she wanted him to stay. She was too proud to ask him. After a while she felt her chest begin to tighten. Sobs were swelling in her throat. She curled on her side and held the pillow against her and sobbed herself to sleep.

And next morning she felt no better. She waited for Andrew to call her, but he didn't.

François Lapierre came after her as if they were on a desert island together. He was sexy and attractive, but she just did not want to get into that with him. At meals his dark eyes kept looking into hers with a pleading expression, like a faithful dog. On the second night she agreed to go to the discotheque with him. She had to admit to herself it might be partly to annoy Andrew. She had had a furious argument with him that afternoon, when she finally called him on the phone. She asked if she could come and see the paintings he was taking to Lennox. She really wanted to see them very much, she said. But he refused to show them to her. He was adamant. She had stormed out and gone to the Winter Garden for a drink. At dinner she had found François's attention enjoyable. So she went to La Cave Napoléon with him.

But François assumed that her going with him was a straight invitation for more than dancing. Corinna practically had to fight to keep him out of her cabin.

"But why do you come with me," he kept asking, "if you do not like me?"

He actually made her feel guilty for wasting his time. One whole night out of five is a high proportion of waste.

Every morning the majorettes practiced on deck. They got no better, but they grew more confident. The passengers never tired of filming them. The girls began to think they really must be good. They stamped across the deck, swinging their hips and trying to make musical sense of "The Star-Spangled Banner."

Corinna did not spend much time there. Nor at playing deck quoits. Or the game of guessing the daily mileage of the ship's run. She found herself more and more frequently gravitating to the bar. The Winter Garden was quieter than The Pub. Corinna would go and sit quietly there among the potted palms, and look out across the sea, and sip her Scotch. She felt at ease there. Perhaps, she thought, she was becoming an alcoholic. Perhaps that was why she had this feeling of detachment, of dislocation.

François had found her hideaway quite soon. He came often and bought her drinks. He looked into her eyes and occasionally ran a beseeching glance over her body. He did not seem to have been put off by her rejection.

But Andrew did not come. Corinna had breakfast in her cabin and never ate lunch in the dining room, so she only saw him there at dinner. And then he was falling all over Enid Roscoe all the time. It was horrible to see him, making amusing conversation and handing her things, like a gigolo. It was partly Corinna's own fault, she supposed. She had been difficult and not very friendly to him, but could he not understand that there were reasons for that, and they were nothing to do with him?

They went about together all the time, Andrew and Enid Roscoe. If Corinna ran into them, Andrew behaved with perfect manners. They would stop, and the three of them would chat about shipboard subjects—the weather or the Dutch majorettes. But Andrew took care not to stay too long. Once he and Enid looked into the Winter Garden while Corinna and François were there together. But Andrew smiled, looked around as if he were looking for someone, and went away immediately.

"Your companion is—er, very friendly with the English widow."

"How did you know he was my companion?"

François shrugged. "I am the purser," was all he said.

"And how did you know he is so friendly with her?"

He smiled. "This is a ship, remember." Sometimes his smile was infuriating. "On the transatlantic run, even the gossip is in a hurry."

On the fourth night Corinna went to bed with

François. It was absurd, but she felt she owed it to him.

François was triumphant. In her cabin, on the narrow bed, he came at her again and again, smothering her under his hairy body. He was insatiable. In a sort of passive way she enjoyed it. He hardly seemed to need encouragement. And somehow, like that, she did not feel so involved.

The final straw for Corinna was Enid Roscoe's party. Mrs. Roscoe gave a party every year on her way back from Europe to the States. The paintings she had bought on her trip were displayed around the walls of her cabin. She was one of those people who was on friendly terms with half the ship before they had been on board twenty-four hours.

She asked everyone who sat at her table, including Corinna and François.

After what François had told her, Corinna certainly did not intend to go. Andrew had been helping hang the pictures. It had apparently been difficult to decide on the best arrangement. According to François, he had been working on it in Mrs. Roscoe's cabin until the early hours of the morning.

"If you will allow me to be with you," François said gallantly, "I too shall not go."

"Oh François," Corinna said. "You don't have to." She blinked away the tears that had come to her eyes. She had never known herself in such an emotional state.

"No. But I should like to."

"I should like it, too," she said. And she meant it. She felt a sympathy with this passionate Frenchman, a kinship with his Latin blood and swarthy coloring that made her feel at home with him. "And there is something I think I might want you to help me with."

François's eyes were sparkling. "Yes?" he said, smiling eagerly. "At any time . . ."

"Not that," she said.

"Ah," he said. He made a face like a disappointed child. "Perhaps after I help, we shall have that? As a reward?"

"I should have thought you had had enough of it."

"But that was yesterday. Today is another day, to start again."

Corinna laughed. She told herself that she must not take François too seriously. He had one of these romances, she was sure, every trip he made. It was probably the way it had to be for him—he was highly sexed and easily bored.

Enid Roscoe's party was an after-dinner affair, starting at 9:00 P.M. François and Corinna did not go into the dining room that evening. Instead they drank for another hour at the bar and then had a hamburger and a milk shake at Le Drugstore. François kept asking what it was Corinna needed help with, but she would not say.

But when they came out she stopped at the head of the stairs and said, "Now. Here is the key of my cabin. I want you to go there and stay until I phone you."

François looked at her doubtfully. "This is very mysterious," he said.

"You have to trust me," she said.

"Of course," he said. "Of course."

Corinna herself went down to Andrew's cabin. At the end of the corridor was the stewardess's cabin. She knocked boldly at the door. Mme. Morin came out, with a suspicious expression on her face.

"Ah, Mme. Morin," said Corinna brightly. "Would you like to open the door for me now?"

Mme. Morin frowned. "Mademoiselle?" she said.

"Mr. Tait's door. Would you open it now for me, please?"

"But Mademoiselle . . . ?" Mme. Morin was mystified. She recognized the girl. She had seen her with Monsieur Tait the first day. His *"amie"* he had said she was. But . . .

"But Madame. Don't you remember? Mr. Tait arranged with you to let me in to his cabin." She lowered her eyes. "Really, Madame, this is rather embarrassing. I know he spoke to you. He told me himself this morning that he had arranged it."

She could see the panic in Mme. Morin's eyes. Had she forgotten? Had she misunderstood something Monsieur Tait had said to her? She did not remember him saying anything about the key. But she did not always catch what they said. . . .

Once in Andrew's cabin, Corinna gave Mme. Morin time to get back to her cabin. Then she called her own cabin on the phone and told François to come down. "But be sure to come from the front end of the ship—yes, the bow—so you don't have to pass the stewardess's cabin. And bring the nail scissors from my dressing table."

While she waited for him, she looked around. The room was exactly the same, yet it seemed quite different. It smelled of Andrew—she had not noticed that before, when he was there.

François shut the door silently behind him and turned the catch on the lock. "Now," he said, as he came into the room. "What wicked schemes have you planned? We're to make an apple pie bed, is that it?"

"No," said Corinna. She pointed across the room. "There," she said. "We are going to investigate that package."

"Only investigate?" François was smiling. "This is not to be a robbery?"

Corinna could not help laughing. She was not at all certain why she was there at all, but it certainly was not with any idea of carrying off Andrew's secret paintings. Though, come to think of it, that might serve him right. She did have some idea of getting her own back on Andrew. It was his idea that she come on this trip, and now he was ignoring her. In a way she was ashamed of what she was doing. But she had learned that lesson long ago, not to be ashamed of the fact that you sometimes do things you are ashamed of.

"No. We won't take anything. I just want to see what's inside. Andrew made such a *secret* of it. I want to know what it is."

François inspected the package carefully. "It's sewn in," he said. "We shan't be able to do it up again. And there are Customs seals. Italian. French."

"That doesn't matter," she said. "I want him to know what I've done." She stood by him and grasped his shoulder. "I'm glad you are here."

She sat on the bed while François carefully cut the thread on two sides of the package with her scissors. "There's three frames in here," he said.

"Right. We'll look at them all."

François slid them out of the bag. He took off the individual packing that was taped to the frames.

These paintings were lined up against the wall of the cabin. That was all. Nothing happened. Corinna was not sure what she had expected, but she had expected something. She shook her head. The paintings were still there, still the same. Three old Flemish landscapes, dirty and in bad condition. She knew enough about painting to know that these were third rate. The only thing in their favor was that they were genuinely old. That alone would make them worth a few hundred pounds. But as far as she could see there was nothing else about them to make them worth any more.

"Well?" François said.

"I don't know. I really don't know what to think."

She stood up and stepped across to the pictures. She peered at them closely. They were exactly as they appeared—three old but bad paintings. She touched the surface of one. They had not even been cleaned.

"What's this?" said François. With his fingernail he was picking at one corner of one canvas. "The frame is too big. The canvas doesn't reach the edge."

"That's impossible."

But François was right. In that one corner a straight edge of canvas was clearly visible. Corinna touched it with her fingernail. She could just lift the corner. But all around the rest of the painting the edge was hidden under the frame.

"It looks as if it's stuck on. I don't understand. What's the point?"

"Perhaps to hide the painting underneath?"

"Yes," she said reflectively. "That's it. There's another painting. Hidden underneath."

"Shall we pull it off?"

"No," she said sharply. "No. We mustn't damage it. . . . It doesn't matter. It's not so important."

"Good," said François, brightening. "So, we put them back. And then it's time for our little reward, eh? You want to put them back first?"

"Oh yes. I think we should put them back."

At that moment the screaming began.

At first there was one thin, high scream, somewhere

outside in the corridor. Then the sound changed. There were sharp stabbing cries. Then the scream again.

François and Corinna looked at one another. "What's that?" they both said together.

They opened the door of the cabin and looked out. They could see a crowd gathered at the end of the corridor. Shouts mingled with the screams—men's shouts. And different screams, at a different pitch.

They put up the catch on Andrew's lock and left the door open, as they went towards the crowd. When they drew near they heard women's voices shouting "No! No! No!" One or two were hysterical. Doors were banging. Men shouted. "Get them! Get them!" one cried. "Help!" from another. Doors were flung open and slammed shut. The cries and shouts came and went, pleading, screaming. . . .

They came up in time to see the Dutch majorette leader wearing a brief, transparent shift, seize one of Jonas Field's boys by the wrist and drag him towards her cabin.

"Help! Help! Help!" the boy was shouting.

The girl called her roommates to assist. Laughing, they came out to drag him in.

"Retreat! Retreat!" came the cry from the next cabin. Two boys came out, waving handfuls of girl's underwear over their heads. "Success! Success!" they shouted.

But evidently things were not going too well in other cabins. The Dutch girls were tough and uninhibited. And strong. They didn't hesitate to use their fists. As well as their natural weapons—tooth and claw. The American boys had been taught that was dirty fighting. Their faces were gouged. There were teeth marks on their wrists.

The girls were screaming from sheer excitement. From one cabin a boy flew out on to the floor of the corridor. A girl was still fastened to him. She bit a piece out of his ear. Another sailed from the doorway and pinned the boy to the ground. Deliberately she ground her knee into his groin. Her mother had given her practical advice before she let her go on this trip.

The boy was moaning under the two girls. Another boy stood over them, crying, "You can't do that. My God, you can't do that."

"Retreat! Retreat!" the boy called desperately. He could see who the next victim would be.

Stewards and stewardesses pushed their way through the spectators. "Mesdames! Messieurs!" they cried. But they hesitated to intervene. They stood at a safe distance and tried to sound like scolding parents. "Boys! Girls! Mesdemoiselles!" But it made no difference.

"For Christ's sake, get these bitches off me!" The boy was recovering. The girl bounced viciously on him again, nightie above her waist, screaming rhythmically.

Jonas Field pushed his way through the crowd. He was wearing a dinner jacket. He had evidently been summoned from Mrs. Roscoe's party.

"Boys! Boys!" he shouted vainly, nervously rubbing his hand over his bald head. "Boys! Get back to your cabins at once. *At once!*" But he shouted in vain. They would probably have been glad to obey, but they couldn't.

Meanwhile the leader and her friends had stripped their victim naked and thrown his clothes out of the porthole. They dragged him out into the corridor. One sat on his head, the other at his feet. They pointed derisively at his genitals, shriveled with fear.

"Leetle boy," they shouted. "Wot a leetle boy." One was beating him lightly with a drumstick. The boy's scream was muffled under the girl on his head.

"Go back. Go back to your cabins at once," Jonas Field was vainly crying. His voice was rising. "*Do* something, for God's sake," he shouted at the stewards. But all they did was shout louder. "Mesdemoiselles! Messieurs!" Nobody took any notice.

Then the leader and her friends spied Jonas Field. He was obviously responsible. They got up from the naked boy. "Le smoking," they cried. "Le smoking."

The boy they left was weeping. He crumpled at the side of the corridor and buried his head in his hands. But another of the girls came up to him, took hold of his hands, and pulled them away. She spat in his face and threw him back his hands.

Now all the girls advanced on Jonas Field. He tried to back away, but the crowd was thick behind him. "Boys! Boys!" he cried. But the boys slipped through the crowd and made their getaway.

"Oh no! Oh no! God! Please!"

The girls were still shrieking. They were determined on vengeance. Perhaps they had understood all the things the boys had said as they watched their daily rehearsals.

"Mesdemoiselles, Mesdemoiselles. *S'il vous plaît. Als tu bleift.*"

"Those boys are nothing to do with me. Stop! Leave me alone! I'll tell the captain. Where is the captain? Fetch the captain, someone."

But the girls surrounded him and began to take him away towards their cabin.

François began to push forward through the crowd. He was laughing. "I'm going to stop them," he said. "This is going too far."

"I'm going back to my cabin," Corinna said. "I'll see you later."

As she turned to leave, she found herself face to face with Andrew.

"Oh!" he said, as if he had just realized something. "It was you?"

"Yes. It was me. Don't worry, you won't find any damage.... Now, if you'll excuse me, I think I'm going to bed. Good night."

**2**

Reaction set in that night, as soon as François had left her. Alone at three in the morning, Corinna was desperate. She decided to phone Andrew. "I am sorry, mademoiselle," said the duty operator. "Number 217 is not answering."

It couldn't be true. She had to speak to him.

"Are you sure?" she said. "I expected an answer. I had arranged to phone. . . ."

"I am sorry, mademoiselle. There is no reply. *Il n'y a pas de réponse.*"

For the second night she lay alone and sobbed into her pillow. Tomorrow they would arrive in New York. She wished she had never come. She had felt unsettled at Boys Hall, but nothing like as bad as this. Now she was frightened. She couldn't face New York alone.

She tossed and turned on the bed. It was so hot in the cabin. At length she slept fitfully.

After breakfast she got the operator to try Andrew's cabin again. This time he was there.

"Andrew," she said, "I'm sorry. I'm sorry. It was such a stupid thing to do!"

"I'm sorry you had to do it." His voice was cheerful. At least he didn't seem angry. "You should have believed me. I told you those paintings weren't worth unpacking."

"But . . ." she began. She checked herself. "No," she said. "It wasn't worth it."

"Cheer up," he said. "You sound miserable."

"Well . . ."

"How's the boyfriend? Are you staying with him in New York?"

"Oh Andrew. You don't understand. He was—well, he has family in New York, he tells me."

"Oh I see. The proverbial shipboard romance. But fun while it lasts, at least?"

"I suppose so." François had been so eager to get away. He had to be on duty first thing, he said. Obviously he had no family. He was bored with Corinna and already looking for the next affair. "Was yours?"

"My what?"

"Your romance. Was it fun?"

"I shouldn't have called it a romance."

"Oh. Maybe Enid Roscoe would." She was glad he could not see her. The tears were running down her cheeks. But she kept up the lighthearted tone.

"Oh no, she wouldn't. Don't get the lady wrong, Corinna. She might not be serious, but she certainly isn't stupid. She took it for what it was. We both did. We should never have been together if it hadn't been for you in the first place."

"Andrew, what do you mean . . . ?"

"I mean, if you hadn't been so damn frigid with me and then started making eyes at that French gigolo . . ."

"Oh, Andrew." She so wanted to believe him. "Andrew. I want to talk to you. Can I see you?"

"Well . . . right now I'm getting my stuff together. I haven't packed a single thing yet, and we dock in an hour. Why don't we have some lunch one day? You're staying at the Foxleys', is that right?"

"Well . . . yes." She thought she would break down. Her hand was gripping the sheet. "Yes. Did I give you the number?"

"No. But I know the Foxleys. Everyone in New York knows the Foxleys. I'll give you a call there. Okay?"

"Yes," she said. She forced her voice to sound cheerful. "Fine. I'll see you later then."

Corinna found a quiet space at the rail to watch as they came into New York. A cloud of gulls had come out to greet them, scavenging for scraps at the side of their wake. The sky was bright, but a stiff breeze blew down the Hudson from the north.

The Dutch girls were warming up. This morning they were nervous. They kept adjusting their braided caps, pulling down on their tunics, shifting from one foot to the other.

The Statue of Liberty rode on their left, her hand flung high in welcome. Corinna felt threatened by the gesture.

But the other passengers were excited as children at Christmas. They weren't going to miss a minute. They thronged the rail at the front of the ship, pointing out to one another every new thing that came into sight and photographing it at the same time.

The *Josephine* slid by the piers. Corinna read their names above the docks—United Fruit Co., Venezuelan Line. Cranes were dipping slowly into the holds of docked ships, emerging with slings of bales. Ahead,

the tugs were waiting to turn the ship's bows across
the river into her berth.

Above Corinna the *Josephine*'s hooter released a
long, deep boom. The New Royal Netherlands Girl
Majorettes started into "The Star-Spangled Banner."

And, as if on cue, Enid Roscoe and Andrew came
up on deck. Enid, in an ensemble of soft heather
purple, looked healthily feminine. Her cheeks were
smooth and pink, her eyes bright, her colorless hair
simply waved. Andrew too was looking spruce in his
blazer. Any woman would be glad to be seen with
him, Corinna thought. Especially a woman of Enid's
age.

Corinna turned back to the rail. She was disgusted
by her own thoughts. She could tell New York was
going to be a dirty city.


"Andrew," Enid called from the dressing table in
her bedroom next to the bathroom. "Andrew, I think
you should hurry. We shouldn't be late, you know."

Andrew pulled the plug from the bath. He had
not realized Enid Roscoe was quite so rich. Her
brownstone was up in the East 70s, right near the
Rothschilds' New York house. On Thursday afternoon
the chauffeur brought the Rolls along from the ga-
rage, and they went out for the weekend to friends in
the country, purring out of New York with a low
swishing sound, like waves breaking on a rocky
beach.

Even in the bathroom you would know right away
you were not in an ordinary household. It had recently been done over by David Hicks, in marble and
stainless steel, offset by feminine colors, rose and dove
gray, especially to match a set of charming Boucher
watercolors that hung on the walls. In the sitting

room, pride of place was given to a superb Matisse collage. "It was my husband's acquisition," Enid always hastened to say. "I don't buy things like that anymore."

"You have to be early and bright," Enid said in a joking tone that nevertheless carried a hint of warning. "This party is being given for you, remember."

Andrew had forgotten that ruthless New York hospitality. "I begin to feel like a performing dog."

"I wanted to show you the art world in New York. I'm going to teach you all about it, my dear. You must let me help you."

"I know all about it. I lived here two years, didn't I?" He took a thick Turkish towel from the warm rail and began to dry himself.

"In the time since then, there have been a lot of changes."

"But I know *that*. London is not exactly a monastery. We do hear what's going on."

Enid appeared at the door of the bathroom with an eyebrow pencil in her hand. "My dear, don't sound so *fractious*," she said. "You must realize I am only trying to help."

Andrew grinned sheepishly. "Sorry," he said.

Enid went back to work at the mirror.

"But I only came over," Andrew went on, "to deliver a painting to Lennox. I didn't come to catch up on the scene."

"Oh, Lennox can wait. There's no hurry for that, surely?"

"He's waiting for it. And it's important for me. I need the commission. I can't live on nothing."

"You can stay here, you know, as long as you like. So that's no problem, is it? But I must say, I think that painting is *very* suspicious. Why don't you show it to me?"

"It's not my secret. I would show it to you, but he asked me to keep it to myself. I told you."

"You ask to put it in my safe, and you won't even let me see it. I tell you, I know you're smuggling it. It's another Raphael. You're going to sell it to Boston to replace the one they had to give back. The Italian police are hot on your trail. You know what they do, don't you? They hold up your luggage at the airport and search it secretly. That's why it was so long coming through. Then they follow you and arrest you in the act of handing it over."

She appeared again at the door of the bathroom, smiling.

Andrew had finished drying. He put the towel back on the rail.

"I must say," said Enid, "you don't look very frightened." She stepped forward. "I think you should stay," she said in a low, intimate voice. "New York is really the center of the art world. Englishmen are rather fashionable. Your friend Wetherby is having an enormous success. I could be a great help, you know. I know a lot of people. I'd like to help you, Andrew. I do hope you understand that." She looked down and smiled. "Unfortunately, I think we should go."

The party was on the West Side. In the car on the way over, Enid gave Andrew a rundown on who would be there.

"Well, Horace, of course. He's the host. You know him."

"Yes."

"He's still drinking rather a lot, I'm afraid. But it's still the best gallery in town."

At Horace's apartment, Andrew soon felt at home.

Enid was right. Not all the usual people were there when they arrived, but most of them turned up in the course of the evening. The room quickly grew hot and smoky. With the heavily shaded lights and green furnishings, Andrew had the feeling of being under water. And he soon realized what Enid meant about the party being in his honor. Everyone in turn, it seemed, came up to him, either to remind him when they had met or to say, "Ah, so *you're* the famous Englishman Enid met in London." Then they waited for him to prove he was worth throwing a party for.

Before Andrew left, Horace insisted that he must visit him in the gallery.

"Come for tea one afternoon," he said.

"He's going to California," Enid said.

"Come before you go. Come tomorrow. If someone is coming, it makes a nice excuse."

"You need an excuse for tea?" Enid asked.

"Well, we have this special tea." He was smiling. "Sparkling. Bottled in France."

"Okay. Yes. Thanks."

"What are you doing in California?" he asked Andrew.

Enid answered for him. "He's taking out a secret painting. I'm sure it was stolen from Italy or France." She laughed.

"There are more secret collections in Texas than in California," Horace said. "There are twenty-five that I know of, and there must be others."

"Oh, there are several in California," Enid said. "After all, they've only got to sit on them for ten years—at least the Italian ones. After ten years Italian law can't touch them."

"But no one's going to put a whole raft of pictures

on display suddenly and defy anyone to try and get them back."

"Of course not. They really buy them only as investments—except for the few real monomaniacs. After ten years they start selling them. Discreetly. They trickle into museums and collections after twenty-five years or so. Somehow it doesn't seem so bad then."

"Well, I'm sorry to disappoint you, but the painting I have has not been stolen. I can assure you of that. I wouldn't risk my neck. It's simply a recent acquisition for a private collector. And I've sworn not to divulge what it is. I don't want to lose my commission. That's all."

At the party, Enid seemed satisfied with this explanation. But later she came back to the subject.

"Are you sure the painting is all right, Andrew?"

"Yes, of course," he said somewhat irritably. "I wish you wouldn't keep on about it. You have to take my word for it."

"I do, my dear. Of course I do. It's just"—she placed her fingers briefly, absentmindedly almost, on his thigh—"it's just that I'd hate you to get into any trouble. I'm very fond of you, you know. Andrew, I do wish you'd think about settling in New York. We could have a marvelous life; I'm sure we could."

She used that "we" rather often. It was beginning to frighten Andrew. And those friendly creases around her eyes—he couldn't help looking at them, they were really scary.

"I think it's time I settled down and invested in a little enterprise here in New York. I have some money, you know," she said.

"Why don't you put it on Wetherby? According to Horace, he's looking for a backer. And he's quite good-looking," he added viciously.

"Yes, he did ask me," she said smoothly. "But I told him I'm not really interested in the downtown galleries. I feel more at home up here. Sometimes I'm not even sure that I can face some of those young mainstream American painters. Their work is so—so aggressive. It's very *masculine*, of course. But you feel they would rather like to be able to attack you with the paint if they could think of a way how. I don't mind being disturbed, but I don't always feel able to withstand attacks. And besides . . ." Her hand was firmly on his thigh now. A breath of scent reached him—the thick, sweet smell of gardenia, rich and feminine, with its hints of oily secretions. "Besides, I don't feel I could have the same sort of relationship with Bob as I could with you."

"You mean he doesn't screw?"

"Andrew, do you have to be so crude? Bob Wetherby is a happily married man."

"I don't believe that."

"Well, don't you think I should be more likely to know than you, perhaps?"

"Perhaps."

"Would you like a drink?" she said suddenly. "How very remiss of me. I never offered you a drink."

"No, thanks. I drank enough."

"Kiss me."

"Of course."

"Again. You're a nice lover. Why do you have to go away?"

"I'm not going quite yet."

"I'm going to the bathroom," she said, almost in a whisper. "I shan't be a minute. Why don't you just slip into bed?"

"All right."

Andrew lay in the bed and laughed to himself. He

wondered how many vitamin pills she took on these occasions.

After a few minutes she came to the bedroom in a blue negligee frogged with bands of lace. She turned out the light and slipped into the bed.

Andrew took her in the dark. She talked all the time. She was a very articulate lover. "Oh," she cried. "It's never been like this before." And "Oh, this is the most wonderful moment in my life." Already, Andrew thought, in the middle of the action, she was turning it into a memory. People like that preferred memories—they were easier to control.

Corinna very soon came to the conclusion that she hated New York. She had known the Foxleys in England—their parents were cousins of Lord de Boys. They were a generation older, but she liked them. And she liked them still. They did not seem changed. But she was amazed by their friends. She understood that "Uncle" Peter was involved in some sort of antiques business. She knew a little about English antiques. But she found it impossible to talk to these people. She had particular trouble with a man called Frank Williams. He obviously thought he had been called in to squire her around. (She couldn't believe that the Foxleys would actually have intended that when they invited him.) He was so charming it was frightening. The trouble was they all talked art the whole time, but as far as she could see they didn't care a fig about it. They were on the art circuit, so they talked about art. They cared only about the scandals and the prices and the reputations and successes—it might as well have been show business, or the stock market.

Almost her only pleasure was to go to the museums.

Without her mother looking over her shoulder all the time and telling her what she should like and what not, she could look at modern art without any inhibitions. She preferred to look at pictures alone. With other people it was difficult to know what she really felt. At the Guggenheim and the Museum of Modern Art she at last felt relaxed and unself-conscious. She began to understand what it was that excited her mother about this revolutionary American art.

She was nervous again when she met Andrew for lunch. But he himself seemed so miserable, she was immediately concerned. It was nice to be with him, she thought. She had wondered that morning if she were going to be able to control her emotions. But it was not the way she expected. There was no strain. It was just that something that had been there before between them was not there any more.

Andrew ordered them a second martini—gin for him, vodka for her. He didn't look any more cheerful. She just had to ask him what was the matter.

He looked at her. "I made a mistake, Fidget. I'm sorry. I was wrong."

"What do you mean—wrong?"

"Well ... because ... I mean Enid Roscoe. I made a mistake going to stay with her. Of course there's nothing like *that*. And it's a great house. She knows a lot of people. It's really fine ... except ..."

Corinna waited.

"She's so *nice*. She's so damned nice. She's such a nice, helpless lady, with all her pills, and those 'pretty' paintings. But underneath she's as hard as nails. And selfish as a cuckoo. You realize all of a sudden that she's taken you over, that you're doing what she wants you to do. All that money she has, it means power. It means she can afford to be nice, because she knows in the end her money will buy what she wants for her. She doesn't have to fight for it."

"Leave," Corinna said simply.

"She doesn't even know I'm having lunch with you. I didn't like to tell her."

"Leave," Corinna repeated. "Surely, Andrew, she doesn't actually lock you in? Move out. The Foxleys have masses of rooms if you want a free bed."

Andrew avoided her eyes as he answered. "Yes. I will. You're right. I should. But I don't want to offend Enid. She doesn't mean to be so possessive, I'm sure."

"But Andrew . . ."

"I've decided what I shall do. I'll wait until I go down to Lennox. I shall have to go soon. I'll stay until then."

"Andrew." Corinna tried to hide the desperation in her voice. "I suppose I sound like a jealous woman . . ."

"I don't see why you should," he interrupted sharply.

". . . but I honestly don't think you should stay with Enid. She's one of those people. She's awfully nice, but she's lethal."

"You're not jealous, are you, Fidget?" he said suddenly.

She smiled. "In a way, yes, I suppose I am. I mean, I did think we were going on this trip together, and I haven't seen all that much of you."

"But you were coming to New York anyway. I just thought it would be fun for us to travel over together."

He looked at her with such innocent, open eyes, she could almost believe he saw it like that.

"Will you be able to see me tomorrow?" he asked.

"No, Andrew," she said slowly. "I don't think so."

# 3

A NDREW REHEARSED THE SALE of the Rembrandt to Lennox like an actor learning his lines. He'd been through it so often, his only fear was that Lennox might not have rehearsed his own part so well.

Lennox played it like a game. For two days Andrew was treated as a house guest on Lennox's fantastic estate. The main building was a vast, genuine Norman castle, complete with moat and drawbridge. It had once stood in England, on the Welsh border. Lennox had had it transferred stone by stone and reerected in the hills behind Santa Barbara.

Andrew flew into Los Angeles and was met by McIntyre. It had been too late to drive to Lennox's estate, so they stayed the night in the Beverly-Wilshire Hotel. Next day, in the chauffeur-driven Rolls Royce Silver Cloud, they sailed along the freeway at a terrifying speed. Andrew had been surprised by the Spanish charm and the sunny streets of Santa Barbara. It was such a contrast to the East Coast.

But he was not half as surprised by Santa Barbara

as he was when he caught his first sight of the castle
towers as they approached Lennox's estate. In the
lush landscape of spreading avocados, of orange
groves and gum trees, the gaunt gray stone battle-
ments seemed doubly severe.

In the grounds, guest bungalows were disguised as
ancient thatched cottages. Inside, they were luxuri-
ously furnished with priceless European antiques—the
walls hung with French tapestries, the floors laid with
Italian marble.

McIntyre gave Andrew a key. "There's no danger
of intruders. The grounds are guarded. The walls are
fitted with double alarms. You know, we have had
some rather unpleasant occurrences in this part of the
world. You never know where they might strike next."

Lennox worked morning and afternoon in his "library." Andrew had visited him there to say hello the
morning he arrived. Three interconnecting rooms
made one unit. There were few books to be seen. But
there was an impressive array of teleprinters, radiotel-
ephones, computers, and other business equipment.
Lennox himself sat in a bare room, at a vast desk with
three gray telephones.

At lunchtime he made a brief appearance in the
dining room. This was the old hall of the castle. The
walls were thick stone and the ceiling was lofty—a
cool and relaxing room, perfectly suited to the California climate.

But Lennox scarcely spoke at lunch. He ate fru-
gally, drank only iced water, and in ten minutes ex-
cused himself to get back to his desk.

Andrew spent the mornings at Lennox's museum.
The castle's north tower had been converted, and additional buildings added, to house the Lennox collection. For the public there was a separate entrance

from outside the estate. This was open every afternoon. Andrew spent the afternoons at the pool, or
walking in the grounds.

But wherever he was, whatever he was doing, there
was only one thought in his mind. Over and over he
rehearsed his part—the story of the discovery of the
painting, the provenance, all the arguments that
would bolster the sale. He was determined not to ap-
pear overeager. He made great play of staying close
to his painting, locking himself in the bungalow to inspect its condition. But he never mentioned it.

On the second evening there was a guest at dinner—Gail Peters. Lennox clearly enjoyed Andrew's
surprise. "It turns out the lady is a neighbor," he said.

"When I knew you were coming, I asked myself to
dinner," Gail said. "I hope you don't mind."

"Mind?" Andrew didn't have to pretend—he was
genuinely pleased to see her. For some reason, her
being there immediately made him less nervous. She
was deeply tanned and shining with health. "You look
great," he said.

The butler served fresh Scottish salmon, with cu-
cumber sauce.

It turned out that Gail knew also why Andrew had
come to see Lennox. Andrew was glad. He was
pleased to be free to speak about it in front of her.

"I'm quite discreet," she said.

"I know," he said. "I should have told you myself if
you didn't know already."

Conversation turned naturally to the painting.

"You know the Rembrandt that comes up at Christie's next month? McIntyre asked. Sent in by a Mr.
Timothy Proudfoot, our information is."

"Yes, I know it very well. I know the family. It was

left to Tim Proudfoot by his father. It's the most important Rembrandt still in private hands."

"*The Nude Diana*—is that it?"

"Yes."

Lennox looked up. "Is that like it sounds?"

"That's right. It's a great painting. One of the great paintings of the world. Without exaggeration."

Lennox's eyes flickered in his impassive face. "Why didn't we buy it, Mr. Tait?"

"It's not available."

"But," McIntyre said, "it's up for sale."

"Sure," said Andrew. "But it happens to be one of the world's great pictures. It's the last great Rembrandt we shall see on the British market for twenty-five years, maybe ever at all. They're not going to let it out of the country. People can get very patriotic about things like that."

"It's not an English painting. Rembrandt was Dutch. It was painted in Holland."

"Titian was Italian. So was Leonardo. They didn't get an export license. After two or three hundred years the paintings get honorary citizenship. They'd never allow the *Diana* out. It's one of those paintings the public knows. They remember the name. It's all right for a painting only the art world cares about. But it doesn't make political sense for any government to let the *Diana* out of the country."

Lennox nodded slowly. "That's what I figured," he said.

"So," said McIntyre, determined not to let the subject die, "may we now ask how you yourself were able to bring a Rembrandt out of Europe—a comparable Rembrandt, you say. Presumably other countries have the same regulations. Or is that a trade secret?"

"It is a trade secret," Andrew smiled. "But under

the circumstances I think I should let you in on it."
He turned to Lennox. "I want to be quite frank with
you, Mr. Lennox, all along the line."

Lennox grunted.

"The reason I could take out this painting, to put it
simply, was that no one knew of its existence."

Lennox and McIntyre were watching him closely.
He felt a surge of excitement. After all the rehearsal
he was on stage at last.

"I'm sure," he said casually, "if they had known
about it they'd have slapped a restriction on it right
away."

"Why didn't they know?" said McIntyre. His slight
Scottish intonation betrayed his suspicion.

"Because no one knows about this painting. No one
has ever known about it. Rembrandt sold it secretly.
It was—well, for those days it was somewhat scandalous. You'll see. Neither you nor I would find it in
the least scandalous, I'm sure. But she is a totally un-
draped nude. And in those days that was considered
rather gamey. But Rembrandt needed the money. He
always needed money. The bailiffs were always taking away the furniture. He painted this picture as a
private commission, at the same time he was painting
*The Nude Diana.*"

There was no change in Lennox's impassive expression, but Andrew sensed a stir of interest.

"It was never exhibited. My guess is that Rembrandt sold it on condition that it not be shown in
public. After all, he and the girl were living together
as man and wife. They were bringing up his children."

"How did you get to learn about it?"

"Ah," said Andrew. "Well, the picture's been in the
family since then. They knew what it was, but they
weren't particularly interested in art, and they didn't

need the money. They passed it on as a family heirloom."

"But how did *you* get to hear about it?"

"Well—how do you get to hear about these things? Luck, in a way, I suppose. A friend of mine gave me the tip. He'd married a Dutch girl. Her parents knew this family. She knew he was in the art world. . . ."

"Why didn't your friend want to handle the sale himself?"

Andrew shrugged. He allowed a hint of annoyance to enter his voice. "He didn't know how to cope with it. He didn't have the contacts."

"It must have been a temptation to try to find them. A financial temptation."

"Well, naturally," Andrew said shortly. "He's not going to *give* away a tip like that. I have to cut him in."

Gail was watching them calmly, taking small sips from her wine.

"But why," McIntyre went on, "didn't the owners sell it in Holland, if they couldn't sell it abroad?"

"Mr. McIntyre, I think you know the answer to that question yourself. They wouldn't get anything like the price in Holland that they could get on the open market."

"What you're proposing, Mr. Tait," Lennox said, "is not my idea of an open market."

"How do we know what you say is true? How do we know—excuse me, but how do we know that this is not a stolen painting?"

"It would be a clever thief who found a painting that no one knew existed."

"And how do we know it is not a forgery?"

"You don't—not yet."

"The beauty of your story, Mr. Tait, is that there is

no provenance—the painting is unknown, the owners anonymous." McIntyre very slightly exaggerated the burr of his accent, and Andrew understood there was some personal challenge in this.

"My 'story,' Mr. McIntyre, is not a story. It's a fact. I realize you have to raise these questions. But I'm sure you realize I'm somewhat sensitive on the subject. Okay, there is no provenance. No certificate of ownership. But you have to realize that this is the only way you're ever going to get your Rembrandt. The doors are closing all over Europe. There aren't many great paintings left, and it won't be long before every damn country in the world clamps down on exports. Coming across this painting is a fantastic piece of luck. *I* know it's a genuine work. You can take my word for it." He smiled. "But you don't have to. If you want it, if we can agree on everything else—then you can call in your own experts to authenticate it. It's an offer to you until you're satisfied one way or another. You can't ask for anything fairer than that."

"No," said Lennox.

"There are three or four Rembrandt people. I guess you've found that out."

McIntyre nodded.

"There's a guy in Boston. There's the director of the Rembrandthuis in Amsterdam. He'd come over if you asked him. They don't come across a new Rembrandt every week. *You* can go to these people. I couldn't. You can say you've been offered it by a dealer, on behalf of an anonymous owner, and you need their opinion. You can produce the painting, because by now it's untraceable to its country of origin. It could have come from anywhere. What government can claim a painting they didn't know existed?"

"Right," said Lennox. "Mr. Tait, when are you going to show us your painting?"

"Tomorrow," Andrew said. "Tomorrow at lunchtime." He turned to Gail. "I hope you will be able to come too!"

"Yes," Lennox said. "You must come, of course."

"Thanks," Gail said. "I'd love to."

She smiled directly at Andrew. He was glad she would be there. He was beginning to think her presence was a good omen.

Later, when Gail had left, Lennox said to McIntyre, "I think Mr. Tait and I will go to the museum. I want to know his opinion of my paintings. Will you have the lights turned on?"

"Right," said McIntyre.

Andrew and Lennox took their brandy with them. The floors of the castle corridors were thickly carpeted, but the walls were bare stone, hung with tapestries and an impressive collection of antique arms and armor.

In the museum Lennox was a different person. He relaxed his tough, laconic exterior, and his face took on a warm, concerned expression. He moved from one painting to another, as if visiting old friends in the hospital. He stood before each in turn, regarding them with undisguised affection.

He and Andrew stood before a magnificent Tiepolo. He gripped Andrew's arm. "Are you a gambling man, Mr. Tait?" he said.

"Not at all," said Andrew firmly.

"Oh," Lennox sounded disappointed. "I should have thought you might have been." He walked away from Andrew and stood looking at a marble Venus. He did not move for thirty seconds. Then he gave the sculpture an affectionate pat and came back to Andrew. "I thought you might be interested in a—a proposition. Not a gamble at all, really."

Andrew waited. He was calm. So far he had not made a mistake. After a long silence he said, "A proposition has to be proposed."

"Yes," said Lennox. "What I had in mind was to offer, here and now, for your Rembrandt, the sale price of the one that's coming up at Christie's, less two hundred and fifty thousand dollars. No provenances, no authentication. We settle it here and now."

"But you haven't even seen the painting yet, Mr. Lennox."

"I don't need to see it to know what it's worth."

"It's worth more than you're offering, Mr. Lennox. It's certainly worth more than the sale price of the Proudfoot Rembrandt. I told you that I consider that that painting is offered on a closed market. It will have to stay in England."

"But no one is going to question its authenticity. Now *your* Rembrandt . . ."

"I have no doubt that it is authentic."

"How do you know that you weren't cheated, Mr. Tait? Sold a forgery? The whole story could have been a put-up job."

"I have made it my business to be an expert, Mr. Lennox. So would you if so much depended on it. *You* need the director of the Rembrandthuis to tell you if a painting is genuine or not. I don't. I can tell as surely as he. Probably more so. He has only a reputation to lose."

Lennox took his arm again. "I can see you *are* a gambler, Mr. Tait."

"There are two views on gambling. Some would say it's no gamble to bet on a certainty."

Lennox chuckled. "Come, Mr. Tait. I have something to show you."

As Lennox steered him by his arm through the galleries, Andrew was thinking. He knew he had done the right thing, but he wondered why Lennox had made him that offer. Andrew obviously could not accept it. It was not just a matter of convincing Lennox that it was a genuine painting. It would enter the artist's listed works. It would be scrutinized by every art expert in the world. If it did not stand up to that, he would have to repay Lennox, whatever the bargain they struck. Andrew had no intention of skulking in some remote village for the rest of his life, not daring to show his face in London or New York. He stood or fell on the authenticity of the painting. Therefore it was worth either nothing at all, or it was worth the very top price. Maybe Lennox was testing him. If so, he had done the right thing.

Andrew liked Lennox. He liked him more and more as he got to know him. Lennox was rich, but he had made it all himself. Every penny he had earned was by his own sweat. Or his cunning. Andrew did not find that kind of wealth offensive. Lennox had a right to it. And he didn't give himself airs. He knew what he wanted, and he used his wealth to get it. He did not boast. He did not patronize. Andrew liked that quiet style. He did not want to cheat him. And he did not intend to. The Rembrandt would be authenticated. When that happened, it would be a Rembrandt. If the greatest experts the world could produce would say so, to the world's thinking it must be a Rembrandt. And that was what Lennox was getting. The fact that this genuine old Rembrandt had been created by Andrew was his secret. And his triumph.

Lennox stopped in front of a large Monet study of

water lilies. He released Andrew's arm and felt along
the bottom of the picture frame. He must have
pressed a button—the painting moved to one side on a
sliding panel. Behind it there was an opening in the
wall.

"In here is our storeroom," Lennox said. He mo-
tioned Andrew to go ahead of him.

The door closed automatically behind them. Andrew looked around. Dozens of paintings hung at the
side of the room, in close racks, just clearing the floor.
They were fixed on tracks on the ceiling so that they
could be run out individually to the center of the
room for inspection. Against the far wall was a bench
and a couple of easels. On one of them was a
painting, half-cleaned. Lennox was making some ad-
justment to the racks at the far end of the room. He
stood back. Four of the racks slid automatically to the
center of the room. Lennox was hidden in the corner.

"Come Mr. Tait," he said. "I said I have something
to show you."

Andrew found him standing in the corner, facing
the blank wall. All the walls of the room were covered with strip paneling of natural wood. At a touch
from Lennox, part of the wall opened into a doorway.

"Come," said Lennox.

They walked into a large room almost the size of
the storeroom. But this room was carpeted, and the
walls were covered with dark red silk. Two Jacobean
armchairs, covered in red velvet, were placed in the
center of the room facing in opposite directions.

Without a word Lennox went and sat down.

Andrew followed the direction he was facing. He
almost gasped. Before him was the Vermeer *Woman
at the Virginals*. It had been stolen from the
Rijksmuseum twelve months before.

Lennox turned and smiled at him, almost shyly. "She's beautiful, isn't she?"

"Yes, but . . ."

"I come here often, you know. I can sit here for hours, just looking at her. No one knows she is here, of course. Except McIntyre. He knows. But no one else. Not even my wife. She would not understand. And you. I feel I can trust you, Mr. Tait."

Andrew did not know what to say. "Yes, but . . . he stammered.

"Like I can trust my paintings." Andrew realized Lennox was not really talking to him—merely talking his thoughts aloud because Andrew was there. "My paintings don't ask for anything from me. They are beautiful and ageless. They never change. They give me pleasure. They give me peace. Sitting here with her, these are the best times of my life. My children— I give them everything, and they spit on me. They take what I give, and they spit on me. They marry the wrong men, they kill themselves in automobiles, they take drugs, they get themselves blackmailed by go-go dancers. . . . But the paintings, they are faithful, I can rely on them. They don't run off. If only my children were like this. People admire my pictures. They are mine, and they stay with me. . . ." He seemed suddenly to remember Andrew's presence. "I'm sorry. Forgive me. A rambling old man, I am becoming."

"Not at all," said Andrew. "What you say makes good sense. I agree. That's the thing that paintings have. In some peculiar way, they can become friends. But this Vermeer . . . she is beautiful. But . . ."

Lennox steered the conversation another way. "Tomorrow, before lunch," he asked cheerfully, "we shall have a glass of champagne, and you will unveil your Rembrandt for us, Mr. Tait?"

"Yes," said Andrew.

"I shall look forward to it."

At least the sight of that secret gallery quieted the doubts in Andrew's mind. He had been shocked. His own deceptions were comparatively mild.

Corinna was surprised to get a call from Enid Roscoe. And more surprised still at her friendly tone.

"Have you heard from Andrew?" she asked.

"No," said Corinna. "Have you?"

"Oh yes," said Enid.

But Corinna was sure she was not telling the truth.

"To tell the truth, my dear, I'm worried about him."

Enid Roscoe really did sound concerned. Corinna's suspicions were reinforced. She herself had been half-expecting to find Andrew was in trouble with the customs, or the police. There was something very suspicious about the disguised painting and the lies he told her. And he had seemed so tense and desperate. Perhaps Enid Roscoe knew what it was all about. Perhaps that was the reason Andrew had had to keep so close to her.

"I wonder if you'd like to come over. Pick up a cab and come over and we can have a talk."

In Enid's elegant living room Corinna discovered that Enid knew a great deal more about Andrew's movements than he suspected. She knew he had seen Corinna.

"Didn't you mind?" Corinna asked.

"Oh no, my dear. Why should I? You young people like to be together. It's natural."

"How did you know? Did Andrew tell you?"

Enid laughed a warm kindly laugh. "Oh no, my dear. Of course not. Men like to have their secrets, don't they? I wouldn't want to deprive them of that.

It seems to be necessary for them. But other people are always very ready to tell you things like that. I don't know why."

She gave Corinna China tea and buttered toast. In New York she played on her Englishness. In the apartment the paintings and sculpture were expertly displayed, carefully spotlighted so that only flattering, reflected light fell on the people in the room.

"I won't beat about the bush, my dear. You know he is taking a painting to that man in California, whoever he is?"

"Yes."

"Have you seen it?"

"Well . . ."

Enid lifted her head suspiciously.

"Well, no I haven't. Andrew wouldn't show it to me. But, I don't know if he told you, but, well, I did do something rather awful on the ship. . . ."

"No. He didn't tell me. What did you do?"

Corinna told her about bluffing her way into Andrew's cabin with François on the last night of the voyage.

Enid laughed merrily. "He didn't breathe a word to me," she said. "Isn't that typical? He wouldn't risk telling his right hand what the left was doing."

Corinna was beginning to feel uncomfortable with this powder-room gossip. Enid must have had something else in mind. She kept leaning across and patting Corinna affectionately on the knee.

But when Corinna told her about the pasted-over picture, Enid's mood changed.

"Ah," she said gravely. "Now that ties up. That's very interesting. I think perhaps I can tell you what was underneath. You see, we have a safe in this house. My husband had it installed. It's quite large.

Of course, everything we have is insured. But sometimes we used to have a painting on approval. Or new things not yet covered. Insurance companies are funny, you know. You can't just get on the phone and arrange coverage for a Van Gogh, like you can for a car. At any rate, I have this safe here in the house. And Andrew asked me if he could put a painting in it. Only one painting, mind you. He wouldn't tell me what it was. He had brought it for this man in California, he said. He had sworn not to tell anyone what it was until the man wanted it made public. Andrew said he would lose his commission if he betrayed that trust."

"That's what he told me."

"At least he told us the same story. He brought it here sewn into a green canvas bag. It was terribly suspicious. And to tell the truth, I didn't think it was fair to me. One ought to know what's in one's own safe. What if it turned out to be—well, say, a consignment of heroin? Who would believe that I didn't know anything about it?"

"Good God. He isn't mixed up in that, is he?"

"No, my dear. Don't worry. But for all one knew, he might have been, mightn't he?"

"I suppose so."

"So I decided to investigate." Enid said firmly. "I had Horace ask Andrew to go around to the gallery for drinks. And I investigated. Oh, I was very clever. I had already had my maid buy some thread that matched what Andrew had used. Fortunately he's not very neat at stitching. That made it easy. . . . Anyhow, to come to the point: the painting that Andrew has taken to California is a Rembrandt."

"What?"

"Yes, my dear, I know. At first I couldn't believe

my eyes. But I do know enough about painting to recognize a Rembrandt when I see one. I don't know where this came from."

"It could have been a forgery."

"Yes, I'd thought of that. But if it was, there wouldn't have been the need for all this secrecy. It makes me wonder if it really is a stolen painting. Do you know if a Rembrandt has been stolen?"

"No."

"My dear, I'm so sorry to trouble you like this. But you can imagine how worried I've been."

"Did Andrew know you'd looked at it?"

"Oh no, I don't think so. I was very careful. I sewed it up again very carefully."

Corinna left Enid's house with a hundred unanswered questions churning in her head. She knew she wasn't going to solve the riddle of Andrew's behavior by worrying at it. All the possible answers filled her with apprehension. One of them had to be the fact. She was scared of what was going to happen.

Next day the problems were driven out of her mind by the Western Union messenger. He delivered a cable at the Foxleys' house addressed to Corinna. It was from her mother: ARRIVING KENNEDY FRIDAY AM TWA 703 PLEASE MEET MOTHER.

From the moment he lifted the cover Andrew could see that Lennox fell for the painting. For a long time he contemplated it in silence, sipping at his champagne. But his eyes burned with a deep light, and Andrew knew that he was hooked.

Eventually Lennox stirred. "It's got class," he said. "I'll say that. It's got real class."

From him that was a high compliment. Lennox did not have a vocabulary of aesthetic superlatives. But his appreciation was no less keen. Under his cool exterior, Andrew was exultant. It had worked. At first sight Lennox had fallen in love with Franco's *Diana*.

He had McIntyre fetch an easel so that the picture could be displayed near them as they had lunch. "If that's all right with you, Mr. Tait."

"Of course. I never tire of it myself."

Andrew and Gail exchanged a glance. Facing away from Lennox, she dared a quick wink.

After lunch, Lennox thanked Andrew rather formally and went to his study.

During the afternoon, which he spent with Gail by the pool, Andrew was summoned to the phone to take a call from New York. It was Corinna.

"Hello," he said. "It's good to hear you. How did you get the number?"

"Well, Andrew," she said, "men like Lennox are quite well known. Even if you don't have the street address."

Andrew laughed. "Okay. You're elected Secretary of the Week. What time is it with you?"

"Evening," she said. "Seven o'clock."

"Good Lord. Yes. What's the weather like?"

"Cold."

"In a city you don't like, it's always cold. Who said that? Hemingway? Raymond Chandler?"

"I don't know. But it's true. I'm freezing. And I hate this city."

"I'm sorry."

"Listen, Andrew. I didn't call you to talk about the weather. My mother arrived here yesterday."

"You called to tell me that?"

"Yes. At least, partly that. I mean, yes, but the important thing is the reason she came. She came to get away from Boys Hall, from England!" She hesitated.

"Why?" Andrew prompted.

"Well . . . Andrew I wish you were here."

"Why?"

"Well. You know Tim and Sally were putting the Rembrandt up at Christie's?"

"Yes."

"Christie's won't accept it. They say it is a forgery. A recent forgery. Not more than twenty or thirty years old."

There was a silence at the other end of the line.

"Andrew? Are you still there?"

"Why did your mother leave?"

"She wanted to get away from all the fuss at home. No one else knows. You mustn't tell anyone. Christie's is being very decent; they're keeping it quiet. They can easily say it's been withdrawn to sort out some tax problem. But you can imagine how she feels. . . . She loved that picture. It was her favorite in the whole house. You know, when I was born, she wanted to call me Diana. But apparently my father—my real father—wanted me to be called Corinna . . ."

"Corinna." Andrew's voice was strained. Corinna knew there must be some connection between the Proudfoot *Diana* and the painting Andrew had taken to Lennox in California, but she still could not figure it out. And she guessed Andrew was not going to tell her. Was it possible that the Proudfoot *Diana* had been stolen many years ago? That would have been during the war, when Lord de Boys was away and no one really knew what was going on. And maybe Andrew had traced it. Maybe it had been smuggled to the Continent and hidden. Anything was possible in those days. Or maybe a copy had been made as a precautionary measure, and the original had never been replaced. According to her mother, Tim was challenging the opinion of Christie's experts. But they didn't make mistakes about things like that. . . . There were a thousand possibilities. The only thing she knew was that there must be a connection somewhere. "Corinna. I'm coming back to New York."

"When?"

"As soon as I can. Tomorrow. The day after. Will you be at the Foxleys'?"

"No, Andrew."

"Where will you be?"

"I won't be in New York, Andrew. That's really what I wanted to tell you. I'm going home. I'm going back to England."

"Didn't your mother come to see you? Doesn't she want you to stay?"

"No. She's with the Foxleys. She hasn't told anyone but me about the Rembrandt. She has a lot of good friends in New York. She's at home here. She doesn't need me. I'm sure she'd rather I went. And I don't want to stay."

"But when shall I see you?"

"I don't know, Andrew."

"But . . ."

"What I mean, Andrew, is that I'm not sure. I'm not sure what I'm going to do. And I'm not sure that I want to see you. I think it might be better if we didn't meet. I shouldn't have come on this trip. It's too late to worry about it now, but I'm going back. I don't know what I'm going to do. I doubt if I shall stay at the cottage, but I'll go there for the time being. There isn't anywhere else."

"I shall come and see you."

"Andrew. Please don't do that. Don't you understand, Andrew? I'm saying that I don't want to see you again."

She put down the phone. She was not crying. A faint glimmer of light had appeared to her, at the end of the long, dark, unhappy tunnel of the last months. She began to understand what she was going to do.

# 4

Q<small>UENTIN</small> G<small>OLD</small> had awakened with a start at five in the morning. His heart was racing. What had waked him, he wondered. Then he remembered—today the Proudfoot Rembrandt would come in to Christie's.

He forced himself to take his breakfast slowly. He found himself carefully selecting a tie, as if he had an important lunch appointment. He was at the office before the doorman had put on his cap for the day.

Sally was late. She had driven up from Boys Hall that morning, starting soon after dawn. Quentin was not the only one who was nervous, she told him. Although it was insured for a vast sum, Timothy was reluctant to let the picture out of his sight. He wanted to travel up with it in the van, but the transport men would not allow him.

And the night before, Delphine had made an eleventh-hour appeal to Timothy not to take the picture away. She had summoned the family to the top of the stairway in the Great Hall. She stood in front of the *Diana* and pleaded with Timothy. The way she told

248

it, *The Nude Diana* was the chief claim to fame for the Proudfoot family. Without it, they would be nothing. Anyone who knew anything about anything knew that this was the family's most important possession. With tears streaming down her cheeks, she told them how much she herself loved this painting, how she had wanted to name her only daughter after it, how it would break her heart to see it torn down from its place of honor and put up for public auction, like a common prostitute.

"It sounds very dramatic," Quentin said.

"It was. But Delphine thrives on drama. She needs it. She lives her whole life as if she were a dramatic heroine."

"But she didn't make Timothy change his mind?"

"Well, we were all terribly upset, of course. But Timothy isn't the sort of man who changes his mind at the last moment. He made up his mind long ago, and that was that. And I think Giles was on his side, if anything, after his mother's performance."

He was sorry Sally had had such trouble. Unfortunately, in their business family disagreements were all too common. He'd learned never to take sides and to insist on the proper authority for every step he took himself. That way he avoided difficulty, if not unpleasantness.

At noon they had a message that the painting had arrived. Sally hurried out to find Timothy. He had followed the van up to London in his car.

A porter was bringing the picture to the storeroom. Quentin hurried downstairs.

As soon as he saw it, he felt a sudden panic. Something was wrong. He was sure of it. For twenty years he had been training his eyes to judge paintings. He had learned to trust their reactions. And they told him immediately that there was something fishy about this picture. He could not say right away what it was—simply that the picture was not "right." He did not have any doubt of that. It was more than a suspicion. Those twenty years had given him that confidence. He was absolutely certain it was wrong.

Sally came into the storeroom. She was flushed with excitement. "Tim didn't come," she said. "His car broke down on the highway." She laughed. "The painting got here anyway."

"When did you last look at it, Sally?"

"I don't know. Last night, I suppose. I look at it every time I go up the main stairs at Tim's house."

"I mean really look at it. Look at it closely."

"Oh, I don't know, really. It's just there all the time, you know ..." She caught a hint from the gravity of his voice. "Why? What's the matter? Is it damaged?"

"No," Quentin said carefully. "I don't think it's damaged."

"Quentin." Her voice was filled with apprehension. "Something is the matter. What are you saying?"

"I'm not happy about it, Sally. It doesn't smell right."

"How can it possibly ... ?" Her voice trailed away.

Quentin peered closely at the surface of the canvas. He picked up his magnifying glass and inspected the flesh of Diana's leg. "It's very good, I must say," he murmured.

"What do you mean, very good?" Sally was frantic, only just in control of herself. She wanted to run away. But she forced herself to say calmly, "What is 'good,' Quentin?"

"The brushwork," he answered automatically. "Rembrandt's brushwork was bold—almost Impressionist, if you look at it. He must have painted quickly. There's nothing finicky about it. Look at that white shift or whatever it is she put on the grass. The paint's really slapped on. That's just how Rembrandt did it. The paint's not built up with smooth layers. You can't get that effect by painting meticulously. You can't keep stopping to see how you're getting on, to check if Rembrandt's brush went slightly to the left or right ..."

"But, Quentin, you're talking as if this were painted by someone else, a copy. . . ."

Quentin turned slowly and looked at her. "Yes, Sally, I'm afraid that's exactly what I am saying."

"But it can't be," she burst out. She turned on him. "How do you *know?*" she demanded angrily. "How can *you* say? It can't possibly be by anyone else. Anyone can see it's a Rembrandt. *You* can't just sit here and say it isn't. You don't *know* it isn't."

"I *do* know, Sally. For myself I'm quite satisfied." His own face was ashen. Up to now he had simply been concentrating on the identification of the painting. Now the implications of what he had said was beginning to dawn on him. "It doesn't quite hang together. It isn't quite confident enough. But that doesn't prove it, of course."

"What are you going to do?"

"I shall talk to other people. The other people here. We shall have to decide. We could refuse to handle it. We could try to persuade your fiancé not to offer it for sale. That's usually the most tactful way out of these situations. We can make some tests on it."

"Quentin, how can you sit there and calmly tell me that this painting is a—a forgery? The whole world knows this painting. Hundreds of people come and look at it. They don't think it's a forgery."

"They don't look at it as closely as I."

"That painting means a whole life for Tim and me," Sally said. There were tears in her eyes. "How *can* you just sit there and tell me it's worth—worth *nothing?* You just look at it and tell me it's worth nothing."

"Unfortunately, it's my job to tell people these things—if it happens to be the case. Look, Sally, I don't enjoy it. It's a terrible disappointment for me too. I wish I didn't think this painting was wrong. But if I do, I have to say so. . . ."

Sally ran from the room.

Quentin called the other directors. At first he said nothing of his suspicions.

"What do you think of her?" he asked.

"Beautiful. Magnificent," said one.

"It's wrong," said the other. "It's a fake."

"Yes," said Quentin, "That's what I thought. What do you think we should do?"

Christie's told Timothy that, in their opinion, it was a suspect painting. He was indignant. How could it be a forgery? It had hung in Boys Hall for three hundred years. He wanted to take it away from them and give it to Sotheby's to auction instead. But they persuaded him it was wiser not to say anything until they had made some tests. While it was still at Christie's, they assured him, the matter would be handled with complete discretion.

Finally he agreed.

First they took the canvas out of the frame. They agreed that the frame was genuine. The stretchers on which it was fastened were also genuine—they were certainly of old wood. But here was the first evidence to support their opinion: the edges of the canvas were almost straight and had not shrunk away from the nails at all.

They took threads from the edges of the canvas. They sent them to the workshops of the National Gallery and asked for a dating. The threads were returned with a report that they were from canvas of nineteenth-century manufacture, or later. There were traces of bleaching chemicals—not used on old canvas—which caused brown stains when treated with sodium hydrate. Furthermore, both the threads and the weave of the canvas were of a nineteenth-century, or later, machine-made type.

X-ray photographs showed no evidence of another painting under the *Diana*. But they did show clearly that the canvas was fixed to the stretcher with machine-made nails. This was imperceptible to the naked eye because the heads of the nails were covered with paint. Further, a radiograph showed that there was considerably less crackle down at the canvas than a direct photograph, or even visual inspection, showed at the surface—an indication that the crackle had been induced artificially from the surface and not caused by the natural movement of the canvas as the paint dried.

From three separate places on the canvas a tiny core of paint was taken off with a hypodermic needle. These, under microscopic inspection, showed four or five distinguishable layers—two grounds, two or three layers of paint, and one of varnish. This was perfectly in line with Rembrandt's known techniques. But chemical analysis of the paints revealed a different story. Some of the blue pigment, instead of ground lapis lazuli, turned out to be artificial ultramarine. This is obtained by heating together kaolin, sodium carbonate, and sulphur. Chemically the components are those of lapis lazuli. But under the microscope the particles are not crystalline, as are those of lapis lazuli: they are smaller and they are all blue, whereas in lapis lazuli there are some uneven and colorless crystals. Artificial ultramarine was first available in the nineteenth century. Further, under test with the microspectroscope, some of the blue pigment revealed traces of cobalt, showing absorption bands in the red and yellow, and a bright red band.

Dirt lifted from the surface cracks was shown on analysis to be almost unadulterated charcoal dust.

The Louvre kindly supplied microphotographs of the brushwork of the flesh and the eyes of their *Bathsheba After the Bath* for comparison with the *Diana*. A painter's treatment of the eye and the mouth are almost inimitable when looked at in this detail. Although to the naked eye the effect of the flesh tones of the *Bathsheba* and the *Diana* were identical, in the photographs it was possible to see they had been built up differently. Bathsheba was much more boldly, irregularly worked, with tiny jabbing strokes of the brush.

"That should be enough for anyone," Quentin said when they had the final report. "I wish to God I had been proved wrong. Proudfoot won't like it. But he'll have to accept it."

Andrew took the local connection from Santa Barbara to Los Angeles, where he would get the New York plane. It was damp and cold when he left. As the plane came in from the sea, the rising sun was shining on the yellowish pall of the smog that hung over Los Angeles. For half an hour they circled, until it was clear enough to land—round and round over the same drab landscape, gray houses, gray yards, and chlorine-blue pools.

Back in New York Andrew again put the painting

in Enid's safe. She seemed glad to see him. But it wasn't easy to tell with Enid how much was politeness.

"Your friend Corinna's mother is here," she said. "She is the toast of New York."

"Really?"

"She's a friend of yours too, is she?"

"I know her. I wouldn't say she is a friend. She doesn't like me at all."

"She sees a lot of Bob Wetherby. They are inseparable."

"That's clever of her."

"Clever of him. I've no doubt she's immensely rich."

"Yes," said Andrew. "I suppose."

When Corinna had called him at Lennox's estate, it had taken him ten seconds to piece together the whole story. He intended to get Delphine to confirm that he'd got it right. If he had, it meant he would have to put his Rembrandt away for the time being, and see what developed.

Andrew soon discovered that Delphine and Bob Wetherby really did make the New York scene. They went to all the openings, of course. But so did Enid and Andrew.

Bob sold paintings to David Whitney, to the Sculls, Norton Simon, and a whole raft of the super-rich (with their private tax-avoidance foundations.) He was a good friend of Barbara Rose, Marion Javits, Leo Castelli. He was everywhere. And he took Delphine with him.

"We shall have to do something about this," said Enid. And she was not entirely joking.

But Bob Wetherby did not like rivals.

He asked Andrew to have lunch with him. "Just

man to man, eh? Make it the Oyster Bar at the Plaza. One o'clock."

Bob Wetherby sucked down a dozen oysters and drank Black Velvet.

Andrew did not like that style. He ordered a Bloody Mary and clams. "How's Delphine?" he asked.

Bob Wetherby ignored the question. "Been to see Lennox, I hear, Andrew?"

"That's right."

"You're working for him?"

"I wouldn't say that. He's in the market for some things. There's nothing exclusive, I'm sure you know quite well what he wants."

"A Rembrandt more than anything. He says you have one. He thinks he can get it from you cheap. I hope you're not going to give it away."

"We didn't even discuss a price. I'm not even sure I'm going to let him have it."

"Quite right. I'm not sure he should be allowed to have a Rembrandt at all. There aren't so many good ones about. Yours is a good one, is it?"

"Yes," said Andrew. "The best. The last best Rembrandt there will ever be. It's worth a great deal of money. I don't know where Lennox got the idea it would be cheap. It certainly won't."

"I see," said Wetherby. "How exciting. You know, I'm not altogether sure I trust our friend Lennox. Tsk. Tsk. He doesn't always quite tell the truth." He shook his head sadly.

"But Mr. Tait gave us to understand that a Rembrandt would not be allowed out of England. Or any other country, for that matter."

Ashton Lennox, his eyes shaded by tinted glasses, accepted a glass of iced Coke from McIntyre.

"That's not necessarily true."

Bob Wetherby, immaculately dressed in a gray lightweight suit, knocked the ash from his Havana cigar into the pool. McIntyre blanched. Wetherby knew he was angry. He had deliberately provoked him. He had flown out to California to teach Lennox a lesson—that doing deals behind Wetherby's back is asking for trouble.

McIntyre had a second glass of Coke in his other hand. He gave it to a girl who was standing by Lennox's chair. She had been introduced to Wetherby as Lennox's niece, a student at Berkeley. Lennox's wife, apparently, was in Europe, and Linda was staying at the castle. She took her Coke and stretched out on her stomach on a towel by the side of the pool. She slid her arms out of the straps of her tiny red bikini and settled down to freshen the tan on her back. Lennox's face was expressionless as stone.

"You mean Tait's a liar?" he said.

"No. I wouldn't say that about a professional colleague. Perhaps he is not so experienced. I have been practicing this trade longer than Andrew Tait. All I will say is that in my experience there are ways and means of moving paintings—perfectly legitimate ways and means of moving paintings from one country to another."

"Your Rembrandt is in Europe?"

"Yes."

"We know that one. The Proudfoot Rembrandt."

"*The Nude Diana,*" McIntyre added. "They'd never allow that out."

"No. I did not mean *The Nude Diana.* The Proudfoot picture will never be sold."

"What do you mean? It's coming up at Christie's. It's been announced."

"Could you give me the date?"

"No Well, I don't think the date's been fixed," McIntyre faltered.

"I say it will never be sold."

"Why do you say that, Mr. Wetherby?" Lennox asked in his deliberate voice.

"Because the Proudfoot picture is a forgery, Mr. Lennox."

"What?" McIntyre burst out. "What did you say?"

"It's a forgery. A fake, Mr. McIntyre."

Lennox took a sip of his Coke. "And how do you know that, Mr. Wetherby?" he asked.

"Because I've seen it, Mr. Lennox. I know the family quite well. I've stayed quite frequently in their house. They have some magnificent paintings. But this is not one of them. It is a forgery. I knew it the first time I saw it, and I've never changed my opinion."

"Is that so?" Lennox said. "That's amazing. Tell me, how can you be so sure?"

"One has a certain instinct, Mr. Lennox. One trains it. One takes notice of it. Our whole system of education, our whole society, tries to persuade us not to trust in instinct, to rely only on such things as proof and logic. In fact instinct is a very accurate instrument. It takes into account all those almost imperceptible clues, perhaps too fine to measure. My instinct is what I rely on, Mr. Lennox. I would back it against a whole lot of documentation, and not a little science. So far, I'm glad to say, there has been no conflict between me and the evidence."

"Do the family know this?" McIntyre asked.

"I doubt it. It's a very good copy. I doubt if there are more than half-a-dozen men in the world who would even suspect the painting without the chance of testing it.' He smiled. "The other five have probably not seen it. Scientific tests, of course, would prove it. If the family did know, they would be running a very great risk, surely, in sending it for auction."

"Lady Delphine is in New York, isn't she?" McIntyre made it sound as if he were scoring a point.

"Yes. I haven't spoken to her about it. She hasn't mentioned it to me. As you say, it is commonly assumed that the painting will be sold."

"Does she know it's a fake?"

"I really couldn't tell you, Mr. McIntyre. I haven't asked her. Perhaps you would like to do so yourself?"

Lennox said, "Have you seen Mr. Tait's Rembrandt, Mr. Wetherby?"

"No. Why?"

"It was painted, Mr. Tait says, about the same time as the Proudfoot painting."

"You must draw your own conclusions from that."

"Yes," Lennox said. "May I ask you if your instinct formed an opinion as to how recently the Proudfoot painting had been made? It has been known for some hundreds of years. It came direct from the sale of Charles II's collection. He bought it from the artist. Did the artist sell him a fake?"

"Without inspecting it, I couldn't say for sure. I would guess that it was a recent forgery. Not more than a hundred years old. Does it make a difference?"

"Yes. You see, Mr. Tait's painting is very similar indeed to the Proudfoot *Diana*. It's not similar enough, however, to be the same picture in an altered state. Mr. McIntyre has checked on this. If the Proudfoot *Diana* is a recent forgery, an original must have existed. Mr. Tait's twin painting therefore seems at least a possibility."

"Did he offer no provenance? No certification? No evidence of ownership?"

"No."

"This really does begin to sound suspicious."

With a deliberate gesture Wetherby threw the butt of his cigar into the center of the pool. "Now, listen, Mr. Lennox. I'm offering you a Rembrandt. Its provenance is indisputable. It's a portrait of his son Titus. Not dissimilar to the one Mr. Norton Simon has in his collection here in California."

"Did he buy that from you?" McIntyre asked.

A shadow of annoyance crossed Wetherby's face. "No," he said. "He chose to buy it himself at Christie's. I offered to obtain it for him. He wouldn't have had to pay so much. But he chose to buy it himself."

"And they let him take it out of England?"

"Exactly."

"How much?" Lennox asked.

"What?"

"How much is yours?"

"It will not be cheap," Wetherby answered. "If you want a Rembrandt, a good Rembrandt, a *genuine* Rembrandt, you must be prepared to pay for it. But consider, Mr. Lennox, what you are buying. What Tait says has some truth in it. It becomes more and more difficult to get great paintings out of Europe. There are very few left. If you have to think about the price, Mr. Lennox, you shouldn't think about collecting that sort of painting." He appeared to be fascinated by Linda's back, as she raised her head to take a sip of her Coke, holding her other arm across her breasts. "You know what the great Duveen, the great dealer, used to say? 'When you pay high for the priceless, you are still getting it cheap.' He was right.

There's one thing you can be sure of—if you try to buy masterpieces in the bargain basement, you will run into trouble. If they're in the basement, it's because there's some reason they dare not show themselves upstairs in the drawing room. You, Mr. Lennox, have a magnificent collection of drawing-room paintings. Many of them, I'm glad to say, purchased on my advice. If there are any of those paintings, if there is even one, that you now regret, I beg you to return it to me immediately. I should, of course, credit you with the full purchase price."

"I'm perfectly satisfied, Mr. Wetherby. In fact, as I hope you know, I'm proud of every single picture that you've found me. I'm proud to possess them."

"And I wonder, Mr. Lennox, if there are any paintings that I have advised you against that you now wish you had bought nevertheless?"

Lennox was about to speak, but Wetherby continued, "If there are, I will undertake to go to the present owner and, if at all humanly possible, obtain them for you—at whatever the price. And I should be glad to present them to your museum as a gift."

Lennox lowered his head. There was a slight smile at the corners of his mouth. "There are none," he said. "Mr. Wetherby, I'm entirely satisfied with—with your help. Without your good advice, my museum would be nothing like it is."

Wetherby stood up. "Thank you," he said. "I'm glad to hear it. I wanted to be sure. I thought it worth coming to see you."

"I am glad you did."

After he had gone, McIntyre said to Lennox, "He didn't arrange to show us his Rembrandt."

Lennox chuckled. "No," he said. "I don't suppose he

could. I doubt that the owner has ever agreed to sell.
Wetherby has some work to do on that."

"Then what was he doing here?"

"He came to warn me off Tait, you fool. It's as
plain as the nose on your fat face."

"What will you do? Will you deal with Tait?"

"I don't know. What we shall do, McIntyre, is wait
and see. Remember, *this* is where the money is. We
call the tune. The worst mistake we could make is to
let ourselves be rushed. I've learned that lesson in the
last forty years. Act swiftly if you have to. Never act
hastily."

Delphine tried to avoid Andrew in New York. If
they were at the same party, she avoided his eyes and
stayed in another part of the room. If he called at the
Foxleys' house, the maid always reported that she was
out, and they didn't know when she would be back.

But Andrew was determined to see her.

His chance came one afternoon in Sonnabend's
SoHo gallery at the Gilbert and George show. Gilbert
and George, two precise Englishmen, very properly
dressed, gilded their faces and sat in the gallery with
impassive expressions. They sat there all day, scarcely
moving. Now and then they sang an old popular
song. . . . This was their art.

When he walked into the gallery, the only other
person there, apart from Gilbert and George themselves and a boy at the desk, was Delphine.

Andrew went straight up to her. "Hello, Delphine,"
he said.

She did not hide her displeasure. She adopted her
most superior expression.

"Hello, Andrew," she said, as if he were a servant
she had had to dismiss some time ago.

"I'm glad to see you, Delphine. I've been trying to catch you. You're very elusive."

"I seem to have been frightfully busy."

If possible, she was thinner than ever, her cheekbones even more prominent. She was dramatically dressed in long boots and a richly embroidered calf-length dress. But she looked ill.

"I wanted to talk to you. It's rather important."

"Oh?" she said, as. if she could scarcely imagine anything Andrew said could be important.

"Yes, I wanted to talk to you about the Rembrandt at the Hall—the *Diana*."

"Why? What do you know about that?"

He was glad she was so insulting. Otherwise he might have felt sorry for her. Those people got away with being rude for so long they never bothered to learn to be polite.

"I hear that Christie's is refusing to handle it, that they think it's doubtful."

"Corinna told you?"

"Yes."

"How dare she?"

"She told me nothing I couldn't have guessed myself. I knew—in a way I knew already. But I'd like to hear the details from you."

"What did you know already?" Her eyes were beginning to shift with fear. "What details? You seem to think you know everything already."

Gilbert or George, whichever it was, began to sing in a thin small voice. "Underneath the arches . . ."

"Wouldn't it be better if we talked about it somewhere else?"

"If you insist."

"Would you have lunch with me?"

Delphine shrugged her shoulders, a tiny movement. "Oh, all right," she said in an exasperated tone.

Delphine was half an hour late for lunch. Andrew waited calmly. He knew she would come. She was scared, and she wanted to find out how much Andrew knew.

And she had evidently decided that her best plan was to be cooperative.

"I'm going to tell you everything," she said, almost as soon as she sat down. "I don't know how much you know. But I have to tell someone. And it's probably better to tell a stranger. It's been such a terrible strain. All these years. It's ruined my health. Look at me. I never sleep. I can't eat. Look at me. I look terrible, don't I?"

"No, of course . . ."

"Oh, don't be polite. Please don't be polite. I've had this bottled up inside me for twenty-five years. It's been eating at me all this time. Like a—like a cancer, it has been eating at me. How many people look at me and say 'Delphine certainly knows how to get what she wants'? But what's the cost? Is what Delphine gets always what Delphine wants?"

"I'm sorry."

"Who else knows?" she asked, looking up suddenly. "Does Corinna know?"

"Nobody else knows," said Andrew. "Different people know different parts, but no one but you and I know the whole story."

"And . . . and . . ." She could not bring herself to say the name.

"And Franco? Yes—at any rate up to the death of your husband."

She watched her own nail marking lines in the tablecloth. Then she said quietly. "It was his fault. It was Franco's fault. You know that?" She glanced up quickly at Andrew. There were tears in her eyes. "He was so proud, so stubborn. After the war I wanted him to stay at the Hall. It would have been quite easy. I was willing to pay for him to be trained. We needed someone to look after the pictures. Some of them were badly neglected. He was very stubborn. He insisted that if I really loved him, I should run away with him. We should get married and live on his painting. It was all very romantic. But neither of us would have been happy. You know. Italians are obsessed with their masculinity. Franco would have sacrificed anything to bolster his male pride. And I wouldn't let him."

"Had he painted the *Diana* then?"

Delphine's answer was almost inaudible. "No. He had started. He had made sketches, but he hadn't finished." She looked directly at Andrew. "I didn't know what he was doing. I knew he had been copying pictures in the Uffizi. I thought he should keep his hand in. I encouraged him. I was ... very fond of him. I wanted to help him. He begged me to let him stay until the birth of the child. I hadn't the heart to refuse him. I didn't want him to go away. Oh, if only I hadn't been so softhearted. If only I had known what he was doing."

"Did he stay at the Hall?"

"No. Oh no. He went to live in an old cottage on the estate. The cottage that we gave Corinna later. It was quite isolated—you remember?"

"Yes."

"It had been empty for years. Franco patched it up. Word did get about that one of the Italian prisoners had stayed in England rather than go home. But the cottage was miles away, and Franco never came to the house, so no one ever knew who he was."

Franco had found work at the houses in the neighborhood, gardening and odd-jobbing. In those days Delphine had horses of her own. She would take them out every day for exercise and find her way to the cottage. She took Franco food, money, and the materials he needed to continue his painting.

He had fitted up the stables beside the cottage as his studio. In the woods to the rear he found an old charcoal burner's camp. He renovated the oven in preparation for the final stages of his work.

"Did he use an old canvas?"

"No."

"Why not?"

"It was a mistake, I know. He should have done. There were some quite important old paintings in the Hall that no one would have missed. Or if they had, they might have been stolen while everyone was away. Things did disappear during the war. But I tell you, I didn't know what he was doing. As far as I knew, as long as it *looked* genuine, that was all he wanted. I bought him new canvas and he treated it somehow. But of course the Christie's people knew at once that it was new."

Franco had boiled the canvas for hours and then laid it out in the sun to bleach and fade. But the summer of 1945 was cold and wet, and when it did shine the English sun was too weak to be effective.

"I couldn't understand," Delphine said, "why he was so keen to get every detail right. Even the back of it. He took old wood out of the rafters of the cottage to make the stretchers. Of course I know why now, but at the time I thought it was just that he was a sort of perfectionist. You know how some people are funny about getting things exactly right."

For priming the canvas after he had bleached it, Franco made glue from rabbit skins. The land around there was infested with rabbits, and he soon grew skillful at snaring them. With the meat he fed himself and the old mongrel dog that came to live with him. The skins he cut up and boiled in an evil-smelling mess that eventually he was able to strain and use as glue.

"But there were some things I couldn't get for him. I couldn't get the blue he wanted. Lapis lazuli. In the war you couldn't get it. It was practically unobtainable. It was fearfully expensive, anyway."

After the painting was completed, Franco baked it very slowly in the charcoal oven. Later, in his studio in the stables, he wet the canvas thoroughly and, with a compass point, marked on the back the lines of the main pattern of crackle he wanted. Then he rolled the canvas, paint outwards, repeatedly and carefully. A convincing pattern of crackle appeared on the surface.

"Why did he do it?"

"I didn't know he *was* doing it. All I knew was that he was becoming very strange. I thought he was obsessed with what he was doing, with the creation of a duplicate masterpiece. It was only when he had finished that I realized why he was in such a state. You see, he thought that, if he could put it in the place of the real Rembrandt and sell the original, he would have so much money I couldn't possibly refuse to go with him. He knew about the secret market. He had come across it occasionally when he was copying in Florence. He was quite sure that this was the answer to all his problems. In so many ways he was quite innocent, you know."

"Where is it now, the painting?"

"I don't know. I honestly don't know. I didn't want to know. Where do these paintings go? You probably know better than I. I always used to think they were all in South America, but one hears all sorts of stories. I was even told there is one secret collector in England. I refused to have anything to do with it. I shouldn't have helped him. But—well, I *loved* him, Andrew. And I was beginning to be *frightened* of him. He was like a man possessed. And then—well, it didn't seem such an awful thing. No one would ever know. I couldn't tell the difference between the paintings myself, from close up, and I do look at a lot of paintings, you know. I know what to look for in a painting. I knew that no one would ever suspect anything while it stayed there on the wall. And why should it ever be taken down? Certainly not in my lifetime. I think I let Franco persuade me that there was no *real* difference in the value of the two paintings. Only for people who didn't matter—investing collectors, and money men. For everyone else, after all, the experience of looking at his copy was the same as looking at the real thing."

She put her hand on his and shot him a pleading glance. "He persuaded me. I know it was wrong of me. But you must understand how it was for me. All the things I had wanted to do, all these years, they all suddenly seemed possible. Not for myself. I didn't care about myself. There was so much I could do for the family, for the Hall and . . . well, I have to say it, for Art."

Andrew shifted.

"But you didn't go with him?"

"I told you, he was becoming so strange. I was frightened of him. I thought he would become violent. He threatened me—literally threatened me. It was a terrible time. When you see someone you have loved becoming . . . becoming so strange. I couldn't talk to him any more. He was a different person. My Franco had been so gentle, so sensitive. This wasn't the same person. I couldn't imagine spending the rest of my life with this man, the man he had become."

"What happened in the end?"

"He went. I thought he needed help. I wanted him to go to a doctor. And he refused. He was furious. He shouted at me, swore and shouted. It was a terrible time."

"And he went?"

"Yes. He said that was what he wanted. It was all he wanted, he said, to get back to his own country. I gave him the fare. He went back to Italy."

"You gave him the fare? The picture wasn't sold?"

"No. I had found a man who said he thought he knew someone. . . . It all takes time, you know. He had to make some enquiries. It was a terrible time. We had already taken the *Diana* out of the Hall. It was at the cottage in the stable, in a crate. It wasn't difficult, getting it there. It was quite common for crates of paintings and things to arrive for me at the Hall. I had Franco bring the copy in a crate in a van on the afternoon of the annual cricket match. The house was empty. I said earlier he never came to the house, but it wasn't quite true. He came that day. It didn't take long to change the paintings. It's not a large picture. Getting it out of the frame was worst, but Franco knew how to do that sort of thing." Her voice took on a dreamy reminiscent tone. "It was like the old times, with Franco in the house. It was a beautiful summer day. He stayed as long as we dared. . . ."

"So when Franco left, the painting was not sold?"

"No," she said sadly.

"But you did find a buyer?"

"Oh yes."

"And that was what paid for the new wing, and the pool?"

"Yes."

"And you never saw Franco again?"

"No. Never. It was cruel of him. I never heard a word from him. Not even an address." She was crying discreetly, with her face averted.

Andrew stretched out and grasped her hand. "I'm so sorry," he said. "Don't cry."

But that was not what he was thinking.

THE BREEZE HAD CLEARED the blossoms from the
apple trees in Corinna's garden, and they lay on the
grass like pink snow. It was beautiful there at the cottage. In the spring it was always beautiful there, but
this year it was specially so. When she rode through
the woods the leaves were such a beautiful green, soft
yet vivid. In the fields the wheat was growing strong.
On sunny afternoons she heard the sinister cry of the
cuckoo. They said the cuckoo throws his voice like a
ventriloquist, and she never caught sight of the bird.

Corinna was aware of the beauty of the countryside. But it did not cheer her. In the sunshine she was
still melancholy. The truth was, she no longer thought
of Boys Hall as home. She had left New York, not
with a sense of going home but of getting away from
a situation. And now she was back in England it was
the same—she didn't feel that she had come home, but
that she had escaped from New York.

She did not like the city. It was not the simple fact
that she was used to living in the country. She often

stayed with friends in London, and she never felt there that she had to get away from the crowds and the traffic and get back to the quiet of the cottage. But somehow in New York, the quality of those elements was different, more desperate, more extreme. The buildings crowded in on her. The traffic came at her, on the wrong side of the road. The whole atmosphere of the city was tense and pressing. But, if she thought about it, at other times such things would have been tolerable. The Foxleys' house was a refuge from the storms of New York. They lived a privileged, easy life, and Corinna could have joined it with them.

She had drifted into a casual relationship with Andrew. A chance encounter, because he was there when she needed someone. A casual encounter for both of them. And then she found herself taking it seriously. And taking it seriously, she guessed, not because her feeling for Andrew was so instinctively one of love, but because she still needed someone she had to take seriously. At that time she was adrift, unsure of herself, and a serious relationship would give her an anchor, a sense of purpose. It was this realization, that she was trying to tailor a casual affair to suit her own needs, that made her leave New York.

When she thought about it, it was a hopeless relationship. Andrew was no more sure of himself than she was of herself. For all his ambition, he lacked direction. She did not even mind that he did not tell the truth. But she did need a man with authority. Perhaps it was a father figure she needed, after so many years of unknowns and substitutes, a man she was sure of, who could fill all the male roles in her life. And Andrew was not that man. She needed a stronger man. She could almost believe she would be content with some sort of brute. There was no point in refusing to face these tendencies in herself. That afternoon in the woods when Andrew was so angry, when he had forced her from her horse and almost raped her—she had to face the fact that she found that episode deeply exciting.

Now, at the cottage, she was still unsettled. She began to think she knew what she wanted, but she needed time to sort herself out, to be quite sure before she took irrevocable steps. The cottage was the best place for thinking. There were no social duties, no demands. To all appearances she took up her old life. She helped Giles on the home farm. She groomed her horses and took them for exercise. Occasionally she joined the family at the Hall for meals. But she knew it would not be for long.

One hot afternoon, as she came back from a long gallop on the black mare, she saw a familiar car at the door of the cottage—a green MG. For the moment she could not remember whose it was.

Andrew was waiting for her. He lay stretched out on the sofa in her sitting room, asleep.

"Andrew!" Corinna's voice reproved him. She stood at the doorway, as if frightened to come into the same room as he. "Why did you come? I asked you not to come."

He rose from the sofa and came towards her. "Fidget," he said.

She turned her head. "Please don't call me that. I'm no longer a child."

"I'm sorry, Corinna." He stood in front of her. Her tense attitude warned him not to touch her. "I had to come."

"I asked you not to."

"But I couldn't—I couldn't just accept that I shouldn't

see you again. I had to see you. I came over on the night plane. I drove straight here. I haven't slept."

Corinna sighed deeply. Her body relaxed. "All right," she said. "I'd say you'd better come in, but you haven't even left me that. I've just been out, and I'm hot. I'm going to have a shower, then I'll make you some tea."

Evidently Corinna had taken up cooking. She brought out seed cake and rich fruitcake for Andrew. But he was too tired to eat.

"I just wanted to see you," he said.

Corinna stiffened. "Andrew, please. Let's talk about something else."

"What?"

"Now you're here you can tell me something. I was going to write to you."

"You were?"

"Yes, I want to know where I can find my father."

"What do you . . . ?"

"Andrew, please don't pretend. My father. You know where he is. You've been out to see him, haven't you?"

"I don't know what . . ."

"Andrew." Her voice was taking on a hurt tone. "Please try to tell me the truth for once."

"How do you know?"

"It's the only thing that makes sense. Andrew, please, I want to see him."

"What do you mean, it's the only thing that makes sense? Makes sense of what?"

"Oh, it's obvious, surely. The *Diana*. Someone forged that so well that no one noticed for twenty-five years. There has to be a connection between that and the Rembrandt you took to New York."

Andrew's mouth fell open. "What are you talking about?"

"Andrew, please. I told you not to come here. But you came, and you forced your way into my house. At least now don't waste my time by not telling me the truth."

Andrew sipped slowly at his tea. It was cool inside the cottage, but his forehead was glistening with sweat. Eventually he said, "But how did you know? I don't see how you know."

"Enid," she said simply. "She told me."

"She looked at it? She opened the wrapping?"

"Of course. You know, you underestimate her, Andrew. You told me yourself she was dangerous; she wasn't the silly old dear she pretended to be, by a long shot. And you expected her not to do a simple thing like that? Of course she looked at it."

"Oh God!"

"But she didn't guess what it was. She saw it was a Rembrandt, that's all. She thought it might be stolen, but she didn't guess it was a forgery. Though that was before the *Diana* was thrown out by Christie's. She may have heard of that by now, and put two and two together. She's very well informed. And she's not stupid."

Andrew buried his head in his hands. "Oh God," he said again. "Oh God."

"You don't have to worry. Neither Enid nor I will broadcast the news. Nothing has changed as far as you are concerned. We might use what we know to get things out of you, but we shouldn't harm you. I don't know what Enid might want. What I want is to know where I can find my father. That's all. I don't really care about the forgery. I don't really care if every great painting in the world is a forgery. People see what they are looking for when they look at pictures. All I want is to see my father."

"All right," Andrew said in a low voice. He did not raise his head. "I'll tell you. Of course I'll tell you where he is."

Crossing to Andrew, Corinna laid her hand gently on his hair. "Thank you," she said simply.

Later in the afternoon they walked in the garden. Corinna took carrots to the horses. Andrew stood by the stall and watched her as she spoke quietly to them.

"I think you should stay here," he said. "I think you belong here. There's one thing I haven't told you. Did you know that it was here that your father painted the *Diana?*"

She looked at him. "Do you mean at the house, or at the cottage?"

"I mean here. Where we are standing. He used these stables as his studio."

She placed another piece of carrot on her palm and held it out. The black mare fumbled it off her hand with her lips. "There wasn't a sign when I came here. No paints or anything."

"I guess your mother took great care to get everything cleared away. She told me he used an old charcoal oven in the woods behind here. To harden the paint. Did you ever come across that?"

She looked up. "Yes," she said. "It's still there."

"Well, that tallies. Your father stayed here after the war. Your mother used to come over on her horse to see him. This was his house. Why don't you stay here? In a way it belongs to you."

"Why did he leave here? Because she sent him away, I'll bet."

"Something like that, I expect. She told me a story.

But she did not quite tell the truth. It's funny, isn't it, how no one can ever quite bring themselves to tell the exact truth."

"Poor Mother." She looked around the stables, as if trying to imagine how they were in those days. Then she walked to the door and the sunshine outside. Andrew followed. "Poor Mother," she repeated sadly. "She sacrificed so much to get the things she wanted. In the end it hasn't really been worth the trouble."

"I'd say she's had a pretty good life."

"Would you? I wouldn't. She's always been in trouble with money. She always spent too much. She had such grand ideas, and she couldn't even pay for them. I bet she's spent far more than she ever got for the Rembrandt. I suppose she did sell it, did she?"

"Yes."

"I wouldn't want to go through life with the debts she's accumulated hanging around my neck."

"It worries some people more than others. You wouldn't ever borrow a lot of money. The sort that do are the sort that can enjoy it like that. They can savor the last glass of champagne while the bailiffs are halfway up the drive. You don't have to worry about them. A lot of us just wish we could get that much credit."

"Mother isn't like that. She does worry. She worries like hell. She's sick with worry all the time. Why do you think she never eats? Her stomach is raw with ulcers. She's in pain the whole time."

"She didn't have to do it."

Corinna shook her head impatiently. "No. Nobody has to do anything. Kleptomaniacs don't have to steal. Liars don't have to lie. Boys don't have to play with themselves. It's known as free will. All you have to do is to stop yourself."

"Okay. I'm sorry."

"You know," Corinna went on, "when she was a girl
in France, Mother was fat. Not plump—*fat*. Her
parents loathed her. They were such a beautiful, elegant couple. They didn't have any money, but they
were beautiful. They got by on that. They went everywhere. In those days there was a terrific social life
in Nice, you know, and Monte Carlo, summer and
winter. All sorts of people had villas there. They liked
to have her father and mother about. They were so
charming, so decorative. That was all they had to
pass on to their children. Beauty. 'My face is my
fortune, sir,' she said. For the girls especially it would
be the passport to a wealthy marriage and a comfortable life. But little Delphine was fat as a pig. They
hated her for spoiling their plans. For ten years her
father did not speak to her. Can you imagine? She
told me. For ten years he didn't address a word to
her. Even when they sat at the same table he would
say to her brother, 'Tell the fat girl to pass the sugar.'
Mother was so unhappy, she only thought of two
things—eating and killing herself. As she was Catholic,
the only thing she did was eat. She got fatter and
fatter, and more and more miserable."

They were walking now side by side in the orchard
on the soft new grass. They turned at the fence and
began to retrace their steps.

"On the morning of her sixteenth birthday she got
out of bed, took off her nightdress, and stood in front
of the mirror. She looked into her own eyes. She suddenly realized that those eyes did not belong to the
fat girl at all. Those eyes belonged to another person,
trapped inside that mountain of blubber she had
thought was herself. And the other person was pleading to be let out. From that moment, for the rest of

her life, she hated food. She ate to keep alive, for no
other reason, and not an ounce more than was necessary."

"God. I'm sorry. Did she tell you that?"

"No," she said, with a brusque change of tone. "Of
course not. I made it up. What does it matter? It
might as well be true."

She broke away and ran into the house.

Andrew found her lying across her bed, sobbing
into the pillow. He sat on the side of the bed and put
his hand on her shoulder.

"Can't we talk?" he said.

She turned on her side. "I'm sorry," she said. "I'm
sorry to be such a bitch. I shouldn't have done that.
But what can we talk about? There's nothing to say."

"We must talk." His voice was plaintive. "You can't
expect me to just get in my car and drive off, without
a word, and not see you again."

Corinna turned on her back. She put her arm across
her eyes. "You might as well, Andrew," she said
quietly. "We both know that's what you're going to
do in the end. It might be better if you did it now."

"But why do I have to go at all? I came to see you.
I wanted to be with you. I hoped we could—we could
understand one another."

"Oh Andrew, I do understand you. That's the
trouble. I've come to understand you so well in the
last month. I've thought about you a lot since I came
back."

"And . . . ?" He took his hand from her shoulder and
laid it on the coverlet between them.

"Andrew, you wanted to be with me because I had
gone away. That's your trouble—I realize it now. You
only want what you haven't got. As soon as you have
anything, you're bored with it. You're always envious

of other people, but you're never satisfied enough to settle down with anything you've achieved yourself. I think perhaps you're frightened to put yourself to the test of actually doing anything. You wanted me to come on the ship with you. But as soon as I was there, you were bored with me."

"My God. You don't think much of me, do you?"

"That's not true. I like you a lot, Andrew. More than that, probably. I don't want to analyze it. There's nothing terrible in what I've been saying. Most people are like that, more or less. It's just that, in a lover, I think I need to look for the exception, the one person in the whole world who that isn't going to happen with. For me, that's not you. And for *you*, it isn't me."

Andrew flung himself across the bed. He lay on his back, staring at the ceiling.

Corinna caressed his brows. "Don't agonize, Andrew," she said. "It's true, isn't it?"

She was praying that he would deny it. But he didn't.

They agreed Andrew should stay the night in the guest room. Corinna made a ceremony of their last dinner together. The table was candlelit. She roasted a pheasant and served it handsomely, as if for a special occasion.

Andrew sat at the kitchen table with a bottle of wine at his elbow while she prepared the meal.

They talked of the *Diana*. After Christie's rejected it, Corinna told him, Timothy refused to accept their judgment. He threatened to sue them for professional negligence. He had the painting brought back to the Hall and hung in its old place on the stairs. He invited the director of the Rembrandthuis to come over from Holland and give his opinion. He didn't tell him about Christie's report.

The man arrived late one afternoon. After half an hour's preliminary inspection, he declared that he was not prepared to give an opinion without having the painting taken from the wall for a close look the next day.

After dinner Giles insisted he be shown Christie's report. The director was visibly impressed. He went off to bed without a word. And the next day, after half an hour with his magnifying glass, he pronounced the painting an undoubted forgery.

After he left, Giles and Timothy had a bitter argument. If Giles had not shown the director Christie's report, Timothy said, he would have judged the painting genuine.

Timothy should never have tried to take the painting from the Hall in the first place, Giles argued. He should have listened to the rest of the family and left the painting where it belonged.

"And what are you going to do now?" Giles had asked. "Pull yourself together, man. What are you going to do?"

Timothy had broken down. He was weeping openly. "I don't know. What can I do?"

"There is only one thing to do. We put the *Diana* back on the wall, and we say nothing. No one but the family and a couple of people at Christie's know that it's not the real thing. No one's noticed before. I don't see why they should notice now."

"But who painted it?" Polly burst out. "How long ago was it put there? Can't we find the real *Diana*? Who did it?"

Giles glared at her. "The *Diana* is not recoverable.

This is the *Diana*. We've thought of it as that for—for long enough. We can go on thinking it."

"But what are Tim and Sally going to do?" Andrew asked when he heard this. "Can they take another painting in its place?"

"Oh no," Corinna said. "Giles wouldn't let them. Nor would the lawyer. They've still got the other pictures, of course, but they won't fetch an awful lot."

"Not enough to finance a gallery."

"No. They've found someone to put up the rest. A funny man. You probably know him. Mel German he's called."

Andrew laughed out loud. "Gerry! Oh yes. I know him very well." Then he said, "And what about death duties? He'll have to pay duty on everything in the house. The rates will be staggering. Giles could save himself half a million pounds—more, if the Revenue agreed the *Diana* was worthless."

"No. No one must ever know. Giles has said we must never tell anyone. You must never tell anyone; you must promise."

"Your brother has a very expensive pride."

"I don't think so, Andrew. It wouldn't make any difference. He could never pay the duty anyway, even without the Rembrandt. The only thing he can do is try to come to some arrangement with the government."

Andrew laughed shortly. "So your mother will have to be an ancient monument after all."

Corinna did not even smile. "Father must have wanted it like this," she said solemnly. "We've all of us assumed we must do everything we can to keep things in the family. Perhaps he didn't agree with that. Perhaps he *intended* it all to go to the nation. He had a lot of time to think when he was ill. He must have known that's what would happen. And," she added quietly, "perhaps he was right. We have been very selfish. Perhaps he was right."

But what was going on in Andrew's mind was some reckoning of his own. If the Proudfoot Rembrandt were back on the wall at Boys Hall, and the fact of its forgery a closely kept secret, his own "Rembrandt" once more became negotiable. When he got back to New York he would contact Lennox again. That was beginning to sound like something. The famous Proudfoot family had to put their Rembrandt back on the wall and he, ordinary Andrew Tait, was able to sell his for a fortune. Hadn't Lennox played into his hands by showing him the stolen Vermeer?

But he had to deal with Enid. If she still thought his painting was genuine, he would be all right. He had to deal carefully with her. He had had to "borrow" the fare to England from her.

"You'll be back?" she had said. "You are coming back?"

"Perhaps. It depends."

"Oh Andrew," she had said. "Don't be so cruel. You must come back. I shall keep your painting as a security. There, you see the things you make us do. But you must come back. I shall expect you."

She had bought him a return ticket and made him promise to use it. But he found her attention somewhat cloying.


Corinna slept with her curtains drawn back. Outside the features of the garden were quite clear in the moonlight.

At two-thirty in the morning she woke with a start. She fumbled for the light.

"Don't put on the light," Andrew said. "It's me."

Corinna rubbed her eyes. As they grew accustomed to the dark room, dimly lit by the moonlight from outside, she could see Andrew was standing by her bed, naked.

"Andrew. What's the matter? What do you want?"

"I've come to say good-bye," he said.

"Oh Andrew, you must be freezing."

"Can I come in the bed? I just want to say good-bye."

Corinna could see him clearly now. "Oh Andrew. Why do you do things like this?" He was standing, pathetic and limp, beside her bed. Her first instinct was to send him away. She hated to see men when they were down. That's why she doubted she'd ever make much of a wife. She understood people's troubles as well as anyone. She sympathized. But she did not want to be there. She did not want to know about Andrew's bad times. She had far rather he had forced his way into her bed and . . . and . . .

"All right," she said.

She moved over to make room beside her. Andrew slid between the sheets, and she held him to her. He was shivering with cold. She stroked the length of his back, like a mother her child.

His head was buried in her shoulder. He clung to her. He was shaking. Corinna wondered if he had a fever. Then he began to cry. "Oh my love," he sobbed into her shoulder. "Oh my love."

Corinna held him close. Her first reaction was to push him away, but she held him close. "Andrew," she said soothingly. "Andrew," waiting for him to gain control of himself.

Even as he sobbed, Andrew's body was pressing to her, working against her. His hands began to move over her. His mouth was at her neck, her ears. "Oh my love, oh my love," he was saying.

He pushed his leg between hers. She could feel him growing hard against her.

She rolled on her back and pulled him on top of her.

She could taste the salt of his tears on her lips. He raised himself. His mouth was on her breasts.

Corinna threw her head from one side to the other. There were tears in her eyes also. "Oh God!" she cried. "Oh God!" Hurt me. *Hurt* me! HURT ME!"

# 6

Andrew flew back to New York with the sense of a new beginning, of being purged of the past. He left England Heathrow Airport, in a Jumbo Jet, with in-flight movies and French cuisine, which was very different from the *Mayflower*, setting sail from Plymouth with the expectation of hymn-singing and ship's biscuits. But he had the same feeling of emigrating, of taking leave of his country and transferring his allegiance to another soil. England, with its old class snobberies still alive and well and living in comfort in the country ... In New York they had that too, but it was less pervasive, and there they had an alternative that could afford to ignore American aristocracy.

He took a cab from Kennedy to Enid's house. He had not told her he was coming.

She was at home.

"How nice," she said warmly. "You're just in time to change and have a drink before dinner."

"Dinner? You know what time it is according to

286

London and my stomach? Eleven-thirty at night. I'm
about ready to go to bed."

Enid blinked. "I expect you'll feel better when
you've had a shower," she said.

And for the next few days it was as if he had not
been away. In the bedroom Enid was volubly passionate. And discreetly demanding. Everywhere else,
even when they were alone together, she was propri-
ety itself. With her pink, powdered face, and her
friendly manner, she gave the impression that the last
thing she thought of was crude physical encounters.
She did not expect sex on the living room rug, or from
the rear, standing up at the kitchen sink. Outside the
bedroom it did not exist.

And so he went around with Enid—to the same
openings, dinners, shows, parties, cocktails, weekends,
theaters. . . .

Delphine was still in town. These days she spoke to
him. She was even friendly. Bob Wetherby brought
over Max Marske for his first New York show. Max
was into sculpture now. He exhibited what looked
like groups of ball bearings, different sizes, highly polished. Andrew guessed that was probably exactly
what they were. Enid had insisted they go along to
the opening. At the gallery Delphine had come on so
friendly that Enid left after half an hour—taking Andrew with her.

Andrew and Delphine had another lunch. She had
heard that the Proudfoot Rembrandt was back on the
wall.

"I'm so relieved," she said. "You can't imagine how
relieved I am."

"Corinna wants to go and see her father," Andrew
said.

"She can't do that."

"Why not? Anyway, she's determined to."

"She doesn't know where he is. Nobody knows where he is. I told you. I never heard from him."

"I know," said Andrew.

"You know where F . . . where he is?"

"Yes. Do you want the address?"

"No," she snapped. "I don't ever want to see him again."

"He was so cruel," Andrew said sarcastically.

"How did you find out?"

"That has to be a trade secret, I'm afraid."

"I see," she said coldly. "And you gave the address to Corinna?"

"Why not? I don't see why she shouldn't see her father."

"No reason for her not to see her father. But plenty of reason why I should not want her to. I should have thought you might have realized that." She drew herself up in her seat and the old haughty expression came to her face. "Andrew, I took you into my confidence about . . . about certain things."

"Delphine, you didn't take me into your confidence. You told me things that you knew I would find out sooner or later. That's not a confidence. That's an admission."

"Oh really," she snorted.

"And don't you try that old haughty snort with me. I've gotten immune in the last year. Like birds get used to the scarecrow—after a while they sit on his shoulder and shit all down his coat."

She began to rise from her seat. "Are you calling me . . .?"

Andrew took her arm and pushed her back on the bench.

"Don't go," he said. "There's something I want to say to you."

She looked at him. "I hope it won't take long," she said.

"No. It's just this. It's time you got to realize that the world was not made for your personal pleasure. You don't want Corinna to go to her father. What about her? Did it occur to you in all those years that Corinna might have needs as well? Did it occur to you that it might be important to her? You never thought. You never looked at her. You only looked at art. You never saw any further than the end of your own Giacometti. Every now and then she passed by and she seemed pretty well together, so you put her out of your head. You weren't a mother for her. No mother and no father. That's not the best start. She made Lord de Boys her father, and she clung to that, though she knew it was only a pretense. It kept her sane. She loved him, because he was the only one in the whole damn family who let himself really love her. Since he died, she's been yawing about like a yacht in a gale. She doesn't know where she is. So she wants to go to her father. I reckon she needs to go to her father. I reckon it's urgent. And just because there's a chance it might cause a little inconvenience to you, you get up on your high horse and look around as if the servants are getting above themselves again. Well, it won't work anymore, Delphine. Not with me, it won't."

"You cheap little ..." Her voice was icy with rage. "You cheap, flashy little ... gigolo."

"That's all right, Delphine. You call me what you like. I told you, I'm immune. I said what I wanted to say. I didn't expect you to like it. It happens to be the truth."

"Well, let me tell you something about the truth," she said, "before I go. If you think I'm impressed by that outburst, you're wrong. I know perfectly well what you are doing, even if you don't. Do you think you've treated Corinna fairly yourself? Of course not. You've treated her badly. You feel badly about it. So you come here and try to transfer some of your guilt to me." She stood up. "I shan't accept it, Mr. Tait." she said. "You will have to deal with your own conscience. I'm not going to salve it for you."

For just a moment Andrew felt uneasy under Delphine's attack. Did he really feel guilty about Corinna? Yes, there was no doubt that he did—at least a little. But there was nothing he could do about it.

Back at the house, Enid was waiting for him.

"You've been lunching with Delphine," she said lightly. But there was an undercurrent of criticism.

"Yes. Does it matter?"

"You didn't tell me."

"Do I have to tell you everything?"

"Of course not." She sounded so reasonable it was maddening. "But you know I'm always interested in what you're doing. I like to hear all about your plans."

"You evidently know, without my having to tell you."

"In this case, yes. Please don't sound so fractious, my dear."

"Fractious! Fractious! You make me sound like a child."

"Oh dear, I can see you are not in the mood to talk. I rather wanted to have a little talk."

"What about?"

"No, really, Andrew. I'm not going to talk while

you're in such a bad temper. It's no pleasure for either of us."

"All right. I'm sorry. I don't like being cross-examined, that's all."

"That's better." She pressed his thigh affectionately. "I expect you ate too much. Why don't you have one of my pills?"

"No thanks. What was it you wanted to talk about?"

"Do you think you could pass my handbag? I suppose I should say 'purse' since we are in New York."

Andrew passed it over. "Here you are. But what is it you want to talk about, Enid?"

"Well." She opened the bag and was feeling inside for something. Her pill bottles clinked as she rummaged. "It was your plans I wanted to talk about. I thought it was time we talked about your plans."

"Oh."

Enid held up two gold keys. "These are the keys to the safe." She held them out to him. "Here. Don't you think it would be nice if you showed me your painting? I do so hate secrets. Apart from anything else, it means you don't trust the person you have secrets from."

"But I told you. It's not my secret."

"Oh Andrew. You know, my dear, it is rather insulting for a woman to be taken for an absolute fool. If I were a follower of Women's Lib—which you know I'm not—I should call you a male chauvinist."

"A male chauvinist *pig*—why leave that out?" Andrew was frightened. He couldn't figure what Enid was driving at, but the whole setup scared him.

"I don't like the word. It's really not a very nice thing to say. And I don't think of you as a pig, An-

drew. . . . Now, please do go and fetch your painting.
I want to look at it."

"You've seen it already. I know. Corinna told me."

"In that case, my dear, why on earth are you making such a fuss? Why didn't you say?"

The safe was in the bedroom upstairs. Enid instruct-
ed him how to open it without setting off the alarms.
He carried down the painting in its canvas bag.

Enid was holding up a pair of nail scissors. "Here
you are," she said. "Use these."

Andrew swiftly slit the threads and pushed the bag
down from the frame.

"Bring it over here. Close to me. I'll take the
scissors. Closer. That's it. It's beautiful. Tell me about
it. Tell me all about it."

"It's Rembrandt. An unknown Rembrandt. I found
it in Holland. It had been in a private collection, one
family, for three hundred years. It's incredible. I got
it out without anyone knowing. Now I'm going to sell
it."

"I don't think so, Andrew." Her blue eyes were
looking up at him as he held the painting in front of
her.

"What do you mean?"

"I mean I don't think you ought to sell it." She
leaned back. "You see, Andrew, I've been making
inquiries. I had a Rembrandt expert come and look
at it while you were in England. He was very
impressed. I think I could say he was excited. It was
not listed. But obviously it was a genuine Rembrandt.
An unknown painting. That would have been very exciting."

"It's fantastic."

"But Corinna phoned me the day after you left her.
And then everything fell into place."

"She *phoned* you?"

"Yes, Andrew. It's quite easy now, with the satellites."

"I didn't mean that," he snapped. "But, God, why should *Corinna* phone *you?*"

"It does sound rather Women's Lib now you mention it ... but seriously, she phoned to tell me—well, there's no other way of putting it: the painting is a forgery. She told me the whole story. Poor girl. I'm so sorry for her."

"My God. Why did she have to do that? The lousy bitch. What a vicious bloody thing to do."

"Andrew. Please. She was terribly upset about it. She didn't do it out of spite toward you or anything like that. She did it from a sense of duty."

"Pah."

"No. You mustn't scoff, Andrew, if other people don't have the same commercial attitude as you. She did it because she cares about what is right. It may sound terribly old-fashioned to you. She's going to her father for the same reason. She wants him to give up all his—other work, and concentrate on restoration. She wants to learn to help him, or look after him so he can devote more time to this work ..."

"But she told me ..."

"Andrew, I'm telling you what she told *me*."

Holding the painting in front of Enid, Andrew was forced to stand still. He wanted to move. He lifted the painting back to lean it against a chair.

"No," said Enid. "Don't move it, I want to look at it closely."

"Look, Enid. Okay. It's a forgery. But it's perfect. Your expert thought it was genuine. It's a far better job than the *Diana*. He's learned a lot. He's got the technique absolutely perfect. Everyone will say it's

genuine. The Proudfoot *Diana*'s back on the wall.
There won't be any talk of forgery. It will be a new
Rembrandt. A great event. It's worth a fortune."

"Andrew, you know I don't like dishonesty. I'm really shocked to hear you talk like this. I refuse to be
involved in anything like this."

"You don't have to be involved."

"But I am involved already. The picture's been
here, in my safe, in my house."

"But you didn't know what it was. You didn't even
see it."

"But that's not the truth. I'm sorry, Andrew my
dear. Even if I could suppress my scruples, it's a risk
I'm just not willing to run. Try to see it my way, Andrew. I'm very fond of you. Well, even in crude financial terms, I've put money into you. Almost literally."

Andrew saw red. "What are you up to?" he
shouted. "My God. You're not the only one. I've been
putting all I've got into you. Absolutely literally.
Which is more than Wetherby could find the stomach
for. Happily married! Happily married, my ass!"

Enid stood up swiftly and slapped her hand across
his face.

"There," she said, almost calmly. "Now look what
you made me do. You really should not provoke me
like this, Andrew. It's all very unpleasant."

"What are you doing? What are you at?"

Enid was standing in front of the painting. "Oh
dear. I'm so upset. My heart. I must take a Valium."

"You can tell me first what this is all about. What
do you want, Enid?"

"Andrew." There were tears in her eyes. "All I want
is for you to stay with me. I told you. I think we
could have fun together. You would make an excel-
lent manager of a gallery. I have money."

"But this picture could get me a fortune—as much as everything you have, more."

"No, Andrew. I don't want you to."

"Why not?"

"I don't like it. I want you to be with me."

She drew back her arm. Something in her hand caught the light. Then, very slowly, she brought forward the scissors.

Horrified, Andrew watched.

With the point Enid made a small hole in the canvas. She inserted one of the blades and began to cut.

Andrew could not move. He stood, holding the painting while she mutilated it.

She cut out a jagged square at the center. Then from the corners of this hole she cut deep lines into the remaining canvas. With the ends of the blades she deliberately scratched deep lines in the paint.

Then she sat on the sofa. "There," she said. She sighed heavily. "Now, we shall never speak of that again."

**THE END OF AN EMPIRE...
THE BURNING HOPES OF TEEMING MASSES...
THE BLAZING DAWN OF A NEW NATION!**

*THE THUNDERING INTERNATIONAL BESTSELLER*

# FREEDOM AT MIDNIGHT

*LARRY COLLINS/DOMINIQUE LAPIERRE
authors of IS PARIS BURNING?*

In a story of epic scope and sweeping grandeur, the bestselling Collins and Lapierre recreate the endless bloodbaths, the frenzied riots and the brutal assassinations that climaxed with the end of British rule in India.

The raging tumult of an era comes alive in the towering figures of Mountbatten, Nehru, Churchill and Gandhi, as FREEDOM AT MIDNIGHT unfolds against the world's most exotic backdrop.

**"The song of India ... illuminated like scenes in a pageant."**
*TIME*

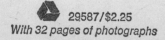 29587/$2.25
*With 32 pages of photographs*

FAM 7-76

A LOVE STORY . . . A HATE STORY . . .
A STUNNING NOVEL
THAT COULD ONLY HAPPEN HERE AND NOW

# THE NEW BODY

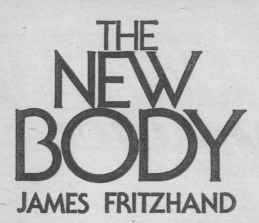

## JAMES FRITZHAND

## WORLD STAND ASIDE. CYNTHIA'S HERE . . .

This is the biggest night of Cynthia's life. It's the tenth anniversary of Nubodies Inc. and thousands of people have gathered to honor and congratulate her.

Ten years ago she was an unhappy, overweight housewife in Brooklyn. Today she's got her photograph on the cover of a national magazine and she's worth ten million bucks . . .

but someone has written a rotten book about her that could mean the end of everything . . .

AVON

27383   $1.95

NB 4-76

*The year's most deliciously uninhibited novel
about the perfect marriage:
Jessica, Jessica's husband...and*

# JESSICA'S WIFE

## *HESTER MUNDIS*

Jessica is a modern housewife with a perfect marriage
... until she returns from a consciousness raising ses-
sion realizing that there's another world outside her
door.

Now her problem is to care for her home, rear her
child, and keep her husband content while she pur-
sues a career.

Her answer?
Get a wife!

Jessica's search leads her through a series of mad,
unpredictable interviews until she and her husband
discover Abby ... great with the children, terrific in
the kitchen, and perfect in bed. Too perfect.

*"Splendid...delicious."*
***Washington Post***

What happens
when the world's
most desirable woman
meets the world's richest man?

# MYRNA BLYTH

Flawlessly beautiful, with legions of
admiring lovers, Suzanne's world is
every woman's fabulous dream come
true. She leads an ultraglamorous life
from Park Avenue to London to Paris.
And when she marries a Greek mil-
lionaire, her every whim is completely satisfied on her very own
island in the crystal blue Aegean.

**"Every woman will love it!"**
Dee Wells, author of *JANE*

 29082/$1.75

CSZ 7-76

# A DAZZLING EXCURSION INTO THAT NEON PARADISE OF UNHOLY PLEASURES

## MORRIS RENEK
# LAS VEGAS STRIP

For Yank it was a dream come true. A tough Brooklyn kid with a thirst for class, he turned his dream into a million dollar empire of vice and corruption . . .

He built the first luxury hotel and casino in Las Vegas, the plush wasteland of the west—where fortunes changed hands at the spin of a wheel, where women were beautiful and marketable, where men murdered casually, and where every human hunger was fed for a price that everyone was willing to pay!

"A STEELY NOVEL OF VIOLENCE, PATHOS, AND ROUGH ENTERTAINMENT . . . ONCE BEGUN, *LAS VEGAS STRIP* ISN'T EASILY PUT DOWN."
*New York Times*

 28332/$1.95